Spam & Eggs

A Johnny Denovo Mystery

By Andrew Kent

For KSM, whose smile lights up each day.

First published by Dog Ear Publishing
4010 W. 86th Street, Ste H
Indianapolis, IN 46268
www.dogearpublishing.net

ISBN: 978-159858-864-4

Printed in the United States of America

Spam & Eggs

A Johnny Denovo Mystery

By Andrew Kent

Enjoy the mystery!

—A Kent.

Chapter 1
Carton

Johnny stared at the email incredulously.

Mad Irma systematically laid out her gripes (". . . a poser who couldn't solve his own lunch, much less solve cases as sophisticated as the Case of the Putrefied Pterodactyl . . .") and her approach to eliminating him from the planet (". . . find you, and then decapitate you with a length of piano wire and a snap of my arms across the front of your body."). It was a pretty cool way to consider his demise, undercut by the fact that it was drawn from cliché Hollywood gangland-murder flicks. Irma was not an original thinker. Judging by the text, she was literate, with full mental capacities, hardly mad in the sense of crazed. Instead, Johnny thought, she was probably in conflict in other ways. Irma was probably a pseudonym, perhaps a stage name of a transvestite. Only a man would off-handedly suggest an approach to murder that relied so heavily on upper body strength. It's what you fail to notice that gives you away, Johnny mused.

Threats like this usually arrived after a case had been solved, sent by someone on the periphery of the action who thought that eliminating Johnny Denovo would put them a leg up in the crime realm.

He forwarded the email to a friend of his on the police force, deleting references to Denovo cases and methods, changing all personal references to the name of a police detective involved with the case, and retaining the source email address, so his intervention was invisible. He also added the contact information for the internet service provider the emailer used, so his friend wouldn't have to work too hard to find Mad Irma. Then he clicked "Send."

Johnny paused to stare off into the middle distance, all the while timing the moves. Eyes poised pensively for the requisite time, brow furrowing for an instant, slight frown, then a look of reluctant acceptance – this was the routine. He sighed and swept his hands through his overly tousled mess of tarmac black hair, pulling it back tight in mock internal agony, as if emptying deep and secret catacombs of stress and anxiety. Actually, he felt fine. It's just that after years of the world reflecting back upon him its expectations of how a cool detective should behave, he couldn't control it anymore. The fiction had become reality. His mental pathways had changed. He'd ceased being John A. Novarro, PhD, and had become Johnny Denovo.

He felt a twinge of pity for the likes of Mad Irma. She was not his focus. She was a worker, a player, an actor. Johnny went after the puppet masters. They worried him more.

He liked his role, being the detective who confounded ambitious criminals at every turn. They couldn't peg him. He had no discernible past, no records predating 2002, and no known relatives. If they only knew. The Johnny Denovo name was like his superhero's cape, his cowl and hood, his disguise. The photogenic front helped distract the curious from his past, his education, his capabilities, and his motivations.

Johnny owed his secret identity to a copy-desk error during the initial coverage of his first case, which became known as the Case of the President's Pianist. A prominent reporter had made the error with some help from spell-check, and Johnny Denovo was born – an infamous case and a strangely inventive typo. The downstream media and blogs had promulgated his new name so widely and swiftly alongside his picture – which had been taken from his best side, no less – he chose that day to embrace the name. It seemed his fate.

He looked and sounded the part, so maybe fate had known something he didn't.

This fate was sealed when the government stepped in to cover his tracks. In one executive order, he'd been separated from a past better left behind, an empty canvas of people who paid no attention to the affairs of the larger world. This fact insulated him further from identification.

Fate was a friend.

As John A. Novarro, a lonely young scientist far from home pursuing an advanced degree in neurobiology, he had become an adherent of the evolutionary insights indicating that humans possess three brains struggling to act as one. The resulting signals could be confusing if you thought people had a single brain. By imposing the model of the three-part brain and other neurobiological insights, Johnny could crack cases and break criminals when others failed. Best of all, they often never saw him coming.

Perceptions, psychology, and behavior were all built on a common biological substrate. No matter the misdirections the physical body might send, ultimately the brain was orchestrating the show. The brain dealt the cards everyone played.

Johnny knew how to cut the deck. He could read marked cards.

Johnny's doctoral thesis had dealt with abnormalities in the limbic system, the dog brain, the metaphor center, where the cards are manufactured and boxed. His research correlated malfunctions in these areas with psychopathic and criminal acts. His work had been published in a reputable journal, but it wasn't linked in any way to Johnny Denovo. Instead, it was the final entry in the scholarly record from John A. Novarro, whose first steps on the academic ladder had been broken abruptly on the same evening Johnny's fate-filled typo changed everything.

But his neuroscientific sophistication, ability to solve crimes, and telegenic looks only accounted for part of his success. His fame was amplified by statements he would often toss off to summarize the metaphorical, almost allegorical outcomes of his cases. In the Case of the Blackened Jack, he'd stated on a talk show that all he'd done was realize that the criminal had a predictable tendency based on a central survival metaphor: "When he was up, he was down; when he was down, he was up. I only had to turn his world over and watch him lose control." Statements like this were fodder for viral marketing of all sorts – clips on video sites, parodies on late-night shows, and appropriation by political figures.

With his scientific theories and strange proclamations making him sound like a seer or a nutcase, he'd been shaped by the media, the public, and clients into something that fit the archetype of a great, handsome, and eccentric detective.

A growl of hunger gurgled through him. It was time for Wei Chou, a great Chinese cook running a busy takeout place on the bottom floor of his condo tower. Something salty and full of shrimp and peanuts sounded good. Noodles, too. He picked up the phone and hit 3 on the speed dial. A few chirps of the ringer in the basement and Wei Chou's brusque voice crackled across the airwaves.

"Wei Chou's, where the chow is way good. Can I help you?" the proprietor answered.

"Wei Chou, it's me," Johnny answered, his voice casual and disembodied. "I'm hungry."

"Oh, I know just what you need, Johnny," Wei Chou answered. "You need the shrimp pad tai, don't you? And some moo-shoo pork?"

"You've read my mind, my friend," Johnny responded.

"Fifteen minutes to cook, five minutes up the elevator," Wei Chou responded. "Give me 20 minutes. I'll put it on your bill, OK?"

"Perfect," Johnny replied and hung up. Twenty minutes to kill.

Johnny let the cordless phone drop onto his desk with a clatter, then yawned and stretched, ending by shaking his head like a dog and making a shivering sound. He had to wake up. This interlude between cases felt like hibernation, a paralysis of the senses. He needed to get his blood flowing.

He needed a case.

Leaning toward his computer again, he noticed that after clicking "Send," his email had begun retrieving another raft of messages.

A slew of junk email messages came across first. These were mostly gobbled up by the anti-spam filter, but one had evaded detection. He'd get to it later. He always marveled at the vagaries of humankind. Why would someone be motivated to create such a poor business as spam email? Misspellings, typos, errors, cartoon curse typography, and all in the midst of a sales approach that was impersonal, tacky, obnoxious, and unwelcome – how did these people make money? He had long thought that spam email would disappear because it failed to work, yet it churned on. A sucker born every minute? Or companies selling spam protection software, creating their antithesis so people would buy their thesis? What concept allowed it to survive as a sales form?

The two dozen emails that remained beckoned for his grudging attention. It was fan mail. "Subject: Love you, Johnny" = auto-response with subject "Thank you for the love, but let's just be friends." It was a nice message about how his heart couldn't possibly be promised at this time in his career, and about how dangerous his work was. Next message, "Subject: You rock, Johnny" = auto-response with subject "It isn't rock, but you're rock solid for believing in me" was a message about how detectives were actually cooler than rock stars, and how he needed his fans' belief and faith to keep forging ahead through the difficult and dangerous cases he solved. Over the past couple of years, he'd developed a number of these kinds of replies based on common slang expressions. He zipped through the rest of the fan mail in a similar manner, and then turned to the handful of legitimate communiqués.

The first ones were requests to pursue cases that fell outside of his niche – the kinds of things that would end up as run-of-the-mill court cases or divorces. He ran the auto-response with the subject

"Mission statement." This message outlined the special nature of his detective work. It read, in part, "The Denovo method is reserved for cases requiring intellectual and reasoning abilities of a special nature, along with a style and air that matches the high-priced clientele who typically involve themselves with twisted pursuits requiring deadly interventions by unique individuals like Johnny Denovo. You should feel lucky your case isn't that kind of case – these cases are truly bizarre and frightening things, and can be extremely expensive to solve, especially with exorbitant travel, lodging, and miscellaneous expenses included. Plus, Mr. Denovo likes seeing corrupt rich people plundered of their ill-gotten gains. Think about it."

Once he'd eliminated the tedious case requests, Johnny was left with two remaining messages. One was from his agent, Mona Landau. She wanted to see him for dinner at Maurice's, a little French bistro with a good bar they frequented. She wanted to discuss the timing of the financial derivatives from the Case of the Unshaven Legs.

Tonight. Dinner tonight.

He could do it, but had the immediate reflex that accepting a last-minute dinner invitation was not something he should consider. It didn't gel with his image. He should be booked weeks in advance, and even then, his dance card should be double-parked. But it wasn't, and she probably knew it, so he accepted the invitation.

He'd disliked the Case of the Unshaven Legs – solving it had required a rather revolting demonstration on his part. Fortunately, the memory had largely receded, so he was ready to discuss how to get the silver lining out of the cloud.

The last email was the elusive spam his filters had failed to catch. He opened it and gazed at it. Why it caught his eye was unclear, yet he examined it intently. The message looked like the majority of spam emails he typically received. It was quite short. Yet something had caused his eyes to hover longer than normal over the nonsensical text, and after a moment, it began to emerge. There seemed to be a subtle rhythm to it, a kind of abstract moiré pattern developing across his neurotransmitters as he peered at the scrambled letters.

Ever since childhood, Johnny'd had a knack for spotting patterns. Whether they existed in the tapping of Morse codes or in fabrics or pictures or melodies, he could discern patterns much more quickly than most of his friends and track sustained patterns longer and in more detail. And this email had a pattern.

At first, it eluded him. The pattern was there, drumming its tympani – he could sense it more than anything else, feel it in the mix of numbers and letters, the spaces, the mangled punctuation. A pattern lurked here.

He let his eyes relax, the focus fuzz. This seemed to elicit patterns, blur the hard edges so that relationships and juxtapositions became clearer through changes in density, saturation, and proximity. The 8's and $'s had a particular relationship, he discovered after a few cycles of focusing and unfocusing. It was a bit of double substitution, where the symbol was substituted one way the first time, and another way the second time, alternating back and forth. These were handy for hiding things from the casual observer, and also allowed relatively rapid decoding by the recipient. Not high security, but enough in most instances.

After a few minutes, the pattern became relatively easy to unravel. He brought up his word processor in a split-pane on his computer, and retyped the first sentence, pushing his hypothesized substitutions through.

The revealed message read, "The summer sun in the south of France makes all the little chickens dance." The unscrambled code revealed a rhyme, a riddle.

It seemed pretty straightforward now. The riddle was obviously giving clues about the location and timing of something involving chickens, if you took everything literally. Johnny thought it reasonable to take the location and timing elements as stated – what else could those mean? But the chickens comment was probably a reference to some shared knowledge of the conspirators. And this looked like a conspiracy.

It was odd that it resolved into a rhyme. That suggested that the participants were fairly far along in their communications, and feeling safe within their protected realm. Not only did they feel safe, but they'd been communicating this way for so long that they were probably escalating the rhyming motif in order to remain entertained. Talk about fat and happy! Johnny's instinctive dislike for corrupt decadence flared for a moment, a shot of adrenaline splashing into his bloodstream.

But why do this? Why hide a message in a spam email? Why not just email the person directly with it? The answer, he quickly grasped, was time-honored – by making the email look like spam, it was likely to be overlooked, in fact deleted, by nearly everyone, including intelligence and police agencies. Most automated software would easily pick up the spam cues left in the email and flush it away. He was lucky his hadn't. Security through ubiquity – if it's everywhere, it's less likely to be noticed, like broadcasting white noise. Poe had made this observation involving real letters. Now, the same principle worked even when shifting to new technologies – hiding email conspiracies in plain sight had a high likelihood of success. It would be too obvious for a secret, and the intended recipient would know what cues to look for to receive and decode it quickly.

Johnny glanced at the neon-lighted clock on his wall, and just then there was a knock on his door. It had been 20 minutes, as promised, and Wei Chou was delivering his meal.

Johnny hopped up, showing uncharacteristic energy, and pounced over to the door.

"Hey, Wei," he said, snapping the door open.

"Hey, Johnny," Wei responded, smiling, his white shirt and apron already stained with the detritus of his work. Johnny and Wei had a very friendly relationship, having been through some harrowing experiences in the past involving difficult cases where the antagonists had tried to get to Johnny. There was nothing better than an observant and quick-witted friend on the ground floor to keep the ticks off the mutt.

"Smells great, Wei," Johnny commented, sniffing the air exuberantly. "I'm starved, starved, starved."

"You seem to have a lot of energy today, Johnny," Wei noted, handing over the paper bag laden with his takeout order. "In between cases again?"

"Yep, it's downtime. It drives me nuts," Johnny growled.

"You need to drag your cases out more, my friend," Wei observed. "You solve them too fast. Bad for the budget, bad for the spirit. Too much churn and burn. You should show more restraint."

Johnny sighed. He knew Wei was right, but he also realized this was the sort of discussion his friend liked to engage in – deep and well-meaning. Wei was sincere, which was probably why he liked to cook. Cooking was a sincere person's activity, Johnny had deduced long ago – unless they become a chef, because being a chef is a cynical cook's activity. Eating was more of an insincere person's thing to do, Johnny had hypothesized. It's about taking and consuming, choosing and rejecting, instead of making, offering, and hoping. Cooking was for sincere people. Wei cooked. He was no chef, just a very good cook, and it came from his heart. Wei was really sincere, and he fretted over Johnny a little, like a mother hen.

A mother hen. That jogged Johnny's memory.

"Hey, Wei," Johnny said, changing the subject. "You know a lot about chickens, don't you? You're a cook, after all."

"I know how to cut them up and make them taste good, get the bones out, keep the feathers out, that's about it," Wei said. "Why?"

"Oh, I just wondered if there were different kinds of chickens in France, that's all," Johnny said in a tone of mock taunting.

"I guess they'd be French," Wei said, not taking the bait. "I don't know even what 'chicken' is in French."

"Poulet," Johnny said, his mouth uttering the word almost before it registered in his mind. "And it's 'pollo' in Spanish and Italian."

"OK," Wei said, barely listening. "Hey, I gotta get back. It's getting close to real people's lunch times, and we'll be busy," Wei said, turning to go.

"Great. Thanks for the grub," Johnny shouted to the departing Wei, closing the door. The food smelled terrific. He couldn't wait to sink his teeth into some sustenance.

Johnny popped open the containers, stuffed a few bites into his mouth, and returned to the little coded email. The sender's address was meaningless, just a nonsense string from a domain he didn't give a second thought, but a quick search of his deleted emails showed that about two weeks ago he'd received another message from the same address, one that his spam filter had caught for some reason. He opened the older message, and quickly noticed the same double substitution scheme at work. The decoded message in this older email read, "The eggs have flown the coop, and soon should be upon your stoop."

More poultry imagery, another rhyme, but this one was more explicitly about an action, something moving from one place to another. Apparently, that place must be the south of France. But what things moved there, and from where did they move? Why did it matter? And whose stoop were they arriving upon?

Johnny sat back and chewed on another bite of savory rice noodles, slowly mulling over the few threads he had in front of him. His main question was, Should I spend time on this? It wasn't as if a client was looking to retain his services, and this hardly amounted to any criminal behavior. But it sure looked like a plot was being hatched, literally, like an egg. Two or more people, communicating through widely distributed spam email using lightly encrypted rhyming riddles, were hatching a plan, following something, keeping track of something.

It felt sinister. Johnny was intrigued.

Chapter 2
Deviled

The more Johnny thought about the emails and what he'd read, the more interesting it all became. Maybe the boredom had lowered his threshold, but he found himself studiously examining the metaphors involved in order to discern the mindset at work. The eggs represented fertility, motherhood, food, fragility, and protection. These were pleasant and affirmative metaphors and images. Obviously, this was a plan to get something desirable and precious. If it had been a murder, espionage, or blackmail plot, the imagery would have been different, the metaphors morbid and dark. It was how the human brain worked.

Yet eggs could also contain surprises. They could conceal their contents, contain secrets. What secret might these eggs contain?

No matter. To get this plot going, Johnny thought, there had to be access to a decent email system, some planning, and active reconnaissance to know when items left one place and arrived at another. Something was being carefully coordinated, and the people behind it were being patient. That could only mean that the payoff was expected to be large, singular, and sudden. They were tracking something of significant value, and something they expected to be transformed into piles of cash.

Johnny added the sender's email address to his friends list so these messages wouldn't be eaten by his spam filter any longer. If the item the conspirators were tracking had arrived, the pace of communication might pick up, and he wanted to see what came next.

The rest of the day passed uneventfully, and in the late afternoon he went out, intending to end up at Maurice's to meet Mona after stretching his legs. It was going to be a breezy summer evening in Boston. Lazy winds from the harbor were already cooling the city's streets. He wore sunglasses and a Red Sox cap pulled low over his eyes to keep out the glaring summer sun and thwart curious passers-by.

The world was proceeding along normal lines, and only once or twice did he notice any illegal activity starting or ending. It was easy to spot now with his experience and observational powers – and of little interest. He knew he catered to a different clientele. His reconstructed industrial neighborhood in downtown Boston had only upscale businessmen and recent stock market beneficiaries. The truly sick and weird rich were not around much. That meant more petty thefts, low-level drug dealing, and run-of-the-mill white collar crime, nothing to match the more convoluted and ambitious exploits of his normal customers. He had to go farther afield to find the rich who cavorted in the realms he frequented.

Boston suited the Denovo mystique in almost cosmic ways – seeking to reinvent itself, it had grudgingly accepted a bargain that transformed major portions of the city into a reimagined and vibrant center. To have a world-famous, modern detective emerge from a city that was simultaneously ascendant in sports, politics, scholarship, commerce, style, and business seemed consonant and appropriate. Johnny was simply another aspect of Boston's transmogrification.

After browsing the windows and crowds at Quincy Market, Johnny began to walk toward Maurice's. It was time to meet Mona, auburn-haired she-devil with the brains and killer instinct of a panther, possessing the great predator's ability to wait for the strike. She was a strong agent, and Johnny was glad she'd found him.

When his first case had been solved and his typographically fated name was appearing everywhere, he'd been beset with business opportunities. He'd settled on an agent who hadn't suited him, and struggled to compensate for the old-school deficiencies the dinosaur brought along. Mona didn't appear until after the initial furor had subsided and more cases had been solved, until a few years passed and other agents had come and gone, until there had been time for Johnny to have experienced some cycles of fame, steadied his attitude, and matured in his new role through calm reflection and repose. Then, with a business-like approach, she'd telephoned and stated bluntly that he was poised at the precipice of an amazingly lucrative business and personal opportunity that could last a lifetime, and that she would help him realize the full potential for a 15 percent share of the gross. She'd finished by stating that her contact information had just been transmitted by email, and that if he were interested he could call her at any of the numbers she'd given. She had then hung up with a cordial, "Any other representation would be inadequate. I look forward to working with you."

Her dusky, rich voice had captured his imagination, her timing and cool approach had provoked his curiosity, and her efficiency and confidence had engendered trust. But his sense of Denovo style had taken hold, and he knew better than to call right back. He knew that Johnny Novarro/Denovo couldn't be seen as needful. He would mull the decision over, perhaps even shrug off the suggestion as too planetary for his comet, make her wait a bit. So, inspired by the fact that this felt like a contract with Satan, he waited six days and sixty-six minutes before phoning back. The devil made him do it.

He recalled how she had answered the phone, her voice dripping with syrup: "Do we have a deal, Mr. Denovo." Caller ID had gotten him, and what had seemed at the time an innocent little set of devil jokes seemed to have stimulated a force in the universe. He had gotten a chill, as if Mona had peered into his soul in that moment. Caught off-guard, he had rather uncoolly blurted out, "Yes, we have a deal." No negotiating – not Johnny's style to haggle, so that was alright – and a deal with the devil. He'd felt as if the road beneath his feet had suddenly lurched forward, dragging him along irresistibly.

Now he stood on a cracked sidewalk outside the trendy little bistro where Mona liked to meet. He doffed his baseball cap, jamming it into his back pocket and rearranging his hair with a scratching and fussing motion as he walked in. Mona was already seated, her silky dark red hair cascading over her ivory shoulders and the spaghetti-strap black dress she wore. She was beautiful, but dangerous. As he removed his sunglasses, Johnny turned up the volume on his act to counter the competing and seductive music she played.

"Evening, Mona," Johnny said, a smart-ass smile on his face and a twinkle in his eye. Mona glared at him for a moment, just like a big sister sizing up her brother and admitting that he was a pain but that she loved him. Assessing her response, Johnny knew he had won yet again. It was an empty victory. He felt like he won battles while she was somehow winning the war.

"Hello, Johnny. Nice to see you still haven't grown up," Mona replied in a world-weary tone. "Have a seat, won't you? I've ordered a glass of wine, but only just glanced at the menu."

Johnny flipped one long leg over the back of his chair and settled smoothly into the seat, fluid and sophisticated. The waiter, happening by with a plate in either hand, caught Johnny's eye and stopped.

"Hello, Mr. Denovo," the waiter beamed. "The usual drink to start?"

"Yes, please, Ivan," Johnny replied. "Gin, tonic, and lemon."

"Right away, sir," Ivan said, and then walked briskly over to a neighboring table to deposit the dinners with their owners.

Johnny glanced up at Mona, as if breaking free of a reverie, and smiled. "So, how are you, my dear agent?" he asked.

"I'm fine," Mona responded curtly as Ivan delivered her wine. "But we're here to talk about how to divvy up the fees from the case before last, the hairy legs case. The payments were sizable, and the client even threw in a bonus of stock options. Very lucrative case, but not a straightforward cut for yours truly."

All business, as usual, Johnny thought, watching her speak. Beautiful nose, lips, and eyes, and that smooth ivory skin offset by hair dark red enough to look raven indoors. Really a gorgeous creature, but completely unapproachable emotionally. He just liked looking, and could easily multitask the auditory and visual downloads.

"Well, I might have another case cooking, too," Johnny noted casually, as if he were noting that Mona's wine was a chardonnay. "So, since I'm busy, I'll propose that you take the stock options and give the rest to my foundation. You don't mind a little risk in your portfolio, do you?" he taunted.

Ivan returned with the gin and tonic with lemon, and hurried away. Mona gave Johnny a condescending smile, as if to convey that his solution's simplicity might reflect his mind's equivalent state. Johnny held his face still, impassive, and sipped from his drink. It was well mixed and tart.

"Johnny, that doesn't help my cash flow," Mona stated flatly. "It's not about risk, but about what I can spend now. I don't want stock options to add to my nest egg."

Johnny startled a little inside, but this only manifested itself externally as a twitch of his eyebrows that could have been caused by almost anything. More egg imagery. This was one of the most amusing things about his pattern-detecting abilities. Sometimes, it seemed as if once a pattern manifested itself in front of him, the entire world reverberated with it. Eggs and France – and now nest eggs in a French bistro. He was living the emails from this morning, the most interesting pattern he had to ponder right now, even if its significance was unclear. He was feeling a pattern begin to mature into a theme. This usually meant that something of some magnitude was going on, not just random noise. He believed in fate, Johnny Novarro/Denovo, whose identity had been cast by fate. Fate was just the history of patterns. His pattern was one of reinvention, which had culminated in a change of actual identity.

Mona closed the menu, having glanced at it again during the silence that ensued after her "nest egg" comment. Ivan approached, pad in hand.

"I'll have the chicken special," Mona said – inevitable, given the theme that was emerging, Johnny thought. "And not too many mushrooms, please. Johnny, would you like anything?"

Ivan looked over expectantly. Johnny was unprepared. It didn't show. He casually asked Ivan to surprise him, and left it at that. He'd eat about anything. The lunch from Wei Chou had been good enough to satisfy his taste buds, so this was just a fuel stop, not a culinary experience.

"So, do you want to go over the numbers?" Mona said, reaching into her briefcase. And the rest of the unremarkable dinner was consumed by the rustle of papers, the clicking of calculator keys, the scratching of numbers on paper, and Johnny's occasional protestations that this all really didn't matter to him. By the time the dessert menus arrived, the math was done, and Johnny's foundation came out with a sizable six-figure donation, even after Mona's cut.

"That will do nicely," Johnny noted. "When will the armored truck arrive?"

"The bank is holding the money and stocks, so I'll have them issue the checks tomorrow. Does that sound OK?" Mona said, beaming him a heart-stopping smile, looking like something between a seductress and a satisfied carnivore. It was unsettling.

Johnny shrugged and smiled with resignation, trying to impart the feeling that he was only doing this because he must.

"Fine then," Mona said. "Now, you said you have another case . . ."

Johnny perked up a little, and his eyebrows twitched again. "Oh, yes, that," he said with feigned disinterest. "It's really rather preliminary."

Mona let out a scoffing and lovely little snort. "Don't play games with me, Mr. Superstar Detective. I know your style. What is it?"

"Just a tremor in the Force, a shadow in the sky, a whisper in the dark," Johnny said in a mock radio voice, deeper and more liquid than usual. "Just two emails that I found today that intrigue me."

"Who emailed you?" Mona asked, genuinely interested. She seemed sincere, but Johnny knew she never cooked. He wondered if his theory linking sincerity and cooking was flawed. But then he remembered that she was a better actress than he was an actor, and probably had her sincerity catered.

"Nobody emailed me. They were spam emails, but with strange characteristics," Johnny continued. He started playing with his dessert fork, which Ivan had just placed in front of him, a prelude to the appearance of his apple tart. "Strange emails, and the more I think about them, the more I want to know."

"Sounds interesting," Mona prodded, stirring the coffee that had arrived with the dessert forks.

"The one I first noticed wasn't intercepted by my spam filter for some reason," Johnny stated. "I opened it because I was bored, and noticed a pattern in what at first appeared to be random characters. It was a riddle hidden by double substitution, and it even rhymed once I decoded it. Then I searched my deleted emails for anything else from this sender, and found another message about two weeks old, coded in the same manner but with a different rhyming couplet. Very intriguing."

Mona seemed transfixed. Johnny liked this part of their relationship, when the cold businesswoman was replaced by an admiring and beautiful fan who knew him well. It almost felt like a romance, but luckily was not. Still, her ability to generate warmth in this manner made him feel especially open to discussions with Mona, and made her a useful sounding board at times like these. Since her success was tied to his, she was like a partner at his virtual firm.

"So, it sounds like the 'Purloined Letter' and secret codes and things like that, right?" Mona asked.

"That's what I get out of it. Hide in plain sight through spam email, but encode just in case, and then use riddles to conceal and keep things fun. I think they've been at this for a while." Johnny paused, and sat up straight. "You know, that's interesting. At first, I was torn, thinking either the rhyming was for fun, or to conceal. But now I'm thinking the layered approach, using rhyming couplets as riddles, has to have a purpose."

Mona tilted her head. "I'm not quite following you," she said.

Johnny paused, and pursed his lips against his tented fingers. "I think there's a concern about their messages being intercepted by people who would know to look for them. As if there is a rivalry here or someone on their trail."

"Well, you have to admit, if you found the code that easily, you can bet the government has, too. But their computers probably dismissed the rhymes as silly nonsense," Mona speculated

Johnny thought about this. The light coding would be fine for speed, and the rhyming couplets could easily defeat automated surveillance. It was probably a balance between some competing concerns.

"I guess you're right," Johnny conceded. "Just speculating."

"These seem to have gotten your attention," Mona noted. The desserts arrived. They'd eaten sparsely during dinner, business discussions dominating the time, so this last course was greeted eagerly. The next comments were muffled somewhat by food in their cheeks.

"Well, the riddles are weird," Johnny said, a fresh bite of apple tart in his mouth. "They talk about eggs, and chickens, and France, and then I've had a day with a few things poultry and French. It's like a thread in the cosmic sweater is unraveling a bit, and I want to tug on it some more."

"I see," Mona reflected, swallowing a bite of profiterole. "Your theory about fate is obviously coming into play."

"Yes, you've got it," Johnny agreed. "Call it what you will, but it has helped me to anticipate things before, you know."

"I know, I know," she said, tossing her glistening hair back as she lifted her coffee cup from the table. Her pale shoulders gleamed at him. "I'm not arguing with you, just noticing a habit of yours. Next, you'll be on about the three-part brain."

"That will come when I get to know some of the protagonists," Johnny commented, swallowing. "I'm not sure what it all means yet, but it seems to indicate a fair amount of planning, patience, and coordination. That's interesting. And the covert communications make it clear it's not legal. That's even more interesting. If it's been planned for a long time, it may feed long-term trends, larger geo-political patterns. Locating events in France puts things smack dab in the heart of Mediterranean intrigue. This could be big."

Mona paused pensively, then looked across the table and asked in a smoky voice, "So, you have two mysteries to solve, from my perspective."

Johnny braced himself. For months, he'd sensed the sexual tension between them, and dreaded the moment it became overt and active. This nice dinner in the intimate surroundings of a favorite eatery had heightened the underlying tension. If it became too great, Johnny feared, it might explode. She wasn't going to pull the pin on this grenade, was she?

His face remained impassive, even though his heart rate had increased. "What *two* mysteries?" he asked.

"First, the one you've identified, namely who is planning what and why," Mona stated, then sipped some coffee. The pregnant pause worried Johnny even more.

"Second," she started, "how you are going to find who you're working for. I need to get paid."

Johnny felt a surge of relief flood over him.

"I see what you mean," he responded in monotone. "I need to find out who would care enough to pay me to protect their goods or save the world if something has already happened. What do you suggest, great huntress?"

"I suggest you wait," Mona said unsmilingly. "If this is big, then the event will occur, you will know about it because it will happen in your client base of power-mad weirdos, but you will hold extra information that will give you an advantage and help you look superior. So, keep watching, keep noting your patterns or predicting fate, and you'll be ready when the time comes."

Damn, Johnny thought, that was pretty good advice.

"Just what I was thinking," Johnny said coolly. They both knew he was lying, and that asking Johnny Denovo to wait was like asking a cake to unbake. They chatted some more, Johnny paid the check, and they went their separate ways, yet again, Mona's tall and lovely form moving elegantly away from him until she turned a corner and vanished. Johnny jammed his baseball cap back on his head as he turned away to start the walk home. He hated waiting.

Chapter 3
Incubation

No new cases crossed Johnny's threshold over the next few days, and activities on other fronts were nondescript. He worked out and found himself doing his tai-chi more slowly, almost as if he had a case. Maybe the fact that he was in the middle of stalking these emails let him believe a case was around him, enveloping him. He was calmer since his mind had something to play with, a toy, an amusement, a worry stone at the least.

And he was worried. Being aware of a plot forming made him hypersensitive to environmental changes. Things were far from normal. News from some of the globe's more unstable areas seemed to be disappearing, he had realized, and silence was encroaching more each day. This was what worried him. It was as if people in volatile places were holding their collective breath, waiting for something big to happen.

And then another email arrived from his mystery sender. He knew it would. It was part of a stack of patterns intricate enough to force fate.

This message was another rhyming couplet double-substituted in the same way as the others. It took Johnny only a few minutes to decode it this time. The message again sounded like another step had been taken by the protagonists behind it: "Night and day, there to see, soon enough they will be free." Nothing about chickens, eggs, or France this time, but Johnny figured that bit of stage-setting had occurred in the other communications. The message confirmed that whatever was being tracked consisted of more than one thing. The rhyme was about parts of a day and what sounded like a heist of valuable objects. The action was heating up. It was time to do a little more work on the technical front.

Johnny took the elevator to the parking garage in the basement of his condo tower, jumped into his stylish European convertible, and sped through the pleasant afternoon air toward Boston's busy wharf, the warm sun glistening on the rippling water, the currents like stains on the surface. He was headed to see Tucker the Technogeek, Tucker the Tigerlily, Tucker the Tenfinger Terror. Tucker the Nicknamed would have some answers.

Tucker Thiesen worked out of his large apartment in a renovated skyscraper near the wharf. It was a rather nondescript locale for a person of such skill and so many monikers. Yet, if Johnny was about projecting an image of style, Tucker was the opposite, and seemed to cultivate an image of not caring about image. In fact, sometimes he was downright annoying, with Johnny's stylish sheen polished highly and Tucker's rough pumice threatening to mar its surface if Johnny got too close. But Tucker could do things nobody else could, and knew that his power lay in his skill, not his style. He did freelance operational activities for some of the world's most secretive clients. He and Johnny had been friends since childhood. Johnny always looked forward to hanging out with Tucker.

Tucker's apartment was different, Johnny thought as he parked his car. It seemed endless in its inner recesses, and rooms seemed to rotate back and forth at will. Perhaps that was because each time he visited a different door was open, so Johnny was always entering without interference into the room indicated, whichever one Tucker happened to be in.

Tucker had repeatedly reassured Johnny that as a master of surveillance and things covert and dangerous, he was perfectly safe in his seemingly open environment. Years ago, Johnny had donated a hair and a few other personal items to Tucker's systems, and afterwards he was told he was welcome anytime. He never understood exactly how this form of carte blanche had been accomplished or how it was maintained.

When Johnny found him, Tucker the Tumultuous was in a deep soul-kiss with a device hooked up to his guitar that transformed his voice in synchronization with the guitar strings. The music he was producing was good, but deafening. In fact, Johnny had heard it coming up the elevator, despite the room being buried inside the building and dampened acoustically, the walls pleated with baffles and grilles.

Tucker stopped when he noticed Johnny and spit the mouthpiece out. "How'd I sound?" he yelled as the last bit of reverb hovered in the air.

Johnny knew he had to yell back. Tucker would be wearing earplugs. "Like Frampton, but with bigger words."

Tucker laughed and swung the guitar deftly down into its stand. "I love it. It frees my mind. It's a great way to start the afternoon. I get so foggy after lunch." He pulled his earplugs out as he spoke.

Johnny smiled at his old friend as they shook hands. "And you do love your lunches," Johnny teased. Tucker the Trucker was portly, as his mother might say, and had always had a robust appetite, even as a kid.

"I do, I do," Tucker affirmed. "Today was fresh steamers at that ramshackle crab house down the road. Delicious with butter! But what can I do you for?"

"Ah, yes. Well, I have a little curiosity for you," Johnny stated, looking around at the paraphernalia littering the room. If it was electronic, it was here. "It's an email thread I'd like you to look at. Have time?"

"I'll make the time for you. Hey, close the door and follow me," Tucker said, wending his way through a door behind the amps he'd been using and into an adjoining room, large and brightly lit, its back wall consumed by computer monitors arranged around a workpit in which a single beat-up office chair resided. Moving into the room, it became apparent that this was really two rooms with a wall missing between them. The brightly lit portion housed Tucker's main computer center, the nexus for his real job, while a more warmly and dimly lit area was filled with comfortable chairs and beautifully decorated walls, one of which supported a large plasma television. The other wall was consumed with a large piece of abstract art, a set of large maroon boxes around a central empty box, all on an background that looked like sand. The inside of each box had intersecting arcs and three lines crossing at various angles. It was a striking piece.

Johnny pried his attention away from the arresting artwork. The unflattering fluorescent lights overhead gave everything in the computer pen a sanitary rinse that left bright surfaces still looking unclean, as if a film of heavy use lay over them. It was a place both alive and depressingly neglected, like a mossy pond in the woods.

"I sent them over to you before I left," Johnny said, following his friend over toward the computer outpost, its cockpit-like arrangement of computers and monitors created for maximum functionality. With Tucker the Turbo's flash and skill with machines, he could play three or four computers simultaneously, like a rock keyboard virtuoso.

Tucker closed the door they had just come through and opened the door on the opposite side of the warmly lit portion of the room. The door opened onto the main hallway. This was now his main portal, Johnny concluded. One at a time seemed to be the pattern to the apartment's exterior door plan. Tucker returned, seated himself with a huff, swiveled the desiccated office chair, and spun toward one of the larger monitors.

"Oh, here they are," Tucker observed, quickly finding the two messages Johnny had forwarded in the long list of email that had accumulated in the quarter-hour it had taken to drive over. Johnny wondered how his friend found time to do anything else.

He had only forwarded the first two emails, wanting to keep the third to himself so that he didn't drag his friend deeply into his theories earlier than necessary. Johnny had imposed a story on these, but it might not be the story Tucker would see. Plus, the latest one was even more provocative, and he knew Tucker could decode them given enough time.

Johnny leaned against a desk while his friend went to work.

Tucker studied the messages a bit, and then pronounced his first diagnosis. "Looks like typical weird spam messages from a well-used spammer account. I don't see anything noteworthy here. Strange domain – miasma.net – but they're probably just spoofing that. Otherwise, nothing unusual."

"Well, the domain is probably appropriate, because I think they are trying to hide something behind a fog," Johnny mused aloud. "What if I told you that the two messages were related, meant to be read by the same people, and used a substitution pattern to hide rhyming couplets. Would you look at them any differently then?"

Tucker studied his friend, taking the information in, and then turned his chair to focus on the emails again. He placed them side by side and hunched forward, his eyes darting between the two, his hand occasionally moving the mouse to scroll up and down.

"If you hadn't told me they were related, I wouldn't have seen anything," Tucker intoned slowly, his cadence speeding up as he spoke. "Now I think I see a couple of things worth noting."

Johnny felt a surge of excitement, and waited for his friend to go on.

Tucker continued. "I mean, these are minor things, but you'll probably be able to use the details later. I know these things can matter. So, what I see are strange times that they are sent. There's an unusual gap in both of them, and it's the same. See here," Tucker concluded, pointing toward the top of the lefthand email.

Johnny leaned in, and studied the timestamps. There was a path noted in the header information, when each node received the email and passed it along. Johnny knew this much. Now, he saw what Tucker was pointing out. In the penultimate node for each email, there was a precise 24-hour shift, as if the email had been plucked out of the network and reinserted one day later.

"So, what does it mean?" Johnny inquired. He could see the pattern, but wasn't certain of the significance.

"Someone is avoiding fingerprints," Tucker said flatly. "They are taking a typical spam message out of the network, manipulating it, and reinserting it. It's a great way to disguise their work – keep the hour the same, just change the day. Most surveillance systems would view these as emails that just got hung up somewhere for a day and ignore them. The email looks like it's from a known spammer, but the content is their own. They get all the benefit of spam without spending years earning the bad reputation and they hide in messages already screened as innocuous. They effectively own an untraceable and free email channel they can use any time."

There was hectic typing and clicking as Tucker flipped through websites and pages at a manic pace.

"Aha, that's what I thought," Tucker announced. "They are likely in the UK."

Johnny shook his head and gazed at his friend. "How do you get that?"

"Easy, my man, easy," he gloated. "There's a pathway of nodes back to the sending node. These emails all seem to traverse the same course, starting in the United States, and then hopping to the Caribbean, and then to various other nodes for more local distribution. Another benefit of the same send time. These people are picking these up at a node in the UK and reinserting them there, and given the local time, they are doing it rather late at night, around midnight in the UK. I'd wager whoever is responsible for sending these along isn't the brains, but the technical brawn, and likes having simple rules to follow. Some sys-op in the UK paid a pittance to do some grunt technical work."

Plus, Johnny thought, it added predictability for simple management. He inferred a ringleader even more strongly now, someone he had not detected directly yet.

"OK, Tuck, now I have to show you something else," Johnny confided. "There's a third email."

"Oh, ho, now you tell me!" Tucker exclaimed, raising his beefy arms in feigned shock. "Bring it on!"

Johnny logged into his email account on another computer, and forwarded the third message to Tucker, who immediately popped it open and studied it.

"Do they match?" Johnny asked.

Tucker leaned back and looked askance at Johnny. "They do more than match. There's another pattern in here."

"What do you mean?" Johnny asked, his pulse racing. "Another pattern?"

"There's a countdown going on here, one with some mathematical precision," Tucker concluded. "Or, a count-up, if you follow me. Look at the days."

Johnny peered over Tucker's shoulder, and studied the three panes that were open on the screen now. The first email had been plucked out of circulation on April 30, and sent along on the first of May; the second had been kidnapped on the twenty-second of June and released on the twenty-third; and the most recent was lifted on the fourth of July and dropped on its final path on the fifth. Johnny saw the pattern immediately with a glance at the screens.

"Primes," he muttered.

"Exactly," Tucker echoed. "This is just like something out of a sci-fi story, communication with E.T. by flashing primes to show mathematical awareness and consciousness," Tucker finished in a mock spooky voice.

"Perhaps we're being invaded by chickens," Johnny joked, his voice remaining grave. "If the pattern is true, then we have their first email. This is such hokey communication at some level," he continued. "But then you have the plucking of spam emails from a server before they are served and smart concealment, which is pretty modern and sophisticated, and speaks of access to some significant Internet leverage point. I'm not sure what to make of it yet."

Tucker was scanning the emails again, and there was a long pause as he studied various elements, the hush of cooling fans from the computers making the room seem far away and secret. Finally, he sat back again, and proclaimed, "Nothing more to see here, folks."

Tucker and Johnny talked a bit more, catching up a little on mundane affairs. Soon enough, he bid farewell to Tucker the Tantrum, Tucker the Tempest, Tucker the Tamed, Tucker the Nicknamed, and headed back away from the wharf and into the city, mulling over the additional details he now had to play with. He decided that technology had shown him everything it could for now, and that it was time to determine why the poultry motif was being chosen.

He headed for the art museum.

Chapter 4
Soft Boiled

Natalie LeSprague was an old friend and an excellent resource. She ran the main information desk at the art institute and trained the docents for the museum, so her knowledge of the art world was second to none. Johnny always checked out flaky notions with her. If art was about taking ideas to a level of abstraction, detection was about taking abstractions and distilling them to their core ideas – motive, means, and opportunity. Like the primary colors of red, yellow, and blue, these three essentials of crime could be mixed in an infinite variety of ways. In Johnny's world, dangerous people with a lot of money could mix them in truly incredible ways and on a breathtaking scale.

The museum was buzzing. Crowds of children were trooping through, and the pace was quickened because the end of the day was approaching. There was an edge of urgency to the voices and movements of the patrons. Natalie was standing behind the information desk, consulting one of the two attendants, both of whom were seated but looking more frazzled than Natalie, who was obviously doing most of the mental and physical work.

Johnny stood up on his tiptoes and caught Natalie's quick eye. She squinted briefly at him as a sign of recognition, and motioned him over to the side of the corral with her eyes. He moved through the crowd with the air of a confidant. The crowd parted easily, some in the awe of recognition (whispering "Denovo" as he passed), but most in acknowledgement that he had been summoned by the local royalty. Even the staff taking tickets seemed to appreciate that he had been anointed by Natalie's flicker of a blessing.

He had to wait but a moment before Natalie could extricate herself from her work. She appeared unfazed and perfectly calm.

"Hello, stranger," she said. "What's cooking? As you can see, I have to be quick. We're wrapping up a busy day."

"Hi Natalie," Johnny responded. "Sorry to bother you, but I have three words for you and just need some free-association. Ready?"

"Ready," she replied, and he felt as if he was the center of her world as he peered into her round face and deep brown eyes, playful bangs framing it all. She had such powers of concentration that she seemed to project a sphere of attention around those who held her interest. It was a comforting feeling, part of what made her so effective and gave her such sway in her work.

"Eggs," Johnny said.

"Faberge," Natalie responded.

"France," Johnny said.

"Major Faberge exhibit about to start," Natalie replied.

"Chicken," Johnny said.

"The flu, bird flu," Natalie responded, a smile lighting her face. "Sorry, with all these people around, it gets to feeling pretty germ-filled here, but you wanted free association, right? Is that it?"

"Thanks, Nat. You're the best. I owe you dinner," Johnny stated.

"Not chicken, though, please" Natalie said, raising an eyebrow. The two professionals exchanged warm smiles and parted ways.

Now Johnny felt he was gathering some major pieces of the puzzle. His limbic brain, the part of his mind that was his homing beacon on the truth – his subconscious Geiger counter, his silent sonar – was purring happily, indicating that he was on the right path. Over the years, he had learned to trust this signal. It sought pleasure and avoided pain, and weaved together preconscious thoughts in meaningful and important ways. Reassured that he was on a productive trail, his concentration moved on, and he realized he was hungry again.

It was time for Wei Chou to work his magic.

Returning to his condo, Johnny rang up his friend and said the magic words: "I'm hungry." He was offered some orange crispy beef, fried rice, and eggroll. It was exactly what he wanted, a high-contrast meal for his palate to explore while his mind sorted out the issues. These meals seemed to help him think.

So, Faberge eggs were traveling to France for a show, and someone was planning to intercept them. That much was becoming clear. He tapped into his computer, and found that the show started on July 22, which was not a prime number. However, 23 was, as was 29, so either date was worth considering. In fact, 23 seemed more reasonable. More information would emerge as time went on, the foggy lens would clear. The criminals were preparing to take a major step.

What should he do? Alert law enforcement and blow his image as an independent detective, a stylish renegade? Hardly an option, he thought. He needed to figure out more about the people behind the scenes, those who were sneaking around and swapping out email traffic to conceal themselves.

His food arrived, brought up by a young college girl Wei employed evenings when the restaurant was busy. She always got a little weak-kneed when Johnny looked at her, so he tried to make the delivery as quick and emotionless as possible, flicking money at her as a tip and barely looking her in the eye as she handed over the food. He knew it was no good. Her level of infatuation was such that any signal was a positive sign. But the food was delicious, so the awkward moments were only to be endured. After the delivery girl left, he opened the steaming containers and sat back to think. Tonight, the meal included an abundance of fortune cookies, likely from the admirer who had just departed, hopeful perhaps that one message would inspire Johnny to take another look her way. He resolved to eat the cookies but not read the messages. This was no time for distractions.

Johnny had researched more than just the dates while waiting for his food. He'd learned that the eggs were traveling from many collections simultaneously, and figured that most had already arrived at their destination in Montpellier, France. That was the eggs' move. The plotters were in the UK – or, at least, one of them was – and some or all were on the move to France, as well.

Johnny started to wonder about this person in the UK, who was just behind the veil the thieves had interposed between themselves and the world. What could Johnny say with certainty about this person? He was apparently near a computer at an Internet node around midnight GMT. Tucker thought he might be a systems operator. So he might work at one of the node hosts in the UK, probably on second shift. Or he was able to hack into a system, and always had time around midnight. Either way, he was predictably nocturnal. But Johnny didn't like the hacker idea – it seemed to not fit the mode of adequacy the group was in – just enough work but not too much, just enough encryption, just enough hiding, and so on. Whatever part of the group he'd detected thus far didn't overexert on the front-end. No inspiration, no imagination. The inspiration resided elsewhere.

Johnny searched out the network nodes in the UK, and found a listing of a few major players in the UK's part of the GMT zone. Placing a bet that his chances were greater where populations were higher, he eliminated the northernmost nodes in his first pass of candidates, and concentrated on three nodes in the south of England – two companies and a university. The next move was his.

It was about the right hour for a little probe, he saw. He quickly scribbled out the words, "Sunny side up and overcooked, it seems as if the rooster looked," and then transposed it into the double-substitution scheme being used in these messages. Typing carefully while checking the final line on the scratch paper, he finished in about 15 minutes. Then he sent the email from his oddly named anonymous email account, which would make it difficult to trace him. He sent a message to "contact@" at each one of the node operators. These emails were sure to go through in an instant at this time of night. Now, he only had to wait to see if he'd set the hook.

After sending the emails, Johnny shut down his email program and concentrated on finishing the delicious meal Wei Chou had whipped up for him, including the mound of fortune cookies he'd been granted by virtue of a teenage crush. The Denovo MP3 score played softly in the background.

About 30 minutes passed, and Johnny logged back into his anonymous account. Four emails awaited him. Three were automated responses, one per node operator. The fourth was the fish he'd hoped to catch. The message read, "Stop farting around! You think this is funny, but if we blow this, we'll never get ourselves set up. Don't do this again. You have no discipline. Bugger off. Lester."

Lester was his man then. Lester worked the second shift of an Internet infrastructure company in the UK. He apparently held a number of strings from which the others depended. And now Johnny knew a name behind the veil of secrecy.

Johnny had gained another advantage. He could continue a discussion with Lester using the anonymous email address and get more information. So he plunged ahead, writing back, "Sorry. I'm just tense. You don't think anyone suspects?"

The reply came back quickly. Apparently, the node Lester monitored was fast-loading and under Lester's obsessive surveillance. The reply read simply, "Stop using this channel, you oaf. Nobody suspects a thing. Trevor's the only odd duck. The daughter's a fool. I'm not responding to these anymore. – L."

Well, Johnny thought, a few more points in the sky, but they didn't form a constellation yet. Who was Trevor? Whose daughter, and why was she significant? He had a long way to go. But he had learned an astonishing amount in just two brief exchanges. His guess was right, this was in significant ways a pretty undisciplined group, or at least part of it had slipped the leash. It seemed from Lester's response that whoever he suspected Johnny to be, this person was customarily sending open messages about the plot in addition to coded ones, and Lester responded openly as well. He had found the soft underbelly.

The summer sun was still blazing, getting lower in the sky, shedding a sulky hot light that seemed to melt the hard edges of Johnny's decor. The day was drawing to a close. Johnny relaxed. He'd made a lot of progress. He knew the names of some of the plotters, the target of their plot to some degree, the geography being traversed, and options around the timing of the apparent heist. But he needed to know the victim's name. Who would stand to lose? Who owned these eggs? It was time to wait. He couldn't do anything until tomorrow, and needed time to let all this news settle in.

The night was calling, and he wanted some gin and a noisy atmosphere. Donning a light jacket, he went to roam downtown and see what the bars had in store for him.

Chapter 5
Half Dozen

Late the next morning, Johnny awoke, a little hung over. It had been a relatively staid evening, just a few gin-and-tonics with lemon, a little dancing, and a nice brunette who'd left early to get home to dress before work. He had used the extra hours for rejuvenating sleep, a luxury his sufficient funds and star stature afforded him. A quick shower and some yogurt and coffee, and he was set for the first part of the day. He checked his Denovo email account and responded to the usual spate of adulatory emails and grim threats. Then, he checked his anonymous account.

An interesting email awaited him there, on this non-prime day of July 6. It was from Lester. It read, "Trevor was a rat. Be on your guard. – L."

The consistently phlegmatic Johnny Denovo knew this was good news. First of all, it meant he had another event upon which to hang associations, namely the known betrayal of Trevor – although he still didn't know who Trevor had deceived, or who'd revealed Trevor as a rat. Second, if the message was sent to him by mistake, this likely meant the intended recipient didn't have word of this development, so would be operating in the blind. This kind of snafu was exactly the snag he was hoping to insinuate, a snarl that could reveal a great amount of detail to the trained eye as events transpired. He sipped some coffee slowly, savoring the touch of chaos he'd injected.

The weather outside had taken a turn for the worse. Thunderstorms were settling in for the day. Already, distant growls of thunder could be heard, the clouds crushing against each other like soft stones in the sky. He grabbed his Red Sox cap and rain jacket, went to the garage, put up the roof on his car, and drove out to see Daniel Mayfair, his friend in the insurance business.

Daniel had a useful perspective on the professions, Johnny contemplated as he steered through Boston's unpredictable traffic patterns. Daniel associated with professionals who were always near things of great value, whether the value was expressed as life, property, or money. That meant that crime was also in the same network — crime shadowed money, life, and property. Johnny and Daniel were symbiotic. They'd shared this link for years now.

Johnny had first befriended Daniel in the Case of the Bulimic Babushka. Over his career, Daniel had accumulated an encyclopedic knowledge about nearly everything of value. He possessed a bottomless memory, and could speak lucidly about any topic. His academic demeanor gave his words a timeless solemnity.

Daniel seemed to appreciate the oddities Johnny introduced into his otherwise predictable workaday existence. Johnny couldn't blame him. From where the famous detective stood, insurance appeared very boring. If he were in Daniel's shoes, any diversion would provide a break from the routine. And Johnny brought him unusual events by the bushel.

He had called ahead from the car to make sure Daniel wouldn't be in a meeting when he arrived. He was in luck, and was able to sit right down with his friend. Daniel was a tall, rangy man in his low 60s, with slicked back orange hair and a bloodhound's face, saggy, friendly, and flappy. He had large, white teeth, and loved to smile. He was happy to see Johnny.

"Welcome, welcome, Johnny my good man," Daniel said, unfolding his long body from behind his desk as Johnny entered the room. The lint-streaked storm sky outside the windows lent a flat and somber light to the room, and made Daniel's red hair stand out even more than usual, like an autumn leaf carried by the wind. From this vantage point, the dim day and approaching storm made the waters of Boston Harbor look like restless, broken asphalt.

"Hello, Daniel," Johnny replied, grasping his friend's outstretched hand. "Good of you to fit me in at the last moment. You know I wouldn't do this if it weren't important."

"Of course, I know you don't waste anyone's time, Johnny," Daniel retorted, half scolding the younger man for thinking such things. "You have one of the most interesting roles in life, the reader of tea leaves. You can see what others are blind to."

"Well, you're being kind, but this time, I need you to set my vision straight about something," Johnny said.

"Ah, yes, and what conundrum are we faced with this time?" Daniel asked formally.

"A matter of eggs," Johnny stated mysteriously. He knew Daniel appreciated the drama of detective work, and making each encounter feel exotic and memorable ensured future indulgences. "Faberge eggs."

"Faberge eggs, is it? Which type are you interested in?" Daniel asked, intrigued.

Johnny didn't know much about Faberge eggs yet, so the question threw him. "I didn't know there was more than one type."

Daniel laughed indulgently. "You are a detective, Johnny, not an art historian or even a Russian historian. You should not be expected to know such things. But after I tell you, I'm sure you'll remember." He paused to gather himself for an explanation. "Fabergé was named goldsmith and jeweler to the Russian Court in the mid-1880s. When the czar, Alexander III, wanted a gift for his wife, Faberge proposed the creation of an elaborate Easter egg as a present to the Czarina. Alexander was so impressed by this first imperial egg that the special Easter creations became a tradition throughout his reign. His son and successor, Nicholas II, continued the tradition. More than 50 were made, and all but a few have survived until now. There are only a handful of collections, one in Paris, one in Virginia, one in Russia, and an egg here and there. As for the types, there are Imperial eggs, Kelch eggs, and modern eggs, if memory serves."

Johnny had listened intently, and was impressed yet again by Daniel's expansive knowledge. He and Natalie were amazing resources.

"So, tell me, if one of these collections were ripe for the pickings by a thief, which one would it be?" Johnny asked.

"Ah, I get to choose, do I," Daniel said, eyes twinkling. "Let me see. I have to refresh my memory. We were just talking about these the other day. There's a show of them coming up in France, and any congregation of objects this valuable makes for water cooler talk amongst us insurers." Daniel had begun typing on his computer, pressing the keys a finger at a time. He peered into the monitor in a bird-like manner.

"Well, the Virginia set is a small collection of wonderful eggs, about a half dozen. They occasionally tour. I'll bet they are quite beautiful. And they are the only ones owned by an individual, which increases the risk to them exponentially. Governments are harder to go up against. So, I'd look closely at the Virginia eggs," Daniel concluded, a note of certainty tingeing his voice.

Johnny nodded thoughtfully, assessing Daniel's logic. "Who owns them?"

"Let's take a look," Daniel responded. "I know who insures them, so it won't be hard to find," Daniel trailed off, typing some characters into his computer with his distinctive syncopated two-fingered style. A moment passed. "Here we go. Insured for a ghastly amount on behalf of a Mr. James Winthrop of Richmond, Virginia. The insurance just had a rider attached for travel. That confirms to me that they are on their way to France."

Certain elements of the pattern were firming up, Johnny could see. Some expensive objects were in play and headed for France. They fit the imagery. He was on solid ground there.

"Interesting. Great information, Daniel, thanks," Johnny said pensively, using his best deep-thinker voice and attitude. "So, tell me," he continued, raising his eyes. "Why would someone want to steal Faberge eggs?"

Daniel laughed a little, a thick chortle that was almost infectious. But Johnny remained impassive, not wanting to seem susceptible to the simple pleasure of social interactions. He was, after all, a cool detective who was focused on solving crime. It wasn't something he was supposed to enjoy, but rather something that he accomplished with effort and daring.

"Well, for a few reasons," Daniel said. "There are collectors who would likely be happy to discreetly purchase the eggs and keep them hidden and secret, simply for the pleasure of owning them. Then, if money were the only object, the gems and gold on some of those in Richmond would fetch a tidy sum. Finally, as you know, often there is a hidden aspect to crimes, which is kept out of the public spotlight. We handle it in insurance all the time – thieves negotiating with the insurance company and owner for a price for the return, which is often less than the full value, but which is paid without the involvement of the law because it is cheaper than settling the insurance claim and results in a happier ending for all involved. So, they can hold them hostage, if you will," Daniel concluded.

A nifty set of options, Johnny had to admit. "Any chance I could get an inventory of the Virginia eggs? Pictures and descriptions?" he asked.

"I don't see why not," Daniel responded. "It will take a little doing, though. Let me see if I can get you something by tomorrow. Can I have a courier drop it by your condo for you?"

"That would be wonderful, Daniel," Johnny said flatly. Inside, he was immensely grateful for the cooperation and trust, but he kept his exterior signals under tight control. He knew this was what Daniel hoped to witness.

He and Daniel talked a bit more about eggs, recent events

around Boston, and the monotony of detective work. When Johnny finally left, he was sure he was onto something and convinced that Mr. James Winthrop was his next stop. He just needed to know a bit more in order to get to Richmond with the right social presence, attitude, and story.

Arriving home, Johnny searched online for clues about James Winthrop, and was able to discern through scattered local news coverage and mentions on a few web sites that Jim Winthrop, as he liked to be called, owned a horse farm in Virginia, was in his late 50s, and had worked in Washington, DC, for a number of years in both a public and a private capacity – the government and the defense industry. He'd been a widower for just about 10 years now, his wife having been killed by a drunk driver while driving alone on a rainy night. The most recent news coverage was also the most revelatory. One story from a local Richmond paper from yesterday had a headline of, "Man arrested in plot against employer," and detailed how the hostler at Winthrop Stables, Mr. Trevor Haines, had been accused of working with persons unknown in a plot to embezzle money from the farm. The charges as described seemed likely to hold up. Another connection in the pattern was made. Lester connected to Trevor who connected to Winthrop who connected to the eggs. Now, he knew the target and the motive.

The phone rang. It was Mona, his agent, the sultry lord of purgatory.

"Hello, Mona," Johnny answered.

"Johnny," Mona said, her voice a flat, blade-like monotone, stabbing him with a command to speak.

He was taken aback at first. This was a person who could throw him off stride and that sad fact reverberated, making him even more susceptible to her. What a nuisance. But the millisecond was over, and he had recovered. "What can I do for you, Mona dear?" he asked.

"I just wanted to let you know that your foundation's bank account will be fatter after 2 p.m. today," she informed him. "The funds are going in from that crazy hairy legs case. Also, the stock will be in my name with your broker, so you may see a transaction fee on your next statement. I'll reimburse you for it. The stock hasn't moved at all since the case closed, so nobody gained or lost otherwise."

"Great. I do like it when these things wrap," Johnny noted. "Is that all?"

There was a pause, and then Mona responded. "What's the status of the new case?" she inquired.

Johnny was glad to have someone cold-blooded and analytical to discuss this with, but didn't want to do it over the phone. "How about we discuss it over a drink later this afternoon?" he asked.

"Is it worth my time?" Mona asked. "Or is this just another excuse to get me to buy you a gin fizzy?"

Gin fizzy, indeed, Johnny thought. "It's worth your time," he retorted coolly. "See you at Maurice's at four, shall we say?"

"Four it is," Mona said. "See you then." She hung up, all business.

Johnny hung up and noted the time. It was past lunch, and he was hungry again, but had no hankering for Chinese food. Wei Chou was not on the menu today. He needed some Italian food. He felt like spinning pasta, untangling his food while his mind tried to untangle this case without a client. Something still wasn't quite right.

Before leaving for the little Italian spot he had in mind, he checked the anonymous email account he had used to contact Lester. There was only one message. It was from Lester, no subject. The text of the message was only one word: "Die."

Apparently, Johnny's little misdirection had been discovered, and Lester wasn't feeling indulgent. But the effect must have been unsettling for the British sys-op, an underling who now likely felt a surge of panic realizing that animals better equipped to hunt had already caught his scent. This little tickle of chaos had already paid dividends, and would probably pay more later, Johnny mused. Lester may even be considered the reason Trevor was revealed as an embezzler, and may now be carrying a discomfiting amount of guilt, a psychological state that would only make him more susceptible to error and discovery.

Reflecting on the overall circumstances that were edging into view, Johnny was happy to see that Jim Winthrop was one of "his people," a rich person with fancy tastes – horse farm, Faberge eggs, and so on. This might just turn into a case after all.

Before he could leave, he had to respond to a series of voicemails and emails with requests for him to take other cases, Again, these turned out to be either mundane cases for rich sane people or exotic cases for poor crazy people. Nothing came across in his sweet spot of rich crazies with exotic, world-changing conflicts or flights of maniacal fancy.

He went downstairs and began walking to his favorite local Italian eatery in the North End, his Red Sox cap and raincoat concealing his identity from those who might seek him out.

Chapter 6
Substitute

The pasta was exactly what he needed. Even from his seat half a floor beneath the sidewalk's level, he could see through the short windows and between the rushed footfalls splashing by that thunderstorms had taken over the day, the streets weeping with rain. Johnny settled into an atmosphere that cultivated thoughtfulness – dark skies full of broiled clouds spitting and bubbling, buttery lighting from table candles, the soothing sizzle of rain. The facts of this new case tumbled through his head, all revolving around the irrefutable truth that so far nobody had asked him to participate. This bothered him only a little.

The reasons to persevere were simple. First, the case seemed to fit his image – a theft involving rich people with high-class problems. Second, he was bored, and this kept him occupied. It was a selfish reason, and out of keeping with professional conduct, but it also fit his image as an unpredictable rebel, as slightly unhinged. Remembering this, he decided it was time to book a flight to Richmond to visit Jim Winthrop and his horse farm. Showing up unannounced would suit his modus operandi.

Johnny settled the bill, slipped into his rain coat, put his baseball cap on again, and dashed out into the wet to hail a passing taxi. It was off to Maurice's for a gin and tonic with lemon with his serpent queen of an agent.

The bumpy cab ride didn't allow Johnny to ponder the facts and patterns of the case, or much else except for his heart rate, as the driver splashed through potholes and evaded other meandering cars in a highly erratic and adrenalized style. Johnny had intended to use the time captive in the taxi to dial up his travel agent and check on prices for a flight to Richmond. But given the deathwish driving style he was experiencing, he wouldn't have dared place a call – he needed both hands to maintain his balance and grip.

To pass the time, he tried to remember how much money he still had on hand for rainy days. He had given all the money from the last case to his foundation. He hoped he had enough cash in the coffers. As he struggled to do the simple math, his concern lessened as he multiplied the final factors. He was fine. He wasn't rich, but he had enough to tackle a case or two before replenishing.

The taxi pulled up outside Maurice's with a bang, smacking into a pothole and from there the curb. Johnny exited the cab with some relief and even anticipation. He was looking forward to seeing the she-devil, he had to admit. Her emotionless ambition was clarifying, even purifying. Observing it and learning from it helped him maintain his aloofness, which was important to his image.

Rain pelted him as he slammed the cab door sloppily behind him. Even though he'd been through Maurice's entrance many times, for some reason the door fooled him, and he pushed when he should have pulled. He was obviously distracted, certainly behaving as if he were on a case. He was nearly soaked by the time he made it into the vestibule.

Given the time of day, the bar area was quiet, with only a few patrons scattered amidst the stools and high tables. There was no sign of Mona, but one particularly boisterous group was carrying on beneath a suspended television set, apparently a collegial gang of traveling business people letting their hair down.

Johnny picked a table visible from the entrance but away from the high density area of the pub. Shaking his baseball cap out and sloughing his raincoat off, he shook his head and smoothed his hair back, then hung his coat and hat from a nearby hook. When he turned around, an attractive blonde waitress was poised right where he turned, a flirtatious smile on her face. "May I help you?" she beamed. She was new.

Johnny was nonplussed, but impressed at the girl's charm and prettiness. Her smooth skin shone beautifully in the stormy day's troubled light, her bright blue eyes all the brighter for the contrast with the dim weather. "Sure, beautiful," Johnny replied. "I'll have a gin and tonic, with a twist of lemon. And pour long on the gin. I like a stiff drink." He held her gaze for an extra moment, but was deadpan in every other way.

He could tell that it got under her skin. He was making progress. She left with a demure smile and sweet, downcast eyes.

"You should pick on someone your own size," a cool voice chided from over his shoulder. Mona had apparently arrived earlier and had been using the restrooms, judging by where she had materialized. He wondered how long she had observed him.

"She can take care of herself," Johnny said, his eyes unblinking, his brow unmoving, his voice flat. "When did you get here?"

"About five minutes ago," Mona replied, placing her coat on the hook next to Johnny's and sliding onto the stool across from where he stood. "It's a lousy afternoon." She shivered slightly, a jarring sight for Johnny. He realized that he had equated ice in the veins with imperviousness to temperature fluctuations. Obviously, he was wrong. Even the devil woman wanted to be warmer.

Johnny sat down opposite Mona as the waitress arrived with his drink. She shot Mona a quick and unfriendly glance, smiled at Johnny, then icily asked Mona for her order. Mona asked for a coffee, black. The waitress turned on her heel and went to retrieve the warm beverage.

"So," Mona began. "What's on your mind? The new case is proving interesting, I'd speculate."

"Yes, it's moving right along," Johnny replied, and then shared the details with Mona, including Tucker's findings after reviewing the emails, the interactions with Lester via the anonymous email account, his conversations with Natalie and Daniel, and his plan to travel to Richmond to visit Winthrop Stables.

"My, my," Mona finally found room to interject many minutes later, getting a refill of her coffee from the waitress, who by now suspected that Mona and Johnny were not an item. She had shrugged off her initial resentment.

"You've been poking your nose around quite a bit. Do you think it's wise to take a case when there is no client?" Mona asked.

Johnny knew she wasn't worried about his safety or sanity. She was worried about his and ultimately her compensation. No client meant no up-front payment, part of which she received as a condition of their overall agreement: some money up front, some through residuals, and some for handling his business matters. With nothing coming in at the beginning, two of the three revenue sources were under threat.

"Not a problem," Johnny soothed. "If my thinking is correct, there are at least two possible financial incentives here. One would be Winthrop – foiling a theft of his Faberge eggs would likely generate a hefty reward. The second would be the insurance company – same reason. So, I might even be able to double-down on this one," he finished with a confident flourish.

Mona shot him a satisfied smile, like a teacher whose student had obviously absorbed the essential lessons and could perform when expected. "So, what's the calling card for the Winthrop visit?" she asked.

"I'm going to buy some horses," Johnny responded. "Speaking of that, can you confirm that I have enough cash on hand to make a decent showing there?"

Mona swirled her coffee a bit, her hands hugging the cup. "You have enough," she stated flatly.

Over the slight steam arising from the brown earthenware mug, in the stormy gray light suffusing the air, and with the red neon bar lights radiating from afar, her auburn hair and dark eyes seemed especially tumultuous and intriguing, glistening with ebony promise and sanguineous highlights.

"You know what you need to make it work," Mona mused. "An assistant traveling with you to handle your business affairs and money. That would give you greater credibility as a businessman, and an extra set of eyes and ears to gather facts."

Johnny paused, slightly stunned at the suggestion but concealing his reaction.

"You mean you?" he responded, controlling his breathing, his cool nearly broken once again by this surprising woman.

"Who else?" she replied, sipping from her coffee, no real expression on her face. "I know the stakes, share the winnings, and I can deal with this crowd. I know a bit about horses, so I can teach you what you'll need to pass yourself off as a buyer. It makes perfect sense."

It sounded logical. And it made good neurological and biochemical sense. Winthrop was a man, and better yet, a widower. Traveling with a woman would give him an edge. Men's brains became slightly unhinged around women, even if they never became aware of the effect. Winthrop would be more likely to be aggressive if there was something wrong, or more likely to be receptive to business if everything was as Johnny suspected. Either way, it was an advantage.

"I don't think it would help," Johnny said thoughtfully, wanting to appear as if no emotion entered into the response. He wanted to continue to repartee. "It's still early in the case, and it would just add unnecessary expenses."

Mona smiled slightly. "But this horse farm has two things going on. One is with the owner, Winthrop. The other is with the hostler, Trevor. You need to match your incursion to the problem. If your interest were only in Winthrop, one person would do. But with two people, we can be two places at once. Besides, if you get his business, I get a share. I'd like to help earn it this time."

Mona still sounded rational, her presentation apparently without ulterior motive. Besides, if anyone was capable of dealing icily with a strong businessman and his employees on what must be a tense horse farm after Trevor's arrest, Mona was the one.

"OK, I'll take your advice," Johnny concluded in a slow drawl, concealing both his cold calculation about involving her as a ploy and the fact that he was a bit intrigued by the prospect of traveling with her for the first time. "Can you be ready to go in two days?"

Mona smiled and tossed her hair prettily. "Book the tickets, Mr. Denovo. I'll be there when you need me." With that, she finished her coffee, slipped on her rain jacket and scarf, and bid Johnny farewell. The waitress approached after a moment, and Johnny ordered another drink. The waitress smiled warmly, seemingly pleased that her perceived competitor had vanished in a puff of acrid smoke.

Chapter 7
Rotten

When Johnny awoke the next morning, it took him a few moments to piece together all the threads that were being skeined together. With two quick calls from his cell phone, he'd had his travel agent book the tickets for the weekend, and had agreed to meet Mona at the airport for the morning flight. Today was July 7, the anticipated day of the next email.

He lay in bed a moment longer, rubbing sleep out of his eyes, then forced himself up. It took some time before he realized that he wasn't alone. A barmaid who made a good gin and tonic with lemon was sleeping soundly next to him, wrapped only in a filmy summer sheet, her contours clear and lovely in the morning light, a sheaf of hay-blond hair atop her shoulders. The storms of the prior day and evening had abated, and a cloudless, hot, and dry summer day awaited them. Johnny only wished he could remember her name. He glanced around the room, and found her uniform shirt tossed on the floor just inside the door. He picked it up and examined it. The name on the badge affixed to the left breast pocket read Gwen. That bit of information would spare him an awkward morning confrontation.

He tossed the shirt back on the floor, slipped on a pair of sweat-pants, and groggily wandered over to his computer. It was earlier than usual for him, much earlier. Before falling asleep next to Gwen, he'd filed a request with his hypothalamus for an early wake-up call, and it had obeyed yet again. He'd had this knack since he was a kid, the ability to reliably set an internal, and therefore silent, alarm. It had come in handy more than once.

Tomorrow, he and Mona would be flying down to Richmond. Or, rather, Johnny Denovo, the renowned detective, and his business manager, Mona Landau, would be flying down. Playing the fame card was a handy option, concealing his background, skills, and relatives from outsiders and enemies. An internal alarm clock and an external projection of star power in a media-driven age – a practical combination for a modern detective.

His anonymous email account yielded nothing. Apparently, Lester was running silent now, having found out that this emailer was untrustworthy. But Johnny's spam filter had fished out the predicted message from the ether, on the right day and, again, around midnight GMT from miasma.net. The coding was the same – a double-substitution pattern – and the rhyming couplet it yielded was on theme, exercising a bad pun to achieve it. This time, it read, "Now fair is fowl, and fowl is fair, two two more days from here to there."

Johnny glanced up at his calendar. There were two possible ways to interpret this message – by adding the numbers to the current date to reach 11, or by reading it directly as 22, adding that to the current date and arriving at 29. Johnny chose the second way to distill the message, even though both resulted in prime numbers. He felt that the strange way to state the number could only be explained by concluding the writer meant to convey 22. The 29th of July was 22 days from now. It was another prime number date. And it was one week after the exhibit was scheduled to open.

Just then, Johnny became aware of the sound of the shower running. Gwen must be awake. She was apparently comfortable making herself at home, he mused. He would have to get her to leave as soon as possible, after a civil cup of coffee. That reminded Johnny that he'd been so eager to read his email that he hadn't even started the coffee maker. He got up, moving swiftly over to the kitchen. In a robotic fashion, he filled the filter with coffee and reservoir with H_2O, and turned the device on with a mindless twist of the switch. He needed a jolt himself. It was going to be a longer morning than usual.

Once Gwen's name badge – blessedly accurate, for the sake of morning peace and quiet – had left Johnny's abode, with Gwen herself tucked comfortably and attractively beneath it, the morning settled down into a more standard routine. This meant dealing with fan emails, case requests, and business propositions – it came with the territory. Most of the latter he forwarded to Mona. Johnny then hit the showers himself, and was toweling off when his buzzer rang. A courier with the inventory of Winthrop's eggs had arrived. Johnny let the courier up, and told him to set the package outside his door. He didn't feel like mingling. He got dressed, at least in a rudimentary way – jeans and a casual t-shirt – leaving his hair tousled and feeling uncommonly unrehearsed. He was letting his guard down slightly on this day before another big plunge into the Denovo mystique. It was a rare indulgence.

After the courier left, Johnny retrieved the package and opened it. Inside was a thin stack of pages, color photocopies mostly, showing pictures of stunning bejeweled eggs on pedestals of varying heights. The eggs were as diverse and imaginatively crafted as he'd expected. He'd seen Faberge eggs before, and had looked at some pictures and descriptions online since this case had started emerging from a fog of spam, but those images had not been nearly as vivid as the pictures that lay before him. He felt himself oddly moved, as if items from another planet had descended into his visual field, inexplicably beautiful and well-crafted, generated by a genius that lay at an upper extreme of human aesthetic achievement.

Withrop's collection was small but impressive. Daniel had also been kind enough to include a pamphlet laying out more about the Faberge eggs in general. It would come in handy, Johnny thought as he studied the information, underlining certain passages and re-reading them. Homework was essential before attempting to impress a potential client, especially one with the financial means and social connections of Jim Winthrop. Johnny thought that at some point in this apparent theft plot, he might need to be perceived as having the background of an art detective in order to fetch the highest rate from Winthrop. A few well-placed art terms and knowledgeable references would make it more likely that Winthrop would empty some coffers on him by the end of this escapade.

He had the encounter with Winthrop already sketched out in his mind's eye. First, they would begin an innocuous discussion about buying horses, until Johnny could size up the man, the horse farm, and the staff. He needed to see if anyone struck him as potentially in league with Trevor, and if there were tell-tale shields that went up when a detective appeared on the premises. Second, once he was able to communicate directly with Winthrop, he would drop pretenses and ask a series of questions about Trevor and the eggs. This was sure to raise Winthrop's curiosity and unease, and let Johnny pitch the business. Once he had a commitment for a funded pursuit of the case, he could proceed. Perhaps a horse would be thrown in as part of the deal, Johnny thought.

The rest of the day was consumed by studying a bit more about Faberge eggs, packing his bag for the trip, and relaxing. He attended a tai-chi lesson, ate some of Wei Chou's delicious fare for a late lunch, and fell asleep early, with the sun still oozing hot summer lava onto the darkening sky. Another early morning awaited him, and his nocturnal habits were set to be disrupted for an extended period if the case took shape. It would all start with a trip to Richmond with Mona Landau.

The next morning, Johnny awoke alone and with a ripple of anxiety. The airport was, for Johnny, a test. To be relatively well-known in a crowd was only part of the crucible. The most trying part was undergoing the dehumanizing security protocols conducted by well-intentioned but ultimately adversarial security staff. Waving their detection wands, hoisting plastic bins, and studying scanner images, these workers were enough to send a super-hip detective running the other way. Coolness was predicated on the ability to subtly separate yourself from the rabble. Yet in the security lines, his smooth signals were jammed with herd noise. His vibes were not only drowned out, but they threatened to create an unmanageable feedback loop right into Johnny's soul. It was coolness kryptonite, this airport of anonymity and animosity. But Richmond beckoned, and Johnny had to suck it up for the sake of his professional duties. He would rather have been headed into a bar fight or a shootout.

Johnny's mode of coping with these trying circumstances involved wearing zero metal, not even in his shoes. In fact, he consistently traveled in leather moccasins – really tacky leather moccasins like the kind tourists buy, with beaded tassles and everything – along with soft and wrinkled cloth pants, a soft cotton shirt, a loose fabric belt, and a single leather duffle. He looked like Lewis and Clarke had collided with surfer culture. But inside his duffle were all the accoutrements of the full-fledged Denovo wardrobe. The airport mode was purely situational.

Mona greeted Johnny on the other side of security. She smiled slightly at his appearance. Gone was the detective decked out in black leather and polarized sunglasses. He had been replaced by organic Johnny. Yet, it worked. He looked cool, stylish, like someone who had slight disdain for but ultimate openness to his environment, someone who made up new answers to old questions or spoke in parables.

"Good morning, mountain man," Mona said, providing Johnny with an exaggerated once-over to indicate she found his get-up rather amusing.

Johnny ignored the obvious baiting. "Good morning, Ms. Landau," he responded, invoking their role-playing assignment early to cut off further good-natured jocularity at his expense. "Is everything in order?" he concluded icily.

Mona realized that this was repartee, and snapped to mock attention, clearing her throat. "All systems are go, sir," she retorted.

Johnny thought this was the most chipper he'd ever seen Mona. Apparently, she was a morning person. He never would have guessed, and he filed this information away for future reference. He felt this might be important to know the next time he toyed with amorous thoughts. This was a potentially murderous incompatibility.

"I take it you've been at the coffee, then," Johnny probed as they began walking toward their gate. The airport was crowded this morning, but people were moving in a fairly orderly fashion so it was easy to stick together.

"Oh, yes, one before I left and one on the way here," Mona said, her eyes twinkling. "Plus, I have to admit that I'm finding the idea of participating in a case rather exciting."

Damn it, Johnny thought. He was in no mood to deal with this, but here was the moment, right in front of him. He had to speak frankly.

"Look, Mona, I wanted you to come because you have ice in your veins and a cool head," he started. "If that's not who is coming with me, then maybe we should rethink this."

Mona was undisturbed by his reaction. "Denovo, just because I'm excited here doesn't mean I'll be a giddy schoolgirl vulnerable for manipulation in Richmond. You're just seeing a side of me I usually hide from you. But I can turn it on and off at will. When we get to Richmond, you'll be in the company of Mona Landau, professional assistant, cool customer, and rational thinker extraordinaire."

"Good," Johnny responded brusquely, and left it at that. Mona squeezed his upper arm to reassure him. She could tell he was grumpy because it was before his usual wake-up time, and her sisterly gesture felt warm, lovely, and anything but sisterly to Johnny. She'd done it again, gotten under his skin. Combined with the jostling the airport gave his psyche, this was stacking up as a tough morning for the world's coolest investigator.

After a quiet wait at the gate, with Mona donning an MP3 player and excusing herself while she enjoyed her favorite songs,

Johnny and his rather redefined assistant boarded the flight. They did not sit together, which was a relief to Johnny. Being isolated was usually one of the benefits of flying first class. He needed some space to clear his head and review some items in his mind.

The starchy businessman seated at the window gave Johnny a withering look, as if someone clad in leather moccasins, rumpled clothing, and a non-leather belt were unfit to be seated next to a corporate stooge in a rack suit. Johnny smiled inwardly. He had come awfully close to that same path himself, only evading it through a few lucky breaks. Choice and chance separated people only very faintly, yet gazing across the divides made people seem very different. Johnny knew it was an illusion.

It was an insight that helped him in his work, giving him a clear compass into the motivations and possibilities of human beings. Appearances didn't matter, brains did. Evolution and nature were indisputable and powerful. Our minds had been billions of years in the making and were wrapped in packages that ultimately were puppets to the cerebral cargo. He knew he simply had to generalize within a given fact pattern, and he could quite reliably predict how humans would behave, especially criminals under stress. It was almost too simple for sophisticates to grasp. Again and again, he'd found that small, nearly inexpressible nuances in how criminals thought, and how those thoughts manifested themselves, made all the difference.

The interior of the plane looked about ten years out of date. The same faux-upbeat color schemes, random patterns to hide wear and stains, and durable fabrics greeted his eye. Everything was a little tired looking from too many cycles of use without replacement – even the passengers seemed to share this trait. Since it was Saturday, he was sure many of the passengers were returning home, likely from overseas flights. The rumpled suits in the first-class compartment bore out his hypothesis.

At least the stewardess was friendly. An older woman still carrying the echoes of superb beauty in her posture and bright eyes, she possessed the bounce and confidence of an attractive woman, but layered on top of that the strength and mysterious sheen of a fading beauty, one whose mind and soul were now more clearly on display as well. Because the business passengers were all immersed in their computers and magazines, she had time to talk with an apparent eccentric flying to Richmond.

"Here's your coffee, sweetie," she said. Her name badge read Miriam. "Is Richmond your final stop today?"

"Mmm, hmm," Johnny confirmed, sipping the hot coffee a bit from the cup. He swallowed, and looked up at her. "How about you? Do you run this route all the time?"

Miriam laughed. "Oh, no, I'm just filling in for a friend today. I usually do trans-Atlantic duty, but I'm dabbling in domestic routes a bit now. The long flights get to be a grind, you know," she concluded with a slight smile.

"But you sound like you're from the South," Johnny noted, commenting on her soft Southern accent and friendly mannerisms.

"Atlanta, Georgia, for years and years," she responded, raising her eyebrows as if impressed and flattered. "I still live there, in fact. But the city's growing so fast, it's losing its identity. Makes me want to hitch up with a hearty old redneck fella and head up into the hills," she finished with a wicked laugh, as if knowing full well she could make this wish come true any day she wanted.

Johnny smiled widely in response, his cold hands hugging the warm coffee cup. The cabin had acquired a chill from being thirty thousand feet in the air. "It's true. The South has been invaded in an entirely different way this generation," he commented.

"Things in Richmond are the same," Miriam observed. Then her eye caught a hand being raised, and she excused herself while she helped another passenger. Returning, she continued. "Where were we? The invasion of Richmond, right? Well, I agree with you, the whole South is being invaded, if you ask me. We lost the war, but the invasion force is just arriving. Computer programmers, retirees,

CEOs, the nouveau rich, you name it." Her voice dropped into a low whisper. "And a lot of cast-offs from DC! I mean ex-government types, some a little shady. In fact, some give me the willies." Miriam sat back up and continued in her normal tone. "They see the South as warmer and cheaper, and they like how nice we are. So things are changing, sweetie, and I don't know if I can change that fast!"

The businessman next to Johnny shifted unhappily and gave a flamboyant shake to his newspaper, expressing irritation that a conversation was occurring in his vicinity, and in first class above all else.

Johnny smiled at Miriam, "Southern manners are in short supply these days, wouldn't you agree?"

Miriam laughed, a sparkling and mischievous sound, catching the sarcasm with ease. "Yes, honey, I'd say you and I are the last vestiges of a far better time." With this, she patted his hand, gave a wink, and moved up to the front of the plane to take care of things in the galley.

The conversation had an effect on Johnny, reminding him that where he was headed was a different world, and he would have to behave politely and formally to broach the first few relationships and days successfully. While economic, technological, and logistical changes had morphed the South in many ways, habits of mind persisted. These changed over generations, if at all.

He had decided to show up at Winthrop Stables unannounced, a risky gambit, but one that was perhaps more likely to succeed. His appearance may be viewed as a signal to Winthrop that there might be more to Trevor's deception than he suspected.

The rest of the flight was uneventful, and the stodgy businessman dozed silently for most of the remainder. After the plane landed and reached the gate, Johnny rose and spotted Mona at the back. Even after a two-hour flight crammed in the coach cabin, jammed between grandmothers and business travelers, she looked completely composed and fresh. She glanced up toward the front of the plane. Johnny averted his eyes before he was spotted gazing at her.

He stood waiting for Mona at the gate for a few moments and marveled at how different Richmond seemed. The air was more humid and smelled better. The sounds of the place were more hushed, even in something as sterile as an airport terminal.

Glancing down self-consciously at his strange outfit, he realized that the Johnny Denovo look needed some restoration before they arrived at Winthrop Stables. They would be checking into the hotel first. He would have time to upgrade to intense urbanity and Denovo flair.

Mona emerged from the jetway flanked front and back by a doddering grandmother smiling in relief at having arrived but slowly trundling through the door, and a family of four with small children fighting their way up through a jangle of kiddie gear and high-pitched requests from the mini members. She appeared unaffected and calm, but Johnny thought he caught a glimpse of deadly impatience in her glare when their eyes met. Mona was not accustomed to being a caged animal, he thought, and sharing the cage with the likes of these was provoking an instinct.

Finally, the grandmother stepped into an area wide enough to allow safe passage on one side. Mona sprinted free of the crowd, swinging easily up next to Johnny with a cockeyed smile and bumping his shoulder with hers.

"OK, boss, shall we go get cleaned up and ready for our grand entrance?" she chided. Johnny smiled slightly, and noticed that more than a few passersby were beginning to glance his way, a warning sign that recognition was not far off. He knew he had to move before someone got up the nerve to ask him for an autograph or to shout his name and point.

"Yes, let's get out of here. I don't like crowds either," Johnny said in a quiet voice, adding the last word to acknowledge that he'd seen her killer instinct surface when she was penned in.

Mona reset her bag on her shoulder with a slight heave, and they made their way to pick up their car and find their hotel. Warm breezes and bright sunshine embraced them outside.

Their rental car was a high-end foreign auto. Tucking themselves into the clean and opulent interior, they activated the complimentary GPS with the address of Winthrop Stables.

The suburban hotel turned out to be more of a motel. The only feature allowing it to be called a hotel was that it had doors facing an inside hallway. Otherwise, it was purely a family motel. They parked outside, the GPS lady sharing their rental car cheerfully announcing their arrival.

"What are you looking at?" Mona said to Johnny as he put the car in park. He continued to stare at the driver's side mirror.

"Nothing," he murmured, but it wasn't convincing. Mona gave him a long, questioning look. Johnny pulled his eyes away from the mirror and turned, giving Mona an implausible smile. "Nothing at all."

Mona groaned, rolled her eyes, and opened her door with exasperated force.

After checking in under assumed names – a caution Johnny took many times to preserve his air of cool and also to retain his privacy – he and Mona went to their separate rooms, agreeing to meet at half-past the hour to head off to Winthrop Stables.

Johnny continued to feel that this was just like working on a case, with the same zing of adrenaline and watchfulness as any other. Yet he was also completely cognizant that he had no client. His own money and volition were driving him forward. He had to tread carefully, or risk getting sucked into a money pit. His emotions could get ahead of him and, like a hyena gnawing a femur, he may not let go if he sensed the thrilling taste of marrow was near.

When Mona and Johnny reconnoitered, he was dressed in stylish black with a gray lightweight jacket, and she was in a tasteful tailored pantsuit with a diving blouse that gave her both the appearance of complete professionalism and enough sex appeal to provide her with the option of bowling over opponents with her looks. It was a good choice, of course, Johnny thought. Mona's killer instinct, even on its lowest setting, was precise in its aims.

As they eased out of the hotel's parking lot, Mona flicked open her cell phone and called ahead.

"Hello, I'd like to speak to the hostler," Mona said when the call was answered. There was a longer pause than usual to allow for what turned out to be a stumbling and slightly angry response from the person who had answered the phone at Winthrop Stables.

"Ma'am, I am not the media, and I have no idea what you're talking about," Mona replied in a calm yet forceful manner. "I am representing a wealthy client who is in Richmond today and would like to consider a stake in your farm, or purchase of a horse. Am I to understand that he is to leave disappointed?" Mona winked at Johnny at this nice turn of rhetoric.

The tone of the response changed, and there was a request for Mona to hold on while another person came to the phone.

Mona covered the mouthpiece of her cell phone momentarily. "Winthrop himself is coming to the phone," she conveyed in a stage whisper, and then lowered her hand and smiled into thin air, expectantly.

There was a pause. "Yes, Mr. Winthrop, my name is Mona Landau. I represent a wealthy client who is in Richmond this weekend, and who has heard that Winthrop Stables has an excellent reputation for breeding and stabling competitive thoroughbred horses. He is interested in discussing investment options with you. Might you have some time today?"

A man's voice was all Johnny could make out, no words or any specific attitude. Winthrop had a soft voice, and was apparently a smooth operator, even if his people were easily flustered.

"Yes, that would be excellent," said Mona. "We understand this is a slight imposition, but we simply couldn't pass up the opportunity while we were in town."

Again, a quiet response of even tone and cadence from Winthrop, final salutations, and the call ended. Mona closed her phone with a snap.

"That's odd," Mona purred, staring straight ahead. "That's very odd."

"Can I guess?" Johnny said, eyes on the road but his peripheral vision firmly focused on Mona's profile.

"Oh, if you were listening, you won't have any trouble with this one. It's very obvious, but odd," Mona said, turning to face Johnny. "He never asked who my wealthy client was."

Johnny thought for a moment. "Yes, that is strange. You'd think even if he knew who you were because he has read your name in connection with mine, he'd at least have confirmed that I was the client," Johnny said. "Did he sound distracted or overwhelmed?"

"No, not at all," Mona replied. "The first person was definitely tense and probably tired of handling the media, so I don't put much stock in that. But Winthrop sounded fine. I could even hear him walking toward the phone across a hard floor, and his strides were steady, not rushed or shifting like he might be uncertain about taking the call. And his manners seemed impeccable on the phone, so I was fully expecting him to go through the motions of asking for names and such. It's baffling."

A moment of silence settled as they drove along. Johnny considered telling Mona that they had acquired a shadow since their arrival in Richmond, but decided against it. There was no need to alarm her, or impinge on her ability to play her part. Before the silence became interminable, the GPS piped up in its pleasant automated voice, "Right turn in point five miles."

Johnny eased the car over to the righthand lane of the divided highway and prepared to make the turn.

"So, his calm disposition can mean a few things," Johnny said, seeking to move the subject away from the odd fact that Winthrop hadn't inquired about her client's identity. "It could mean he's able to cover being overwhelmed by what's going on at his farm, but is under that veneer just hanging on. Or, he might consider the arrest of his hostler for embezzlement to be the end of his troubles for the time being, and is working hard to get everyone else back to a sense of normalcy. Or, it could mean he's a great liar. We'll just have to wait and see."

"Yes, those seem like the options," Mona slowly responded, and before there was time for a downbeat, she added, "Johnny, I think he knew you were coming."

Chapter 8
Egged On

"Turn left now," the GPS sang, and Johnny turned down the shady lane bordered with white rail fences. Winthrop's horse farm was impressive and beautiful, green and shaded and vibrant, with dappled light falling on well-tended meadows and stunning horses grazing here and there like installations of immense picture postcards set up in the grassy areas.

Johnny was a little uneasy, despite the soothing setting. Waiting for Mona at the Richmond airport, he'd had the sensation that another set of eyes weighed on the world around him. It was a funny thing, but since becoming famous, these situations were easier to detect. He'd always been able to sense the subtle cumulative double-takes that signal someone is staring at the back of his head – when enough people glance at you and then at the person staring at you, a human's limbic brain knows to realize that a potential threat looms behind. But being famous made the signal stronger. More people stared at him harder, so anyone watching him was registered a bit faster as these glances would triangulate more quickly on the offending party. Fans didn't see each other as stalkers, but they knew a stalker from a fan, and their double-takes and darting eyes pointed them out more efficiently than any surveillance system he could hope to devise.

During the drive from the airport, Johnny had taken time to consider privately Mona's insight that Winthrop knew he was coming.

Johnny doubted there was a trap waiting. There was nothing at stake between them. Yet the professional surveillance was unusual, and hinted at a layer of decrepitude and power well beyond the norm.

The question in his mind then shifted to how long this had been going on. Had it truly started in Richmond? Or had it been occurring in Boston, as well? He was better known there as just a typical resident, so his fame-enhanced detection system was compromised to some extent. Was it since Trevor had been discovered?

Was it that Winthrop was more involved in the plot than Johnny had thus far perceived? Had Lester had somehow ferreted out that Johnny was on the other end of the emails? If so, he might be entering dangerous territory today. The horse farm was far from any town authority, and police in this area would likely be slow to arrive and predisposed to believe the rich horse farm owner over the interloping and flashy big-city detective. So, if a trap were being laid, he'd have to think of other options than calling the police to fish him out.

Or was it simply that Johnny was being watched before Winthrop hired him? Johnny'd had experiences like this, where wealthy clients would evaluate him using other detectives before approaching him themselves. It made some sense for cautious types. If so, then the surveillance may be a good sign and Johnny might have a client before the day ended. Then this nagging sensation of freelancing for himself would disappear.

It was going to be a worthwhile day in either case, Johnny concluded.

"OK, here we are," Johnny finally said over the GPS announcement. The car emerged out of the fenced drive and into an open plaza, with a fountain trickling in the center, a large house off to the right, and a horse barn set straight ahead. Johnny circled the car to the right and parked it near the house. He could see activity in the corrals through the open barn doors. Through the shadows, silhouettes in the barn and distant figures were walking horses to and fro, lifting saddles and moving somewhat listlessly. It was the end of the morning for these people, Johnny realized, and they were probably finishing up their early duties.

Inside the house, he could see figures through the windows, again silhouettes. It was a busy horse farm going about its normal routines. There were no signs of the press and no heads turned their way in suspicion or doubt.

Johnny and Mona climbed out of the car, Johnny keeping his sunglasses on and Mona smoothing her suit and tousling her hair in an attractive manner.

"Can I help you?" sounded a voice from behind them.

Johnny hadn't noticed it, but beside the house under a copse of trees was a smaller barn structure, apparently to store the modest and more mundane tools needed to care for the gardens and lawns in the immediate vicinity. The person addressing them was a young woman, dressed in dusty but stylish work clothes, her right eyebrow pierced with a gleaming silver stud.

Mona took the lead as Johnny affected an air of distracted indifference, sniffing the sunlight and gazing up at the high trees as if he hadn't noticed the girl approach.

"Yes, hello. I'm Mona Landau, and this is my client, Johnny Denovo. We're here to see Mr. Winthrop about some investment opportunities," Mona said, extending her hand to the young woman.

"Hi. Welcome to Winthrop Stables," said the young woman, taking off her leather glove and extending a hand to Mona. "I'm Justine Winthrop, Mr. Winthrop's daughter. It's nice to meet you both," she concluded a bit pointedly, hoping to engage Johnny's attention with a slight barb. Johnny glanced down and smiled at the young woman.

"Nice to meet you, as well, Ms. Winthrop," Johnny said, and strode forward to shake her hand in greeting. She had a strong grip and her palms were calloused. She was a hard-working young woman, Johnny concluded quickly. "This is a lovely place. How many acres do you have here?"

Justine wrinkled her tanned brow a little, then replied, "We have slightly more than 250 acres. It's a big horse farm, but it came this way. The land was purchased by another family back in the early 1900's. We've been here for a few years now."

"It's beautiful," Mona said, smiling at Justine. "Is your father available? We spoke with him on the phone not too long ago, so he should be expecting us."

"Oh sure," said Justine. "Just follow me. I think I know where he'll be." She led them toward the large horse barn at the head of the large circle delineating this part of the property.

"You've had some excitement here recently," Mona said. "I read something about it online before we came down."

"At least you've done your homework," Justine replied a little defensively. "We had a hostler who turned out to be a thief-in-waiting. But we caught on before he could do too much damage. The money will be recovered some day. The real damage was that he dragged our names into the public eye. That could prove to be helpful in the long run, really, though, don't you think? The newly famous Winthrop Stables?" Justine sounded truly optimistic.

"Potentially," Johnny said mystically. "Unless the spotlight brings unwanted attention."

Justine's head jerked toward Johnny, and her tone took on a note of belligerence. "What do you mean? Are you trying to scare us, Mr. Superdetective?!"

"Not at all," said Johnny calmly. "There is a lot of money here, and now more people know about the place and people. They've seen pictures. Probably nothing will happen, but there will be more awareness of the place within many groups of people. My line of work makes me especially aware of the unsavory types who might now turn attention your way. But I don't dabble in those types of intrigues. I was just making a comment. Take it for what it's worth."

"Well," Justine responded, struggling to regain her composure, "I hate, and I mean hate, dishonest people. Sorry, but if I have a raw nerve, it's with liars." Justine gave a sharp exhale, squared her shoulders, and led them on, muttering something unflattering under her breath. Johnny didn't blame her. His feigned arrogance would have annoyed him as well, but he had accomplished what he needed to – he had seen more of the real person. She would be easier to talk with later, after her defenses stopped resisting the truth of what he'd said, and he now felt that she was a trustworthy person.

Mona jumped in. "Tell me, Justine, are any of these horses yours?"

Justine perked up. "Oh, I ride most of them, but my favorite is Nugget. She's a great mare, with a beautiful coat and the soul of a mother and champion. She's the horse I could ride the rest of my life. And she's still young, so we get along great. In fact," she said as they entered the shade of the barn, "here she is."

The third stall to their right was occupied by a gentle-eyed horse with a coat that, even in the dim light, glistened with striking copper striations. The horse seemed to smile at Justine's approach, her eyes sparkling and head tossing slightly as Justine cooed a greeting.

"Hello sweetheart," Justine said. "How are you this afternoon? Folks, this is Nugget. Nugget, this is Mona and Johnny. Johnny's a famous detective who solves weird cases for rich people."

Inside, Johnny laughed at hearing his occupation so accurately infantilized for a horse, and at the slightly sarcastic tone this allowed Justine to use in his presence. He liked Justine's attitude – she was strong and smart and unaffected.

Justine was stroking Nugget's mane and neck, and smiling up at the horse's eyes. This was a strong relationship.

"She's a remarkable horse," Mona agreed, and Johnny nodded. There was a calm strength emanating from Nugget, a feminine strength but backed up by hundreds of pound of assured muscle and agility.

"Well, we'll have to get you two out on horses before you leave," Justine said. "I have dibs on Nugget, though." Justine winked at them, the time with Nugget having readjusted her attitude. Johnny liked young women this age, because their moods could go from graven and angry to delighted and spunky many times in the course of an hour. It was very entertaining to navigate the emotional gates and moguls. But you were always skiing downhill with females at this stage of their lives, and could crash out if you weren't careful.

"Justy, we have company?" a smooth male voice spoke from the shadows at the other end of the barn, and a lanky silhouette approached them. He was wiping his hands on his pants as he approached.

"Hi Dad," Justine said. "Dad, may I introduce Mona Landau and Johnny Denovo. They just arrived, and I was coming to find you for them."

Winthrop approached out of the shadows, and smiled at them. He was a man in his mid-50's, tall and thin, balding, and dressed in jeans and a work shirt.

"Welcome to you both," he said. "I'd extend a hand in greeting, but I was just doing a dirty job out behind the stables, so I'll have to rely on eye contact and smiles until I'm able to clean up."

They smiled in response and said their hellos. "It's good to meet you, Mr. Winthrop," Mona said. "My client here would like to discuss a possible investment opportunity with you."

"Ah, and I'd like to discuss some things with him," Winthrop responded. "Let's adjourn to the house, I can clean up, and we can have a nice chat over some lunch. I'm hungry, and I know there will be a spread for us to enjoy in about a half hour."

"Dad," Justine said. "I'm going to check on the outer stables and then I'll be in."

"OK, love," Winthrop replied. "Don't be too long."

Justine left with a smile to each of them, and walked briskly through the barn and out into the adjoining corral, the sun striking her brown hair intensely as mid-day approached.

"Come this way," Winthrop said. "And please call me Jim. I'm much more comfortable being on a first-name basis with everyone I meet."

As they walked toward the house, slowly circling the perimeter of the barn and inner corrals, Jim Winthrop gave them a brief history of the horse farm. It had been founded in the early 1900s as a mixture of a horse stable and working farm, but the lucrative nature of horse racing soon transformed it into a horse farm. By 1920, the entire acreage was devoted to horse racing, stabling, and breeding. He told them that he purchased the land about eight years ago after receiving an inheritance and a terrific retirement package from his employer. He'd worked in the US government for years, but went into the defense industry before a string of management blunders put the firm in financial difficulties and he got a golden parachute.

They marched up the steps to the broad porch. Johnny noticed a good deal of boisterous conversation coming from inside. As they opened the front door, the sounds of dishes, cutlery, and laughter greeted them. It was lunchtime for a hungry crew. There were hearty men and women gathering themselves around tables at which food was beginning to appear. They were politely making chit-chat, their eyes darting tellingly at the plates being set out. These people were hungry, and the air was vibrant as the energy of hard work dissipated.

Jim Winthrop quickly steered them away from the main dining room and down a side hall.

"Let's meet in my office," he said. "I sometimes eat with the crew, but they have a better time if the owner isn't around. Plus, we have things to discuss, I believe."

Mona and Johnny were directed into a large wood-paneled office with a bay window jutting from the end of the house and over-looking a harbor of green lawn, bejeweled in the sunlight. At high noon, this was a blindingly beautiful scene, contrasting the cool inte-rior of the house wonderfully.

The office was well-appointed, but a little disorganized. Photos of horses adorned the walls, and stacks of papers lay about the window sills and main desk. Behind the desk, there was a picture of Winthrop holding a woman close and smiling, a little girl about nine years old between the two of them. It was apparently a picture of Winthrop and his wife before she was killed by the drunk driver.

The little girl was clearly Justine, and even then, she possessed an aura of self-confidence. But there was a seriousness in the woman Johnny had just met that wasn't in the face of the girl in the picture. While maturity alone might account for this, perhaps the death of her mother brought about a change in the young woman. Johnny knew the death of a loved one could be a life-changing experience.

"Here, take any seat you'd like," Winthrop said. "I think the couches are the best, but some of the chairs are nice, too. I'll sit at the desk, if that's OK with you."

Mona strode over to a hard-backed chair near the desk, apparently unwilling to relax and drop her businesslike demeanor just yet. Johnny chose to sprawl on a couch nearby, a little aloof but close enough to be civil. He also made sure he was in bright sunlight so that keeping his sunglasses on would seem more of a natural choice.

"Any preferences for your meals?" Winthrop asked. "Any dietary restrictions or forbidden foods?"

When he was assured that both Mona and Johnny were omnivorous, Winthrop picked up a desk phone and asked that three lunches be delivered to his office, along with lemonades.

"There, that should just take a moment," Winthrop said hanging up the phone. He sighed. "It's been a busy couple of weeks, I must say."

Johnny decided it was time to spring his first disorienting question.

"Why is someone following me?" he asked casually, to nobody in particular. His sunglasses concealed that his eyes were fixed on Jim Winthrop's reaction. Peripherally, he could see Mona as well from his perch, and she turned to face Johnny with a stoic face, nonplussed by the ploy.

Winthrop was just beginning to lean back in his chair when Johnny posed the question, and reversed into an upright sitting position.

"Someone is following you?" he asked in a startled voice. "Did they follow you here?"

"Possibly," Johnny responded airily. "I wasn't keeping very careful track. But it just started. Any idea who it might be?"

Winthrop rubbed his cheeks. "We've been having all sorts of strange people around here with the news media and all that. You surely heard the story about the Trevor character's attempt to embezzle from me. Could it be a reporter trying to get a story about your next case? They are a tenacious bunch, I can tell you that. They've gone to all ends to discover something more sordid than an embezzler in our midst."

Mona knew her turn had come. "Can you explain why you didn't ask me who my client was when I called earlier? It seemed as if you knew."

Winthrop looked askance at Mona, his face still resting in his hands. There was a long pause.

"Are you here to talk horses, or are you here to play detective?" Winthrop finally asked in a flat, cold voice. "Just why are you on my land?"

"That all depends," Johnny responded coolly, taking stock of his interlocuter. "Which of the two do you prefer?"

Jim Winthrop leaned back slightly in his chair and placed his hands on his knees, sitting very stiffly, his eyes downcast.

"Well, forgive my poor manners, but then I have to ask you to leave," Winthrop said icily. "I would have preferred to have shared a nice lunch with you both, but I am not a man who likes to play games, especially other people's games. I have enough on my plate as it is. So, if you please, I will show you the way out." Winthrop had stood up as he spoke, and was heading toward the closed office door.

"You have eggs on your plate, as well," Johnny said quietly, not rising from his seat.

Jim Winthrop stopped just shy of reaching the office door, and seemed to seethe for a moment.

"I guess I have my answer," he said. "You are here to play detective. Well, then, let's play detective." And, with that, he turned around and strode back to his desk. "So, Detective Denovo, when lunch comes, you'll tell me what makes you bring up the topic of eggs."

Chapter 9
Shell Game

Lunch arrived soon afterwards. The intervening time was smothered by an awkward and unbroken silence. Winthrop kept his back to the room, staring out over the green expanse of lawn outside his windows. Johnny thought the lack of manners was significant in two ways. First, as his conversation with the southern stewardess had reminded him, lack of manners was a sign of arrogant outsiders deeply unable to adjust to their new and chosen locale. Second, some deep fear had been disturbed, and Winthrop was struggling to control it.

After a knock on the door, a middle-aged woman of sturdy build brought in a tray of sandwiches, salads, sweet corn, lemonades, and cookies. The three of them spent some time wordlessly arraying their own version of the small feast on the practical plates that accompanied the meal.

Johnny took a bite of salad, chewed it quickly, and washed it down with a small sip of lemonade. In the palpable silence that had entombed them, even these small sounds emanated uncomfortably. He wiped his mouth with a deft motion, and sat back again, setting his salad fork down on the cloth napkin without a sound. Jim and Mona each were chewing some food of their own, looking at him expectantly.

"How long was Trevor here as your hostler?" Johnny asked Jim Winthrop, staring into his eyes with unblinking intensity.

Winthrop didn't back down. "Three years. He started in the stables, but had a background that made him suited for the position. When my former hostler left, Trevor was the obvious choice. So, he had been hostler for about a year before last week's events."

Johnny sipped his lemonade again, and smacked his lips insouciantly after the last swallow. "Three years. And where did he come from before that?"

"England. He hailed from England originally," Winthrop answered. "He has a strong British accent, very nice, and it stuck out here. People liked it, he liked beer, and I think both these things elevated him a bit in the eyes of the others. He was very likable."

"Yes, I'm sure he was," Johnny agreed. "Did he like computers, as far as you know? Did he do a lot of things online?"

Winthrop had taken a bit of his sandwich when Johnny asked this question, so the answer was slow in coming. "Well, he didn't have much need in his job with me, maybe some online supply sourcing or the like, but nothing routine. He lived in a small quarters we provided him, nicely appointed, and it had a computer with high speed access, but I don't know about his habits in using it."

Johnny thought this over for a moment. "Certainly, the police must have taken his computer as evidence in their investigation," he spoke into the air, as if expressing a mental note.

Winthrop choked on a bit of sandwich, but then haltingly responded, "Yes, certainly." He coughed a bit more, until a long drink of lemonade helped to settle the irritation.

"Could you or Justine show us where his quarters were?" Mona asked politely.

"I'm sure Justine would be happy to do that," Winthrop replied. "What exactly do you know about Trevor's crime here? And why do you care? They've arrested him. The evidence is very solid."

Johnny was quick to answer. "Are you sure he committed the crime he's accused of? How do you know?"

Winthrop seemed taken aback for the first time since their arrival, and the slip in his control made much of his authority melt away, revealing someone who looked much more vulnerable and less competent than he had been thus far. Mona thought that she might have seen the real character of Jim Winthrop in that brief instant, and she found it a bit repellent.

"Well, his bank account drew the first suspicion," Winthrop stated. "The police tell me that the personnel at his bank were becoming alarmed at how quickly his account balance was swelling. And much of it was coming from sources they knew to be fraudulent or suspicious, the kinds used as shell accounts for criminals. So they alerted the sheriff."

Johnny knew too well how local law enforcement could be quick to use a simple fact-case to draw conclusions, not adding in the dimensions of human behavior that often made facts line up differently. "So, how did they conclude that this flood of money was coming from embezzlement from his employer? It seems like there could be many other explanations, doesn't it?"

Jim seemed a little shame-faced as he munched a bit of salad in the bright sunlit room. He looked briefly out of the window behind his desk and framed his next words carefully.

"Well, you have to understand, I have a lot of bank accounts," Winthrop said, scanning the pastures before him. "Some come from my years in government, some from my years in the private sector, some to do with this business. I don't keep a close eye on all of them, and my business managers are tasked with their own areas. Things were missed."

"What do you mean, 'missed'?" Mona asked.

"Well," Winthrop responded, turning to face Mona. "When the police asked for bank records, they found transfers from various accounts here matching the amounts and timing of deposits into Trevor's accounts, if you adjusted for the laundering activities of the shell accounts. It's pretty damning evidence."

"Yes, it certainly is," Johnny agreed, with a slight growl. He decided it was time to return to the eggs. "And you were worried that the Faberge eggs might be next?"

Jim Winthrop sighed. "Yes, that was my fear. I have only a few, but they are my treasures, and I don't have extremely high security for them here. It's good, but not foolproof. Losing money is one thing, but seeing one of these swiped and hidden away or, God forbid, melted down, would break my heart." Here, his emotion seemed authentic.

"Will you get the money back?" Mona asked. "How much was it?" Money issues always got Mona's full attention.

"It was a healthy six-figure amount," Winthrop revealed. "I can't go into particulars. The case is still pending, and actually the full amount isn't known exactly. I probably won't see the money back for a few years. It will be held up by the courts until this is all sorted out."

Johnny was interested to watch the bluster and arrogance of Jim Winthrop turn into milquetoast helplessness as his story unfolded. He was also noting that Winthrop's interest in Mona's physique was consistently high, so that while he was coming off his proprietorship's haughtiness, he was consistently a hound. This led Johnny to believe that he was witnessing more of an act than anything else. When one attribute remained stable in a shift of emotions, Johnny had learned through scholarship and experience that someone was extending a façade, attempting to manage their environment. Real emotions were too overwhelming to allow for that kind of split devotion. Now, all he had to do was figure out the motivation behind the act, the reason Winthrop was working some misdirection. Johnny had an early idea, but it wasn't nearly specific enough.

"Well, Mr. Winthrop," Johnny sighed, pushing back his tray of half-finished food, "I think it's clear that you don't need a detective. And I certainly don't need a horse. You discovered my ruse. I was without a case, and thought perhaps there was more to this and you might need the assistance of my special agency."

Jim Winthrop seemed very relieved to see Johnny preparing to leave the scene, but glanced furtively at Mona, as if hoping she could remain behind.

"Please, don't be in a hurry to leave on my account," Jim hastened as he rose from his chair. "If you and Ms. Landau would care to stay and tour the grounds or take a horse for a quick ride, I'd be happy to arrange it. I don't mean to be as inhospitable as it might appear."

Mona was about to accept the invitation, but Johnny cut her off. "Actually, no. We should be leaving. If there is no case here, I do need to return to my routines as well. Time is money for many of us, as I'm sure you'll understand."

"Yes, certainly," Winthrop agreed, chagrined. "Here, let me show you out."

When Mona and Johnny had reached the end of the long road out of the horse farm and turned back onto the rural highway, the warm sun beating down in blinding cascades of light on their car's hood, Mona turned to Johnny.

"Why did you leave in such a hurry?" she asked him pointedly. "He seemed devastated."

"Give me a break," Johnny said bitterly. "He's up to his eyeballs in something, and I want to find out what it is."

Chapter 10
Caviar

"Well, let me see here," Detective Timmerman murmured as he leafed through a sheaf of papers bound by a large clip at the top, his soft Virginia accent giving a special poignancy to every word. "We searched the accused's quarters on Winthrop's farm the day of the arrest, and confiscated bank records – a check register, monthly statements, things like that. But, no, we didn't confiscate or inspect any computer. But you said you were told the suspect had one? That's odd. Normal procedure would be to inspect the computer for financial transactions and personal records, contacts, that sort of thing. That's noteworthy."

Despite his minimal age and maximal size, Detective Sergeant Timmerman was far sharper than Johnny could have hoped, at least in the sense that he was exquisitely well-organized. He built this solid base up alongside his above-average intellect and achieved surprising effectiveness and awareness. Fortunately, he was also very impressed to have the world-famous Johnny Denovo in his postal zone, needless to say his offices, so he was endlessly accommodating of the freelancer's requests.

Johnny was not surprised. "Yes, it is noteworthy, isn't it? But that's our job, right Detective. We note things that are odd, out of place, or divergent, and try to make sense of those things alone. By focusing on what doesn't fit, we learn the criminal's path of action."

Behind his calm exterior, Detective Timmerman seemed to be taking a mental movie of this encounter with Johnny, and Johnny was hamming it up for the cameras. Quotes like that were pure camp, fodder for a public looking for stars, but ultimately only useful if they helped him finish a case or get another. His living was more hand to mouth than he cared to admit, especially since he was committed to avoiding extravagant wealth. It was a source of purity for him, and feeling superior to his clients and more akin to the victims gave him a natural advantage.

After a brief moment savoring the great detective's latest wisdom, Detective Timmerman continued. "Yes, that is well stated, Mr. Denovo."

"You can call me Johnny, please, Detective Timmerman," Johnny replied.

"And you can call me Aaron," Detective Timmerman offered in response, obviously pleased to be on a first-name basis with the famous sleuth.

"All right, Aaron," Johnny smiled, the bond sealed. "So, we have this statement from Mr. Winthrop about a computer you didn't know about and haven't inspected. What are our options? If there are pieces that don't fit, we need to examine them."

Detective Timmerman leaned back in his creaky desk chair and closed his eyes. "Well," he almost whispered. "A search warrant could be secured, and we could search the entire property for the computer. But we'd have to seize every computer and inspect every one, because there's no telling which one might have been Trevor's. It could be any one on the farm, if it is on the farm still. But let's assume it is. It's a big farm. We don't have that many men for a quick search. And you probably don't want this bogged down. Am I right in guessing that something needs doing now?"

Johnny liked the detective's attitude and abilities. He may be stuck in a small town police district, but he was obviously capable and loved his work.

"Instead of brute force police work, maybe there's a simpler way," Johnny speculated. "Let's do a little more deductive reasoning, shall we?" Detective Timmerman nodded. Johnny went on. "If the computer is being hidden, concealed, there are a few basic approaches. One is as you've surmised, hiding it in plain sight, mixing it in with the rest of the Winthrop Stables' computers and relying on security through obscurity. But the shifting around of computer resources might be noticed by staff. They would wonder why a new computer suddenly appeared or was swapped. We could ask a few key people if there had been some computer changes recently, but it would only raise alarm bells at the stables, and that might not help us."

Detective Timmerman, his head tilted back in his chair, nodded in ascent. At least, Johnny thought he nodded ascent. With his thick neck contorted as it was, it was hard to tell.

Johnny continued. "Another approach would be to hide it on the grounds, but then it could be discovered by the police using a search warrant. So, that leaves us with the third option. It could have been taken off the farm. This would go unnoticed by the staff, and would conceal it from the police until the heat was off."

Detective Timmerman had listened to this, his head still tilted back. As Johnny concluded his thoughts, Detective Timmerman's eyes banged open and he leaned forward excitedly.

"Ted," he said loudly.

"Ted?" Mona said, perched on a nearby desk's corner. "Who is Ted?"

Detective Timmerman was already punching buttons on his desk phone. "Local computer guy. Fixes all the stuff around here that isn't bigger than a server, which is nearly everything nowadays. The most normal way to take a computer away is to take it for repairs. If it's out for repairs, Ted would know." He pressed the phone to his ear. There was a long interlude in the room as all waited for the phone to be picked up on the other end.

Detective Timmerman sagged visibly. "Hi Ted. It's Aaron Timmerman with the sheriff's office. I've got a couple questions for you if you have a moment. I'm wondering if you've gotten any repair jobs from Jim Winthrop's place lately. Nothing urgent, but please give me a call direct at 2302. Thanks."

He hung up the phone. "He must be busy. Ted's a little eccentric and not always easy to reach, but he knows his stuff. This would be a good shortcut if it pans out."

Johnny and Mona nodded in agreement, and a silence suffused the room, the distant bustle of the rest of the office barely penetrating the late afternoon lull. An antique clock ticking on a bookcase nearby punctuated the passage of time while also reminding Johnny of how unusual the setting was, a very genteel police office indeed.

Detective Timmerman was first to feel the weight of the quiet. He stretched noisily, rising from his chair. "Well, I suppose you'll be wanting to talk with Trevor then," he said.

Johnny shot Mona a quick look of suppressed but happy shock. He hadn't indicated any desire to speak to Trevor, nor had he expected to be given the privilege as an outsider just in town. But Detective Timmerman nonchalantly began leading them out of the offices and down a short hallway.

"Now, I probably shouldn't really be doing this," Detective Timmerman said over his shoulder once they were out of earshot. "But I figure he'll be as happy as anyone to see you. Trevor is a real fan of mysteries, and of you in particular, Johnny." He smiled at Johnny as he said this.

"Great," Johnny replied. "Has he been cooperative?"

Detective Timmerman snorted. "Ha, that's a good one. Trevor is one of the most mule-headed people I know, and I've known him a few years now. We used to talk quite a bit when I was out to the Winthrop place on rounds or if there was ever some trouble out there. That's how I got to know his tastes in literature and the like, you see," he concluded with a wink. Detective Timmerman used a pass card to release the magnetic locks on the door into the holding area, and led Johnny and Mona through.

As with the rest of the building, the holding area was clean, modern, and well-appointed, given its function. Bright sunlight entered through small windows along the ridgeline. There were three cells on either side of the main passage, each recently painted and very clean, the bars unchipped and the floors unstained. The only occupied cell held a man who was quietly reading a thick book, his attention focused. He seemed oblivious to the sound of visitors coming down toward his cell.

"Trevor Haines, stand up please," Detective Timmerman nearly shouted, at which Trevor smiled without looking up and jumped to his feet in a rigid pose, mock militaristic.

"At your service, commander," Trevor replied in a brusque British voice, the heavy book pressed to his side.

"At ease," Detective Timmerman said more quietly. Apparently, he immediately felt the pressure to explain this seemingly bizarre exchange, a flush of embarrassment stealing across his ruddy face. "You see," he said in the tone of a confidant, "Trevor was in the British navy, and I was in the army here, so this is how we greet each other. We know each other as former soldiers, and this routine developed over the years. Old habit. Sorry."

Mona merely smiled. Johnny nodded, taking it all in. This was a close-knit little couple, and the word "incestuous" crept into his mind. He also wondered whether the closeness could lead to blindness on Timmerman's part, or open him to manipulation by Trevor. The fact alone was noted. It wasn't clear that it meant anything yet.

"Trevor, I brought you a visitor," Detective Timmerman continued, turning back to the man in the cell. "Trevor, may I introduce my new friend Johnny. Johnny Denovo, this is Trevor Haines."

Again, Johnny only smiled at the man, who immediately lost every hint of insouciance and acquired a sincerity that was immediately winning.

"You're Johnny Denovo!" Trevor exclaimed excitedly, jumping to his feet, a look of sheer adoration and curiosity firing his countenance. "You are, you are effing Johnny Denovo. Un-effing-believable! It's grand to make your acquaintance, sir."

Trevor extended his empty right hand through the bars of his minimum security cell to shake Johnny's. His grip was firm and hands weathered, obviously a strong man accustomed to working outdoors. It was a reassuring feeling, steady and solid, to receive a handshake like Trevor's.

"Hello, Trevor," Johnny said coolly. "May I introduce my assistant, Mona Landau, who is helping me on an assignment."

"Pleasure," Trevor said, tilting his head downward slightly in a very formal, old world manner. "It must be an exciting job you have, Miss."

Mona could not retain her edge of cynicism in the presence of Trevor. "It is quite exciting," she admitted in a quiet voice, looking from Trevor to Johnny as she spoke. The afternoon sun was making the area warm even with the air conditioning blasting strongly. Her gaze added a bit more heat to the room as their eyes met.

Detective Timmerman cleared his throat to interrupt the sexual tension that suddenly became apparent to everyone in the room. "Well, Trevor, Mr. Denovo is here on a case, and thought you might be worth speaking with since you are also involved in a bit of a mystery." Detective Timmerman stepped behind Johnny and Mona to make it clear that his role in this facilitation was receding into the background.

Trevor looked hopefully at Johnny. "My mystery is to find out exactly what I've done that has caused me to be under arrest and in this cell, Mr. Denovo," Trevor blurted out. "I never embezzled funds from Mr. Winthrop or anyone at his farm. Yet here I sit, accused and without bail, waiting for a trial, and all this supposed evidence is against me."

Johnny paused and appraised the situation. Trevor's indignation was genuine, so his first question couldn't be too obvious. He had to approach this delicately. There was more than one mystery in front of him here, he realized.

"Yes, you seem to be in a bit of a fix, if what I've read online is correct," Johnny said slowly, punching the word "online" a little to see if this created a reaction at all – contracted pupils, a dart in the gaze, a flinch of a finger. Sometimes, the slightest physical reaction could be the tip of a neurological iceberg.

Trevor reacted sincerely, with no signs of evasion or reaction to a key word that might activate his deeper mind. When he spoke, there was a note of disgust in his voice. "So, it's all over now is it? I suppose that I shouldn't be surprised, should I? We're in the information age solidly. Nothing is kept in the family anymore. But I tell you, I didn't do anything."

"Yet there's evidence that you did," Johnny responded calmly.

Trevor grew more agitated. "It's a frame-up is what it is! I've been framed, and that's all there is to it, but I don't know how to break the frame, you see?!" Trevor paused to look at his visitors. "I've been wracking my brains, trying to think of how I can prove I didn't do anything, but I don't know how to prove a negative. Don't physicists say you can't prove a negative?" he concluded imploringly.

Johnny thought he was seeing only an innocent man, a former soldier, and a well-read individual backed into a corner, and decided to proceed accordingly. Nothing was setting off his instincts for suspicion here. Trevor's use of language and metaphor was without taint, words like "solid" and "break" were not the kind that indicated a scheming mind. As if seeking contrast, his mind's eye returned to Winthrop's farm and the odd lunch they'd had there.

"Trevor, tell me about your relationship with Mr. Winthrop," Johnny asked directly.

Trevor gulped and looked down remorsefully. "That's hard for me to talk with you about," he said in a subdued voice. There was a long pause while Trevor gathered himself and set his jaw.

"Right," Trevor crisply stated, pulling his head up and pushing his chest out as if with artificial courage. "Let's talk about Mr.

Winthrop. See, I came over from jolly old England many years ago after being in the navy. I'd run into some US naval officers once ashore, and we'd gotten a little bit of a friendship going, seeing each other during our stints in various ports and on the seas. I worked the communication deck at times, too, you see. So, after I left the navy, I came over to visit some chums in Baltimore, and then decided I'd try to stay. I looked for work, and found some odd jobs, finally landing at the Winthrop place. I'd worked with horses for years as a boy, and even had some real jobs at stables in the UK and Ireland before joining the navy, so it came naturally to me."

Trevor paused, having drifted into a bit of reverie recounting history. He shook his head a little as if to clear it, then proceeded.

"Mr. Winthrop and I hit it off immediately, which was what made it all happen," Trevor said, his eyes clear and staring straight into Johnny's, obvious emotion beaming out. "We were friends and colleagues, and worked to make the farm better. I became an American citizen during all this, too. And the farm was really growing. Winthrop was becoming known as a great breeder and caretaker. His place is thriving. Up until the police came, I never spoke a harsh word with Mr. Winthrop, nor he with me. We were friends and colleagues, like I said."

Johnny felt the sincerity from Trevor again, and believed the story to be true both factually and humanistically. He was confused by this, having expected to meet in Trevor a disgruntled, paranoid embezzler. He thought he'd find someone who knew a good deal about electronics and computers. But instead, he had an honest ex-naval officer from England who migrated to the United States, found work, succeeded, and had a trusted employer.

"Thank you, Trevor," Johnny nearly whispered, his mind racing. "I'd like to ask you a couple more questions, if I could."

"Anything you'd like, Mr. Denovo," Trevor replied.

"Your computer. Where did you keep it in your quarters?" Johnny asked.

Trevor looked from Johnny to Mona to Detective Timmerman. "Computer? I don't have a computer. What are you talking about? Who said I did?"

Johnny was unflustered on the outside, but surprised by this answer. "Oh, I just assumed you had one, being so far from England and given the day and age. I guess I was wrong."

Trevor shrugged. "I don't know computers, Mr. Denovo. I've never had time to learn them. I'd like to, but I knew radio and ships and sailing, then spent years with horses and the farm, you see. Computers sort of skipped over me, or I skipped over them, however you look at it."

Johnny smiled at this. "Well, no problem. I shouldn't have assumed anything. Now, one other question. Mr. Winthrop owns an expensive collection of Faberge eggs. Do you know anything about them?"

"Mr. Winthrop owns a few collections of expensive things, Mr. Denovo. The Faberge eggs he got a few years ago after selling some sculpture he'd gotten on a trip when he worked for the government. I only saw the eggs once, and then they went into safe keeping, I don't know quite where. But he has some fine art, a few pieces of sculpture still, and some antiques. Like I said, the farm was doing well. He could afford some indulgences."

Mona squeezed Johnny's bicep, indicating it was time to go. Detective Timmerman jerked his head toward the door. Their time was up.

"Trevor, thank you for talking with me," Johnny said. "Detective Timmerman did me a great favor in letting me speak with you. Please keep this our secret. I will see what I can do to figure out what has happened."

Trevor brightened perceptibly. "Thank you, Mr. Denovo. If anyone can figure out this injustice, it'd be you, sir! You give me hope!"

Johnny smiled softly, shook Trevor's hand once more, and left, trailing behind Mona and Detective Timmerman, lost in thought, his requirement for a pattern demanding that he reestablish a way of thinking about this case that made sense. The encounter with Trevor had given him a completely different perspective on the motivations and predilections of those involved. He felt adrift.

Chapter II
To the Market

When Detective Timmerman, Mona, and Johnny arrived back at Timmerman's desk, a red light was flashing on the phone. Detective Timmerman dialed in to retrieve the message. With the phone pressed to his ear, he translated out the contents of the voicemail.

"It's Ted," Detective Timmerman said, covering the mouthpiece out of habit even though nobody was listening on the other end. "He did get a computer from the Winthrop place just the other day. Winthrop himself dropped it off, said it was his, and that the hard drive had gone bad. Wanted it swapped out for a new, bigger one. Nothing unusual. Ted said he'll get to it some time in August, that there was no hurry since Winthrop said he'd be traveling."

Detective Timmerman listened for a moment more, and then pressed a button, deleting the message, and hung up the phone.

"Odd thing, though. Ted said Winthrop wanted to pick up the old hard drive before he left. Something about recycling it properly so the data didn't fall into the wrong hands. Ted thought that was strange."

Johnny felt his mind's eye shift back to focus on Winthrop. It was like an insinuation at first, and then the feeling firmed and coalesced in his mind. An image of a cross-section of the center of the Earth came to mind, with a volcano protruding from the smooth sphere like a pimple, and a lava tube going down to the Earth's core. There was a center, and the volcano was just one outlet. The magma at the center could find other paths, explode through the crust at other points. Trevor. The computer. The accomplice tailing them. All volcanoes.

Johnny pondered the metaphor. It was clear that his mind was synthesizing the information into meaning he should attend to. There was a center to the patterns he was observing. He couldn't see all the patterns emanating from the center quite yet, but he was sensing a center, and that center was Winthrop – he was like a caldera fueling these volcanoes and he could provide energy to many more. Johnny had traced his way to Winthrop after detecting some outlying pattern days ago; it was here he had traveled, a telling fact. Activities and people flowed from this center, forcing Johnny to linger, assess, and analyze to see how another pattern might emanate from the hub. Winthrop was the center, Johnny felt certain. The volcanoes metaphor summarized it well enough.

"Well, Aaron, thank you for all of your help this afternoon," Johnny said suddenly, ignoring Mona's choke of protest and surprise. "We'd better be getting around to finding a place to stay tonight, and then we'll be on our way tomorrow. I wish there was something I could do to help Trevor in there, but he seems to be in denial. I'm not a psychologist."

Detective Timmerman stood stock still for a moment, surprised at Johnny's unexpected departure speech, but he quickly recovered. "Oh, all right, yes, it was good to meet you, Johnny. You're a busy man, and I'm glad to have made your acquaintance. If you ever need anything, just let me know."

"Definitely, Aaron, definitely. Ms. Landau, shall we?" Johnny said, offering his arm formalistically to Mona. She rolled her eyes and pushed him forward by the crook of his elbow.

"Thank you, Detective," she said charmingly, looking lovely in the afternoon sun and fluorescent lights. "My boss is a bit of an eccentric, so please excuse our sudden change of plans." She gave Detective Timmerman a soft handshake, and followed Johnny out of the police station.

Once they were in the car, Mona lit into Johnny. "Not a psychologist?! In denial?! What kind of crap was that, Denovo?!" Mona snarled at him, fastening her seatbelt by yanking it hard across her body, jamming the buckle into the latch.

"In a minute," Johnny replied gently through a ventriloquist's lips, starting the car and backing out. "I'll explain once we're out of Timmerman's sight." Suddenly, Mona remembered that Timmerman's office overlooked the parking lot. She looked abashed at her outburst. She sat still and said no more.

They proceeded down the road about a mile, and then Johnny cleared his throat.

"OK, Mona, here's the plan, then I'll explain why," Johnny started.

"Hoo boy, no, you explain first, then I'll help you plan," came the retort from his bewildered passenger. "I'm not going to be condescended to like that. No siree, Bob."

Johnny smiled secretly at Mona's sudden bout of down home spunk. He wasn't sure where it came from, but it beat the cold, businesswoman demeanor she assumed much of the time in the city. Maybe the Virginia landscape was eliciting a deep inner personality in her. He noted that while Mona may have an overdeveloped cerebral presence, beneath it her true self was much more down to Earth and fun-loving than he'd imagined. He was impressed and reassured they had this set of traits in common.

"All right, I'll try to do both, and you should certainly feel welcome to help me out," Johnny replied. "First, Trevor is innocent and is being framed. It was abundantly clear after talking with him, don't you think?"

Mona nodded enthusiastically. "I'd bet my bank account on it," she replied.

"Well, that would be a tempting wager," Johnny joked in response. "Let's say he's innocent. I can't do anything about that just yet, so I had to appear to be uninvolved and uncaring about it, or word would get around that Johnny Denovo had taken an interest in the case, and that would change things, make some things an uphill battle, and we don't need that." Johnny felt good using the word "we" suddenly.

Mona nodded again, relieved. "I'm glad you explained what you were doing, and why you acted that way. I was ready to beat some sense into you. That guy is completely sincere and innocent."

"I agree," Johnny said curtly, then decided he should elaborate. "The computer is my next line of attack. Winthrop panicked when there were police around. He's made a mistake sending his computer out. He's identified what he wants to protect, where his secrets reside. So, we're going to a computer store after we go to an ATM, and we're buying a cheap hard drive with cash. Well, you are. I can't be seen doing it."

Mona looked perplexed, and then clicked her tongue to signal she understood. "Oh my, we're going to have a busy night, aren't we, Mr. Denovo?" she said in a playful voice.

"Yes, Ms. Landau, we are going to have a very busy night," Johnny replied.

Johnny took out plenty of money from the ATM. He wanted to be able to pay for another night at a hotel, their meals, and the hard drive, and still have plenty left over. Cash was a good way to conceal tracks in this age of swipe-strip convenience. Slashing a card through a transaction slot was quick and marketed as the way to pay, but it created an electronic trail that could be fairly damning and dangerous.

Once he had the cash, he dropped Mona off at a big box electronics store. The heat of the day washed in through the open door, receding immediately as the door closed. Johnny parked the car well away under some trees, in the midst of what was likely the employee's cars. Here he waited, glancing in the rearview mirror to watch for her. When she emerged a few minutes later with a small box in a bag, her auburn hair glinting in the fading sunlight as the afternoon softened into evening, he noted that his heart leapt a little at the sight of her. The swinging shopping bag accentuated her silky walk as she approached the car, striding with grace across the parking lot. She was a lovely woman even in this mundane setting.

"All right, Mr. Denovo, stage one complete," she said as she settled back into the passenger seat, her voice a mock tone from a rocket launch sequence.

"Stage Two, Ms. Landau, is to lose our shadow," Johnny replied in the same tone, putting the car into gear. In the hot summer of Virginia, he'd left the car running so he could keep the air conditioning blowing. "You may not have noticed, but he's still with us. He stayed out here with me."

"What's the plan?" Mona asked, resisting the temptation to turn and look over her shoulder.

"First, we have to check out of our quote-unquote hotel," Johnny said. "He's seen that, and we need to erase our bread crumb trail in case the second part of my plan doesn't work, or he has accomplices."

They returned to the hotel and checked out. Mona made sure they paid only a small cancellation fee since they'd merely deposited their bags in the rooms and changed clothes. Then they returned to their car and got back on the road.

"How do we lose this guy?" Mona asked as they left the hotel's parking lot.

"Easy," Johnny said. "We get him arrested."

Mona laughed. "You can do that here, in a town you don't know, and where you have no connections?"

"Oh, Mona my dear," Johnny reassured her. "I have connections."

Johnny popped open his cell phone and called Tucker.

"Tuck, old man," he said when the phone was answered. "Care to help me out of a jam?"

"Sure, I guess," Tucker replied. He sounded distracted.

"What are you doing?" Johnny asked, intrigued by his friend's tone.

"Um, I do have a job, you know. Hacking and spying for that glorious federal assistance program we otherwise call a government," Tucker answered sardonically.

"Oh, right, I forgot," Johnny said in mock absentmindedness. "Hey, I just need an APB in the Richmond area for suspected drug smuggler. Think you could do that."

"Sure," Tucker responded, laughing. "Those are the best. They hold the person for two days, and take apart their car or bust into their house or probe their cavities. Which kind is this?"

"Car and cavities," Johnny replied, deadpan. He then proceeded to describe the vehicle, giving its license plate number and a verbal sketch of the driver. He also suggested Tucker add that the suspect was last seen in the vicinity of the electronics store they had just departed.

Johnny bade Tucker a fond farewell, and closed his phone. Mona was laughing.

"Remind me to stay on your good side," she chuckled. "That's too funny. How can he do that?"

"Jurisdiction," Johnny answered. "I don't know Tucker's full range of responsibilities, but he can somehow have jurisdiction just about anywhere he wants to. I've seen it a dozen times. Believe me, I'm going to stay on his good side, too!"

Johnny continued to drive down the main street of the suburb, straight and true. When the road threatened to become less densely populated, he made a U-turn and doubled back. He wanted the police to have every opportunity to catch their newly minted drug smuggler. He didn't have to wait much longer.

"Look," Johnny said to Mona, arching his eyebrows at the rearview mirror. "Tucker does it again."

Mona turned in her seat to witness a blue sedan being pulled over by a police cruiser.

"He won't be a problem anymore," Johnny noted. "Now, let's find another place to stay."

They settled on a chain motel just off the main drag of the suburb they found themselves in. This facility was even less inviting than the first. It had the same central hallway tempting them to call it a hotel but was clearly a motel all the way. Yet it had a few advantages, including an entrance that was only monitored by a security camera. They were careful to check in using Mona's information. This meant sharing a room, but it gave plausible deniability if anyone asserted that Johnny was there or anything went awry.

With only one change of clothes left each, they then went shopping for some casual clothes, settling mostly for exercise togs in anticipation of the evening ahead. They changed into their new outfits, Johnny donning a baseball cap he first stomped all over to give it that lived-in look, and ate a quick dinner at a fast-food establishment, squirming uncomfortably on plastic furniture. By the time they were done, the sun was setting, and they decided to spend the rest of the time driving around town.

"Should we check out Ted's a little?" Mona suggested as they settled in the car once more. Oddly, they hadn't really discussed the plans for the evening, operating rather on mutual understanding about both the intent and execution of their itinerary. It seemed imprudent to discuss it, as if keeping it quiet would protect the plan from reality. Carrying it gently without looking at it seemed the best approach, as if carrying a full bowl of steaming soup in both hands across a wide kitchen.

Johnny didn't respond to Mona's question. He'd looked up the location of Ted's while Mona had checked into the motel, and knew it was close by. It seemed that this little section of Richmond had a local gravity, with horse farms bounding its western edge like an ocean of grass. Suburban sprawl washed up on the shore of this pastured sea, creating a spit upon which the suburbanites beached. There wasn't a need to voyage far for what you needed, and Ted's computer shop was part of a little retail jetty.

They drove through the fading light, occasionally startled by a car without its headlights on or a shadow on the sidewalk. It was the time of the evening when humans are ill-adapted to see and sense. It was Johnny's favorite time. There was something about the transition from easy daylight to the struggle against darkness that he found philosophical, and he always thought he sensed behaviors changing as the light faded, as if criminality, identity, and possibility emerged as illumination dimmed.

In the flashing glow of passing headlights, Johnny shifted his attention to his peripheral vision occasionally, watching Mona's lovely profile in the warm twilight. She was staring at the world outside, apparently untroubled by Johnny's silence or their plans for the evening. Her hair looked raven black, the auburn subdued by the night. It made her even more ravishing than usual, Johnny thought. Perhaps his own sense of possibility, identity, and criminality was about to shift. He knew at least one of the three would drift into new territory tonight, or the evening would be lost. He wondered if others would follow.

They were approaching the intersection Johnny had in mind, and he eased the car over into the left lane. Traffic was thinning now. They turned down a small two-lane side street, quiet and nondescript. About halfway down on the right there was a small building set off from the rest by a parking lot and a small yard area. This was Ted's Computer Service, the sign advertised, and it was deserted. Bars on the windows and front doors attested to the level of security they could expect to encounter.

Johnny passed the store and drove farther down the street, until they found a grocery store with a large parking lot. He parked close to the entrance.

Mona turned to face him, putting her face closer to him than usual. "Now what, oh great detective? Do we walk right over to Ted's and throw a rock through the window?"

Johnny cleared his throat gravely. "I didn't realize crime brought out the best in you, Ms. Landau. If I'd known, I'd have started knocking over banks years ago, just to get your attention. No, my dear, we're going shopping."

The aisles in the grocery store were quiet, just a handful of shoppers trudging through their routines and somewhere the cry of a frustrated child. The few cashiers on duty were looking a little bored, and the stockers were slouching around with palettes of merchandise. It was a typical summer's evening in a suburban supermarket just off the beaten path.

"And what are we buying?" Mona inquired.

"Some CDs, some tape, glass cleaner, paper towels, and WD-40," Johnny replied. "And some gloves. And then a bunch of food to bury it in the midst of."

They took a cart from the cart stand and walked the aisles, enjoying the frivolity of buying odd, nostalgic, and indulgent food items while also getting the few things they needed for Ted's. Mona paid in cash at the register, a hefty sum given how many superfluous items they ended up purchasing. They had apparently hit all the high-margin items by buying mainly cookies, chips, candy, and soda.

Returning to the car with bags of groceries, they separated out the needed items from the rest. Placed in the trunk of the rental car, the number of bags looked obscene.

"What are we going to do with all that food?" Mona asked indignantly.

"Eat it," Johnny stated. "You'll have the munchies after doing something illegal. Believe me, that's something to know about criminals. They usually eat or drink a lot after a crime."

Mona looked at him through slotted lids. "How gullible do you think I am?"

"You should read the literature," Johnny responded seriously. "Crime gives you the munchies."

Mona abandoned the discussion with a groan, and went to get into the car.

Once they were buckled back into their seats, Mona finally asked, "OK, Johnny, so let me get this straight. We're going to somehow break into Ted's, find Winthrop's computer, swap out the hard drive, and leave, undetected."

Johnny nodded. "Yes, that's the plan. There's something going on here with computers as a main theme, and this particular computer is the variable that didn't fit into the stories we were told today. Now, I could discuss all this with our fine Detective Timmerman, I could ask our histrionic Mr. Winthrop, or I could operate per Denovo protocol and be a fly in the ointment while also solving the puzzle. Sound like fun?"

Mona laughed at the verbal assault she had unleashed with her simple question. "OK, OK, settle down. You'll get us busted for sure with all the nervous energy coursing through your veins!"

It was Johnny's turn to laugh. "You're right, that was pretty impassioned for me. Sorry. I'm finding myself intrigued by what's going on here. There's more than meets the eye. And, don't worry, I realize that I still have no client, but you have to agree, there is something worth investigating here."

"Yes, there's something going on here, but now that you mention it, I certainly hope that whatever it is has some financial upside for both of us. We both live hand to mouth, you know. At least these are rich people we're dealing with," she concluded.

"Agreed," Johnny said, turning off his car's headlights and coasting to a stop. They had parked along the street a few buildings down from Ted's. "Do you have the stuff?"

"Yes sir," Mona confirmed hoisting two bags, one holding the relevant items from the grocery store and the other containing the new hard drive.

"Let's wait until the street is quiet, then go for a walk," Johnny said.

They sat silently, observing their new locale. A car would turn onto the street occasionally. Johnny was trying to get a sense for the timing. He'd learned from experience on stake-outs that the traffic lights in the surrounding area lent a certain timing pattern to all local traffic flows, and he could guess a gap after a short period of observation. So he watched, and soon said, "OK, get ready." A car drove by, loud bass tones banging past as it went. "Now."

Both he and Mona exited the car, closing the doors quietly, Johnny locking the car with the remote. The turn signals flashed quickly, Johnny noting this annoying behavior as a liability he should avoid in the future. Light was to be avoided at all costs tonight. He forgave himself for the oversight. It was a rental car, after all.

The pair crossed the street and walked the short distance to the yard around Ted's shop, the nearby streetlight illuminating it clearly. No other people were out walking, and the street was abandoned, but Johnny knew they had at most a few more seconds. They quickly passed out of the streetlight's beam and stopped.

"Hold on a second," Johnny whispered. Positioned as they were, he wasn't concerned about being seen from the street. They were far enough away from the streetlight to have it work in their favor, creating contrast that would hide them as opaquely as a white wall. From this vantage point, he could assess the store close up.

He gazed at the corners of the building and was relieved to see no security cameras, at least on the three corners he could observe from his position. There was a dumpster near the back of the building, positioned fairly close to what he supposed had to be the back door.

"OK, let's go again," Johnny whispered. A car went by, but Johnny decided to ignore it. They were quickly behind the building and on the other side of the dumpster, facing the rusted metal back door of Ted's shop.

"Johnny, that was a police car that just went past," Mona whispered. "It just went by, slowly."

"You're kidding me," Johnny whispered. "This is not a time for jokes."

"No joke, it was a cop," Mona hissed a little urgently, her eyes darting over her shoulder to indicate where the car had gone.

Just then, the wail of a nearby siren punctured the night's silence.

Chapter 12

Free Range

"Just great," Johnny fumed. "All right, let's just cool it. Maybe it has nothing to do with us." Instinctively, he reached out for and held Mona's arm, which felt soft and warm in the cool night air.

They both held perfectly still, frozen in anticipation. The siren's tone was blaring. It was obviously nearby.

"What should we do?" Mona finally breathed.

"Well, we should proceed," Johnny replied, relaxing. "That's an ambulance siren. It's not the cop." And with that, Johnny released Mona's arm and dug into the grocery bag, pulling out the latex gloves, CDs, and WD-40. Mona sighed with relief.

The heavy metal door looked intimidating, like a relic hatch from a sunken battleship. It had been painted gray at one point in its existence and had a hefty deadbolt lock high up along with a standard doorknob lock. Johnny took out his cell phone and used the light from it to examine the seam between the door and its jam. Oddly, the deadbolt wasn't fastened. As he looked more closely, he noticed that the deadbolt lock was heavily rusted and likely non-functional. This was going to be easier than anticipated, Johnny thought.

The doorknob lock wasn't difficult to work free, using the WD-40 to lubricate it while forcing it with one of the CDs. Ted must have had bars on the window for show. The back door seemed to tell the whole story about the true level of security at his store. As the door snapped open, the ambulance's siren stopped. It was an unsettling coincidence.

Mona and Johnny slipped inside the small building to find themselves in a dimly lit room. It looked like a computer morgue, with stacks of hardware, devices, and peripherals from floor to ceiling, each with a tag on it carrying an alphanumeric combination in no discernible order. Johnny stopped and held Mona by the shoulders to indicate she should hold still. He needed to see if they had tripped a security system or were about to. There had been stickers in the front windows of the store indicating that the place was wired for security, but sometimes these were just a bluff. As he glanced around, he became convinced that like the heavy metal back door with the simple lock, the security stickers were all show.

A work table to the side supported the carcass of an open computer, its cover off and its cables exposed. Ted apparently worked at his own speed. There was a small corridor past a bathroom which led from the back room into the front of the store. Its doorway was covered with a heavy velvet curtain.

Once out of the rear of the establishment, they were in a much more orderly area, with some display cases, sales racks, and a cash register. Johnny concluded that Ted was like many small businessmen, putting on a front while struggling to make ends meet behind the scenes.

"What do we do now?" Mona whispered. Johnny ignored her, looking around instead for any signs of an alarm system in the store. There was still nothing. Judging from everything he had seen, Johnny felt confident concluding that Ted spent his money on something other than security for his store. Reassured, Johnny answered Mona in full voice.

"Now we find Winthrop's computer," he said.

Mona cleared her throat. "I know that, but how?"

"He probably has a log of work orders somewhere," Johnny said, casting his gaze around for just such a thing.

"But won't it be on a computer?" Mona asked. Johnny paused. Of course it would be, he suddenly realized, and probably a password-protected computer as well.

"Hadn't thought of that," Johnny muttered.

Mona's eyes widened. "Hadn't thought of that? What? Are you kidding me?"

"Well, I can't think of everything," Johnny said in his own defense. "Let's go back into the back room before we do anything else."

Behind the velvet curtain, Johnny felt better about using his cell phone. Having seen how his car's turn signals had illuminated the dark street, he was conscious of how bright a cell phone screen might look in a dark store. Seeing a floating light in darkness would grab someone's attention. He didn't want to get busted by a passerby's innocent observation.

He scrolled through his directory and selected a number to call.

The phone on the other end rang. It was answered quickly. "You again! What do you need this time, Denovo?" Tucker asked.

"Tucker, I have a question for you. What if I needed to get into a computer but didn't have the password?"

"Oh, I don't know Johnny, let me think. Hmmm, maybe you could, I don't know, tell me a little more!" Tucker said testily.

Johnny winced. "Well, here's the deal. As you probably guessed, I'm investigating the same case that those emails touched upon. I'm doing the Lord's work at this very moment. And I need to get into a computer so that I can deliver the innocent from evil and prosecute the guilty. Is that good enough?"

Tucker laughed on the other end. "I meant, tell me more about the technical setup, but it's nice to hear that you haven't fallen from the roster of angels yet."

Johnny blushed. "Oh, right." He lifted a finger to Mona to indicate she should stay put, and poked his head outside the curtain, holding the cell phone behind the curtain with a straightarm gesture.

Pulling his head back inside, he said, "Looks like a standard PC with a high speed connection."

"Good," Tucker said. "Can you turn it on?"

"Yeah," Johnny replied. "Give me a minute." He set his cell phone on the floor.

Johnny went out front and turned the computer on. The monitor flashed to life, illuminating the store and causing Johnny to have a minor cardiac event in response. He quickly shut off the brightening screen, plunging the store into darkness again. He stood stock still, gazing around, frozen in place, fearing the worst. Nobody was to be seen and all was quiet. After a few loud heartbeats he relaxed. But he was left with the problem of not being able to see the computer's display. He ducked back behind the curtain and picked up his cell phone. This was not going well.

"OK, Tucker, here's the deal," Johnny explained. "I'm in a place where darkness is a blessing, where the walls are transparent, and the monitor is bright as the sun. What should I do?"

"Are you telling me you can't use the monitor?" Tucker asked.

"That's what I'm telling you."

Tucker was silent for a moment. "We should be OK," he finally said. "You just have to be a great typist. I need you to ping the IP address here in a certain way from that computer, and then I can get into it and gain remote access. Should be pretty simple if you don't make any typos."

"OK, I'll be careful," Johnny pledged. "Will this leave a trace?"

Tucker chuckled. "Only if you forget to turn the monitor back on when you leave."

Johnny handed the cell phone to Mona. "You have to tell me what Tucker says. I can't take this lighted phone out front or someone might notice."

Mona took the phone. "Hi Tucker," she purred in her sexiest voice. Johnny could hear Tucker clear his throat uncomfortably and mumble a hello to Mona.

Tucker recovered his composure quickly, then via proxy led Johnny through a few commands at the keyboard. Once done, Johnny went back behind the velvet hanging and took the phone from Mona.

"Did it work?" he asked.

"Just a moment, your highness," Tucker replied in a distracted tone. "Much typing now happening. Can't talk." The sound of rapid keystrokes confirmed his statement.

There was a grunt of triumph, and Tucker nearly shouted, "Done! OK, chief, what do you need?"

"There should be a work order for a Winthrop," Johnny said.

"Uh huh, let me see, yes, Winthrop, James, number 7843W, with a notation that reads, 'Hold until August 1. Owner coming for drives by July 21' Is that what you're looking for?" Tucker asked.

Johnny smiled. "Yes, that and then some. Thank you sir, you may now disconnect."

"Righto, sire. You and your lovely lady friend have a good evening. And don't forget to power down that computer!" Tucker said, hanging up the phone.

Johnny hung up. "7843W is what we're looking for," he said aloud to Mona. "I've got to go out front to put things back how they were. You start looking."

Johnny turned off the computer, but decided against turning the monitor back on. Its earlier flash of light had left him skittish. He didn't want it revealing him unexpectedly. Besides, if Ted was such a great computer repairman, he'd only spend 30 minutes diagnosing the power being off as the reason his monitor was dark.

Johnny ducked back into the workroom and found Mona studiously looking for the Winthrop computer. He joined her. It took them both a couple of minutes to find the item in question, a standard computer case tucked into the midst of many other items. They carefully unstacked the surrounding hardware and removed the Winthrop machine, setting it on the floor.

"OK, let's open this bad boy up," Johnny said, reaching over to the table for a screwdriver. After removing a couple of screws, he opened the case.

"This is just not my evening," he muttered, staring inside the case. "Winthrop had two hard drives installed in this beast."

Mona peered around his shoulders. "You're not serious. What'll we do?"

"Drives!" Johnny spat. "Tucker even said 'drives' when he read the note to me. I've got to pay better attention. I've got to sharpen up!"

Mona stared at his outburst, unsure of what to say.

"Well," Johnny deliberated, calming down, "it may be all right. Tucker said the work order had a note that the drives won't be picked up until July 21st. That's a couple of weeks from now. Judging from Ted's back room, he's both busy and a procrastinator. I would say we have until then before the problem is discovered, and by then attributing it to us will not be a natural thought. Actually, I think we're OK here." And he began pulling the hard drives out of the case.

Mona shrugged. "If you say so. We're already guilty of breaking and entering, hacking a private computer, and now theft. I guess I should just accept the kind of woman you've made me – tainted, wayward, and devious." She smiled in a way that indicated to Johnny that she was anything but.

They replaced one of the hard drives with the new one purchased just hours before, sealed the case again, and replaced it in the equipment menagerie. After making it back safely to the car and from there to the motel, they were laughing with excess nervous energy.

"OK, it's time for some chips, cookies, and soda," Mona gasped as they pulled into the motel's parking space, referring to their groceries of indulgence. "I need to pig out for a while to get over this."

"I told you crime gives you the munchies," Johnny laughed, the tension being released slowly. "Let's go upstairs and fill our faces."

Chapter 13
Plant

Johnny awoke the next morning to the sound of Mona in the shower. The two double beds had proven useful. In the catharsis after the successful break-in, they had consumed so much sugar, salt, and soda that each needed a place to collapse for the night, bloated bellies, stomach aches, and headaches swamping any romantic tension that might have otherwise developed on a crime-filled Saturday night. For two cultured city folk with expensive haircuts, fancy cars, and sparkling reputations, they had in one evening become thieves, nutritional fugitives, and cultural outcasts.

Johnny gradually realized he had fallen asleep with his clothes still on. If the headache pulsing across his scalp had been caused by alcohol, at least he could have explained it to people with a sense of adult pride or camaraderie, but the night of childish debauchery they had enjoyed could not be shared in polite company without justified ridicule. It had to be another little secret from the night before.

The shower stopped, and Johnny rolled over with a groan, then stretched, a long, much-needed extension of sinew to start the day. Turning on the television, he instinctively flipped to the weather channel, the soothing and familiar adult contemporary music of the local forecast helping him wake up slowly and reducing the intensity of the headache a slight degree.

Mona emerged from the bathroom wrapped in two towels, one for her body and the other for her hair. Johnny found himself suddenly much more alert, the way any male animal would be in the presence of an attractive female. He began preening just a little, too, smoothing his hair and wiping his eyes.

"Good morning, Ms. Landau," he said, his mouth a bit heavy with remnant crud.

Mona smiled a million-dollar smile. She had brushed her teeth, he guessed. "Good morning to you," she smiled, and then began toweling her hair. "How are you feeling after imitating the Cookie Monster and downing a liter of soda?"

Johnny had forgotten those details, but his stomach was upset enough to help him recover the memory. It was a physical memory – chewing, laughing, daring, eating more – he didn't want to linger over.

"I'm going to get cleaned up so we can go," he replied in a very business-like tone. He was suddenly Johnny Denovo, detective, and he had evidence to assess.

The two junk-food-addled adults skipped breakfast, and returned to their normal behaviors, wearing nice clothing and looking well-groomed and respectable. They headed for the airport, two hard drives tucked into Mona's large purse. They made it through airport security without any questions, and were back in Boston just after noon.

At the airport, it was clear their adventure together was over.

"Well, Mona dear, I hope you enjoyed your first taste of detective work," Johnny said as they stood awkwardly at the junction of two hallways.

"Oh, I did very much. I think I'm a natural, don't you?" she smiled sweetly. "And, now, if there are any fees for this supposed case of yours, I get more than an agent's share, don't I? I get a straight 50-50 split as co-detective, risking life and limb for the cause?"

Johnny was not laughing at this. There was something in the tone that indicated she meant business. Mona was back to being a hammerhead shark of an agent, and he felt he'd been outsmarted.

"Fine, my friend, you win this one," he replied coldly. "It was nice traveling with you, and thank you for your help. I'm off to see Tucker to decode hard drives. I'll call you when I have some news."

And with that, the two detectives – one male and professional, the other female and amateur – walked down their separate halls, in opposite directions, their thoughts and feelings contained by their practiced, hardened shells.

Around a corner far down the hall, a shell cracked. Johnny walked angrily, fuming inside at the attitude Mona had exhibited, cold and calculating, before gathering himself and dismissing the emotions with a muttered cuss word. Then, his demeanor restored, he flipped open his cell phone and called Tucker.

"Mr. Denovo, did you have a good evening?" Tucker asked, picking up the phone and dispensing with formalities.

"Yes, Tucker, we had a nice time," Johnny replied.

"Care to tell me about it?" Tucker inquired mischievously.

"No, Tucker, what happened in that motel room is our little secret," Johnny drawled, wanting to drive his friend up the wall with curiosity, or to at least make him jump to the wrong conclusion.

Tucker laughed heartily, then said, "What do you need today?"

"I have two hard drives, Tucker. I need to know what's on them."

"Bring them by, and I'll take a look," Tucker said. Johnny found his car, and headed over to Tucker's to drop off the hard drives.

When Johnny arrived, Tucker was not indulging in an extended guitar solo with voice box, but instead was sitting in the middle of his computer studio, lotus-style, reading a magazine on the floor. It was impressive that even with his solid mass, he looked comfortable in this contorted position.

Tucker glanced up when Johnny entered.

"Hey Johnny, you know I don't lock my door, but you could have knocked," Tucker said irritably, then uncoiled from his lotus crouch with great agility. This was obviously a common stance.

"You should reconsider that practice, you know," Johnny cajoled. "I keep telling you that someday this will lead to something ugly."

Tucker patted his friend on the shoulder. "Not to worry. I have defenses here, hidden and secret, that provide me with great comfort." The bank of computers seemed to hum in anthropomorphic agreement.

"Fine, I won't bug you about it," Johnny conceded, noting the magazine Tucker was reading. It was a gardening magazine, yet there were no gardens worth tending in the vicinity.

Tucker caught the observation. "Yes, I'm reading a gardening magazine. Is that a problem for you? Discursive reading is my pleasure. You never know when something you've read will matter."

"Not a problem, Tucker," Johnny pleaded. "I was just a little surprised, expecting music, computers, or, judging by how you were sitting, yoga."

Tucker snorted. "Can I just have those hard drives?"

"Right," Johnny replied, reaching into the courier bag he had slung over his shoulder. "I didn't mark which one was in the top bay versus the bottom bay, but I guess that doesn't matter."

"Well, it does matter, but I can deal with it," Tucker said. "If it's a master-slave arrangement, I'll need to figure out which one gives the orders. But let me have a couple of days with these. They'll be safe, and I'll protect them from snoops, too. Nobody will know where they are. Any idea what I'm looking for?"

"Oh that," Johnny responded. "Something weird is going on here. So, you remember those emails?"

Tucker nodded.

"Well, the guy in Richmond I thought must be behind it, a gentleman named Trevor, was arrested for embezzling from his employer, the owner of these, James Winthrop," Johnny explained. "But I'm convinced Trevor is innocent, and Winthrop lied about the fact that Trevor owned a computer, and then tried to hide these drives by sending a computer out for service as soon as the police became involved. See if you find anything like those emails, I guess, or anything about Faberge eggs, France, or Trevor. Other than that, I haven't a clue."

Tucker had listened patiently, and remained silent, peering at Johnny.

"If you find anything juicy, let me know," Johnny continued. "It seems Winthrop wanted to hide the drives until July 21st for some reason, so maybe look for things referring to late July or August? Be brilliant. Maybe you'll find instructions for making a nice topiary?" Johnny laughed as he dodged a fake punch from Tucker in response to the wisecrack.

Johnny left feeling satisfied that the case, or whatever it was since he didn't have a client yet, was moving toward some sort of expansion or resolution. He couldn't figure out how the pieces fit yet – France, Faberge eggs, the emails, Winthrop, Trevor – but he felt it was at least now what his philosophy professor might have called a bounded reality. Cause and effect were more tightly related, even if he couldn't draw the lines between them yet.

When he returned home, he was starving, having skipped breakfast in Richmond and lunch getting over to Tucker's. He called up Wei Chou and ordered a nice late lunch of fried rice and egg rolls. It would keep him filled up for the rest of the day.

Johnny unlocked his computer and checked email. There was a lot of the normal stuff, more than usual since he'd been away for a couple of days. He handled it all while he waited for his lunch. He didn't expect to find another rhyming couplet email since today was not a prime number date, so he was surprised to have his filter signal that it had retrieved one message matching the criteria he had set up. It was another double-substitution scheme, and a rhyming couplet. Johnny started to decode it, when the doorbell to his condo rang. Lunch had arrived.

When he opened the door, there was nobody there, just an envelope on the pristine tile floor outside his door. He looked up and down the hallway, but there wasn't anyone in sight.

He heard the ding of the elevator arriving, and realized that whoever had delivered this was leaving. If this was someone from the outside, he should have been notified, or Wei Chou should have performed his handiwork. Johnny dashed out of his condo and around the corner, only to see a grungy courier standing there waiting for the doors to open, the down arrow lit red above his head. The courier gave Johnny a puzzled look.

"Who sent this?" Johnny asked, waving the envelope at the courer.

"I don't know," the courier responded, looking annoyed, his youth and skeletal build underscoring the attitude. "Dude, I get paid double because it's a Sunday, and I don't ask questions. Why don't you open it and find out?" With that, he stepped into the elevator and was gone.

Johnny strode slowly back to his condominium's entrance, opening the sturdy envelope as he walked. The cardboard was difficult to unglue, and there seemed to be nothing inside it. He reached inside and retrieved a simple fax page, with a typewritten note on it.

"Give me my hard drives back," was all it said. There was no signature.

Chapter 14
Scrambled

Johnny was stunned. Nobody had seen them at Ted's the night before. Yet here he was, just over 12 hours out from the events, and an unnamed person, most probably Winthrop, correctly identified him as the perpetrator who had purloined the two hard drives.

His doorbell rang again. This time it was the young woman from Wei Chou's delivering his lunch. It smelled great and he was starving, but he was too preoccupied to have a hunger response.

"Where is Wei Chou?" he demanded.

The girl looked stunned.

"H-h-he's downstairs at the restaurant," she stammered.

"How did that courier get by him?" Johnny demanded.

The girl looked confused and frightened. "I . . . I don't know!" she said in a burst. "You have to ask him." Despite appearing intimidated and scared, she stood her ground.

Johnny's demeanor changed in a flash.

"I'm sorry," he uttered. "It's not your problem. Tell Wei that I need to talk with him when he has a moment."

The delivery girl nodded vigorously.

Johnny smiled. "Thank you." And with that, she left slowly, Johnny attempting to create a bubble of calm around himself to reestablish the crush he'd just damaged.

As soon as she was out of sight, he thought only one thing – he had to call Tucker.

He dialed the phone frantically, and Tucker picked up quickly.

"I told you, Denovo, I needed some time," Tucker said smartly. Johnny was glad to hear his voice and get some attitude. The fax note had spooked him, making him feel like Winthrop's reach might be long indeed.

"Tucker, those hard drives might have some sort of tracking device on them," Johnny gasped. "A courier just delivered an unsigned fax from someone telling me they want their hard drives back. It has to be from Winthrop."

"Oh, that's a good one," Tucker said. "Well, chances are he couldn't track them all the way up here, but let me check." He set the phone down, and there was a pause, with some sounds of devices being turned on and off and some banging. "Yep, little RFID trackers attached inside the cases, limited range, and currently inactive. Probably local tracking only, unless the satellite was repositioned and they were activated in just the right way."

Johnny swallowed. "Have you done anything that might have activated them?" he asked carefully, dreading the answer.

"Well, I just did," Tucker answered, and Johnny's heart sank. "But don't worry, my place is like a bunker. They couldn't transmit out of here. The only reason my phone works is that it's a land line. An unpermitted cell phone can't even receive calls here. You're one of the few who has privileges, you know."

Johnny felt relief surge through him. "So Winthrop knows I have them, but probably hasn't been able to track them in Boston. I was worried about you for a moment."

"Shouldn't be an issue, they were inactive," Tucker reassured his friend. "But he did follow them to the airport, and he guessed correctly they're in Boston," Tucker elaborated. "Here's what we do. I'll make a copy of each drive, bring down the data, and then we send them back. He seems to want to play a gentleman's game, so let's play it his way. I'll have the data, but I doubt he knows about me. I'm pretty invisible in this world we inhabit. I work at it. But I'll add a little tracker of my own to each drive that will record the files he opens. If there's ever a need for evidence, we can access that should the day come."

Johnny liked this idea, but still felt a little paranoid. "He won't be able to detect it?" he worried.

"It will look at worst like a corrupt data file, and if he tries to probe it too hard, it will unleash a virus that will keep him busy for a few days," Tucker said almost giddily. He obviously loved his work and was good at it.

"When can they be ready?" Johnny asked.

"If that's all I'm doing, I can be done in about two hours. I have some other stuff to finish up first for my real job. You could have them in the express down to Richmond before closing time. The place down the road stays open late since it's closest to the airport," Tucker noted.

"Great, let's do that. I'll be over before four," Johnny replied, and the call was over. Hungrily, Johnny turned to his food, his appetite restored by his friend's competent and diabolical nature.

The phone rang before he could tuck in to his meal.

"Johnny," a worried voice greeted him. "It's Wei. My delivery girl said you are angry with me. What happened?"

"You tell me," Johnny said. "A courier dropped an envelope at my door, and didn't buzz up first."

Wei groaned. "Damn," he said. "He had a few things to drop off, so I let him buzz the first person on the list, Mrs. Childers. I didn't know he had something for you, too."

Mrs. Childers ran a collectibles e-commerce enterprise out of her condo and was always getting or sending packages via courier and otherwise.

"No problem, Wei," Johnny reassured his friend. "I have a hot case now, so please be on high alert, OK?"

"You got it, Johnny," Wei responded, relieved to be forgiven. "It won't happen again."

Johnny spent the next couple of hours unpacking and doing the few chores he still maintained. His cleaning service would be over to do the laundry, and they'd already changed the bedding, but he still liked to empty the garbages. It fit the detective motif somehow.

He also spent some time pondering what he might be up against. Apparently, Winthrop was more than he appeared. Johnny reviewed his biography in his mind, and recalled Winthrop's time as a government employee, and then his move to the private sector in the defense industry. Perhaps there was more to that than was publicly available. Winthrop certainly had technology that went beyond the norms, and knew how to both lie convincingly and intimidate effectively. The image of Winthrop as a genteel horse farm owner and cultivated Virginia gentleman had lasted a very short time indeed. Now, in Johnny's mind, Winthrop seemed a powerful, manipulative, self-interested thug, capable of sending an innocent man to jail, if not more.

Suddenly, his thoughts turned to Mona. If Winthrop had figured out that Johnny had absconded with his hard drives, Mona was also vulnerable. He quickly dialed her cell phone. She answered sleepily.

"Mona, how are you?" Johnny asked.

"I'm napping is how I am. Or I was," she said, her voice groggy and languid. "What do you want?"

"Nothing," Johnny said in an apologetic tone. "Just call me if anything unusual happens."

There was a loud sound of throat clearing on the other end. "You know, that's not going to lull me back to sleep. Tell me what's going on?"

Johnny explained about the couriered fax, the tracking beacons, and the plan to return the drives. Mona listened intently, an occasional exclamation interjected in a low voice.

When Johnny was finished, Mona summed it all up. "Winthrop is the mastermind."

"My thoughts exactly," Johnny agreed. "But mastermind of what?"

"The only crime thus far has been framing someone for embezzlement, and we don't even know if Winthrop framed him, if someone else framed him, or if Trevor has us fooled," Mona stated. "And, worst of all, we still don't have a client!"

"Yes, that's all true. Well, be on your guard. I have a case to solve, and one that's gotten a little bit personal," Johnny said. "Think about things while I deal with the hard drives. Why don't we meet for a drink at Maurice's around 7 tonight, and we can compare notes?"

Mona agreed. Johnny completed his few chores and drove over to Tucker's to get the hard drives. The day was dank and hot, no discernible breeze coming off the harbor. Johnny kept the top up on his car. The air conditioning blasted, as did his car's stereo. He wanted to shut down his mind for a few minutes.

Once he arrived at Tucker's, he walked in after knocking. Tucker was putting the drives into a large padded envelope.

"There you are. The beacons have been deactivated, so Winthrop can't ping them, even in Richmond. I have all the data files, and there are some doozies to unravel. Now that I see the data, the fact that he has homing beacons on his hard drives doesn't surprise me in the least." A tone of respect had entered Tucker's voice as he talked. Johnny felt his concern about Winthrop grow.

"What do you mean?" Johnny asked.

"Sophisticated encryption, big files, complicated data underneath. This stuff emanated out of a major technical infrastructure, not some mom and pop computer shop," Tucker elaborated. "I'm eager to see what's inside."

Johnny nodded solemnly. "This gets deeper and deeper," Johnny mused. "I'll send the drives for early morning delivery, and to be signed for, so we can get this one behind us as quickly as possible."

"Roger that, boss," Tucker said, and Johnny went on his way to the express mail offices.

When Johnny showed up at Maurice's, the day was draining of color as clouds rolled in from the west, obscuring the ruby sunset. It gave the buildings a strange wintertime look, low contrast and washed out. If the evening hadn't been so warm, Johnny would have shivered. A low rumble of thunder sounded in the distance as he opened the front door.

Mona was seated at the bar, looking surprisingly sullen, slowly stirring her drink with a red swizzle stick. She barely glanced up in recognition as he approached.

"You'll have to up the wattage on your smile, doll," Johnny growled in poor homage to a dimestore detective.

Mona remained somber. She looked up, tossing her hair slightly and setting the swizzle stick down on the napkin.

"Johnny, this is serious," she said mournfully. "Tracking beacons, threats by courier, breaking and entering. I'm not sure I can go farther with this."

There was a touching vulnerability in Mona's admission, a glimpse of the girl beneath the tough veneer defining the woman, the hard shell of the business agent. A new type of beauty emanated from her features, the gentle grace of innocence and simplicity. It made it all the easier for Johnny to assume the strong role in this pivotal moment.

"Ms. Landau, this is your first case," he briskly stated, taking the seat next to her. "It's natural to feel uncertain, to make more of events than is warranted, to attribute danger to mere intimidation. But trust the worldly Mr. Denovo, who has faced perils untold in the pursuit of truth and justice and vengeance, all while maintaining an air of detachment and *joie de vivre* that would make even the most cold-blooded viper envious."

Ivan, today tending bar, stood nearby, smiling. He was accustomed to Johnny's breathless soliloquies, and knew to wait until the end before approaching. Johnny ordered a gin, tonic, and lemon while Mona sat silently, fretting over the corner of her napkin.

"Is this really nothing unusual for you?" Mona asked quietly.

Johnny laughed. "Has Winthrop freaked you out? He's nothing. He's probably just an ex-government official with some contacts in the spook brigade who thinks he can use those to commit some type of fraud or crime. He's most likely just a windbag who grew accustomed to bullying people over the years from his perch, and now mistakes wealth for power. I run into these types all the time in my line of work. In fact, it's what my line of work is all about. If I don't have my life threatened on a case at least a few times, it means I'm on the wrong scent. To me, a death threat is like someone in the kids' game saying, 'warmer.'"

Mona's posture and body language improved noticeably throughout this monologue, and by the end of it, she was sitting erectly, her eyes making full contact with Johnny's. The vulnerability was gone, but the carapace of the business agent had not manifested itself. Johnny found himself face to face with a strong and beautiful woman. The air charged with electricity as their relationship pulsed with mutual understanding and commitment.

"All right, then," Mona said softly. "Count me in."

Johnny smiled, and touched her cheek in a reassuring manner. The moment may have continued to a deeper level of intimacy, but Johnny's cell phone rang. It was Tucker.

"Johnny, this is some deep doo-doo you've found here," Tucker said excitedly.

"What do you mean?" Johnny asked.

"Well, you get over here and I'll show you," Tucker finished, and the shortest conversation of the day was done. Johnny took Mona by the hand and they left to visit Tucker the Tongue-tied.

Chapter 15
Egghead

Tucker the Twisted was buried in stacks of computer disks and hardware when they arrived at his apartment. Mona had never been to Tucker's before, and had only seen a glimpse of him on an earlier case, so knew him mostly by name. She was entranced at the strange combination of technology, musicianship, comfort, and sloppiness that summed up the areas of his apartment he was currently occupying. It was an expensive and expansive apartment, and Tucker moved about it like a coyote shifting territories through the seasons, adapting and foraging from one zone to the next. This area was new to Johnny. Somehow all the musical affordances, equipment, gear, food, and overstuffed chairs made it seem like a combination of a bunker and a movie set.

Before Mona had gotten far within the apartment, a beeping noise started. Tucker jumped from his chair as if his feet were on fire, leaping over to his desk with a wild-eyed look.

"You brought her!" he shouted at Johnny. "You should have told me! Quick," he said, looking wildly at Mona, "I need a strand of your hair, and then I need you to breathe and speak into this," he said, jamming what looked like a hollow microphone into her hand. The beeping was louder now, and more insistent, picking up its pace moment by moment.

Mona reached up, plucked a hair from her head with a wince, and handed it to Tucker, who deftly wiped her neck with a small piece of white cloth and ran back to his desk with the hair and the little rag. Then, taking the microphone, she exhaled sharply into it, and then, momentarily confused, said, "What should I say into it?"

Tucker gave a shout. "That's enough! Perfect!" The beeping suddenly stopped as he shut the lid on a little box on his console, and Tucker settled back into his chair, sweat glistening on his brow.

Johnny was nonplussed. "I'd forgotten about that," he reminisced. "It's been a long time since I had to do that."

Mona looked bewildered. "I think I just got keys to the place?" she said uncertainly.

Tucker smiled beatifically. "She's a smart one, Denovo," he said generously. "That's about the best way to put it. My security system is triggered by all sorts of things – pheromones, voice, DNA, temperature, you name it. But in those few moments, I was able to get your DNA from your hair follicle because you really gave it a good yank, your voice, your breath, and your sweat and your pheromones, and it's all in my security database now. So, yes, you have the keys to the place. You don't want to know what would have happened if I'd been 10 seconds slower," Tucker concluded, a serious scowl on his face. He glanced at the ceiling and walls apprehensively, then let out a sigh.

"Remind me to ask you about it sometime when I'm totally bored," Johnny said languidly, and Tucker muttered something under his breath. "If I recall, the reason we're here is that we're waist-deep in manure or something like that."

"Precisely," Tucker replied. "This guy Winthrop, he's neck-deep or more, though. We're just downstream from him. I've only been able to get to some of the larger files on these drives, but those are enough. And, by the way, I think he's also your embezzler, but I can't verify it yet. Those are the smaller files, but there are some signs." Tucker paused to catch his breath. "Suffice to say, this guy is dirty."

"Is he tied to Lester, our friend in the UK?" Johnny asked.

Tucker blinked. "Good question. Not sure. I'll look into that, too. Making a mental note. But let me show you this," he said, spinning a large monitor around on the table so that Johnny and Mona could see it.

There were large schematics in CAD style, green net-like 3D renderings of things Johnny hadn't seen before, military-industrial prototypes it appeared.

"You see these?" Tucker asked. "These are top-secret plans for next-generation military equipment. These are, I emphasize, top-secret. Made to fight the new wars – local, drone-driven, targeted, anonymous. I only know about them because there are rumors of hearsay of speculation that they exist. These are so secret that the people working on them probably don't know what they're building all the time. They probably think they're making military toasters. These things are supposed to give the U.S. a lock on worldwide military and surveillance superiority for the next 50 years. If they're in circulation, it's very, very bad news."

Johnny and Tucker sat in silence while these last few words hung in the air. Mona watched them silently.

"But the interesting part is what's not here," Tucker muttered hoarsely.

"Would you care to elaborate?" Johnny prodded.

"What's not here are the insides," Tucker said, reaching over to a large stack of papers covered with numbers and symbols on closely spaced lines. "These are the exteriors only, proof that Winthrop has access to the most secret and advanced plans of our military hardware and armaments, but far short of enough for anyone else to do much with. In this day and age, hardware isn't the secret. Materials and software are the secrets."

Johnny lowered his head pensively and pursed his lips. He didn't know quite what to make of this, but knew that looking thoughtful would buy him time and force Tucker to continue explaining things to him until it was simplified enough for him to understand.

"Don't you see?" Tucker asked, shaking the papers as if they clearly demonstrated how obvious it all was. "Winthrop is showing some leg here – pardon the expression Ms. Landau – but that's all he's doing. There's a little twist to the story."

"You are being awfully melodramatic," Johnny observed dryly.

"Yes, well, I've been doing this pro bono, so let me have my fun," Tucker countered. "The twist is that the exteriors are being presented to you from only a fraction of the file. The rest of the file is locked down in a way I can't crack."

Tucker fanned the papers out so that Johnny and Mona could see that the dozens of pages were covered with the same dense alien language.

"I've pored over these for the last hour," Tucker admitted. "I've thrown everything at them, and had to resort to just printing them for pure brain work. Nada. I got nothing. There's no encryption key to it that I can figure out, no way I can unscramble it. If it's cryptography, it's like nothing I've ever seen before. But I would wager that the interior schematics, materials science, and software specifications are in that file space, inside that encrypted vault."

"So, Winthrop is dealing in stolen military plans," Johnny concluded.

"Apparently," Tucker agreed. "But not just any military plans, Johnny. World-changing plans. Big, big money, crucial national shit."

"Yes, I understand," Johnny replied impatiently. "Still, that's not too unusual, and not all that twisted compared to some of the sickos I've seen in the past," Johnny noted. "But now that we know it, we can't stop. A lot hangs in the balance. So, let's put together the scenario of where he is in his little plan. He needed these hard drives, so chances are that these held, until earlier today, the only copies of these plans. That means he hasn't distributed them yet. But why encrypt the most valuable part of them?"

Tucker rubbed his stomach for a moment, lost in thought.

Mona was the first to pipe up. "Maybe he can't unlock them," she speculated.

Tucker gazed up under his heavy brow and shook his head. "No, I don't think that's the situation. I tried all the military cryptographic and security protocols available, and nothing unlocked this. And the military locks entire files, not just portions. This is someone else's handiwork, and it's damn strange and effective. My bet is that he had these files open at some point, and was able to isolate the most valuable parts, encrypt those somehow, and have the best of both worlds – proof that he had the goods, but the power to hold on to the best part until payday." Tucker set the stack of pages down on his desk in a heavy pile.

"So, let's assume he hasn't distributed these to anyone yet," Johnny stated. "He needed his drives back, but not before late July or thereabouts. Whatever is going to happen, it is going to happen in late July."

"Sounds right," Tucker agreed.

"And he's going to France at the end of July to show his Faberge eggs," Johnny said.

"If you say so," Tucker replied.

Johnny shook his head violently, like a wet dog leaving a sprinkler. "It doesn't add up," he said, frustration coating his words. "There's a big gap here. We are missing something."

"Perhaps," Mona volunteered, "we should begin preparing our trip to France."

Chapter 16
Outfoxed

Johnny and Mona had to wait a few days before there was room on a flight to France. It was peak travel season, and flights were booked.

If their speculation about the timing of Winthrop's moves were correct, the delay was perfectly acceptable, and allowed Johnny's travel agent to find them hotels in Paris for a few days. In addition, his travel agent booked lodging in Montpellier for he and Mona covering what he assumed would be the critical span of time, when the Faberge eggs were due to be exhibited.

To while away the idle hours, Johnny found himself doodling, drawing little geometric pictures while puzzling over the aspects of the Case Without a Client. Invariably, his drawings emerged as circles with empty centers, confirming that indeed there was a central mystery yet to be solved, something linking together the disparate parts, a hub from which the spokes emanated. Winthrop may be the mastermind, but the play he was directing only had a protagonist, with gaps in the plot and an unclear motivation.

Tucker had left on a long trip, drawn away from further analysis of the hard drives by some pressing work that actually paid. Tucker's clientele had always been obscure and secretive, and Johnny thought they most certainly came from the military-industrial complex. Tucker had worked for some of the larger defense contractors over the years, creating weapons systems, encryption schemes, and large-scale software systems for surveillance. Now, as a freelancer, he was formidable and reliable, and often worked for the government as well. Johnny was amazed that he was able to get his services from time to time, and usually without compensation. Tucker had a true do-gooder streak in him. Since they'd been childhood pals, and had both ended up solving puzzles, Johnny counted himself as extremely fortunate to have Tucker as friend and ally.

The 11th of July came and went, but no rhyming couplets from Lester appeared in Johnny's email filters. It must have been an off-day. When Johnny noticed this lack of communication on a prime number date, he wasn't discouraged. The 13th was coming hard on its heels.

As he pondered the facts in his possession, he began to wonder if Tucker's absence from the analyst's chair was a major setback. After all, the amount of information gleaned from the hard drive data thus far was isolated to the largest files. He needed to know more about what else Winthrop might have stored on those drives.

And then it dawned on him – he could walk over and get the printouts Tucker had been analyzing the day before. Maybe with own his pattern-seeking skills he might be able to discover the key that had eluded his friend thus far. Tucker's apartment knew him, and would let him in. He could go retrieve the papers and look them over while he waited for the trip to Paris to begin.

Johnny parked his car on the street, and proceeded up in the elevator to Tucker's floor. It was a tall building, and Tucker lived near the top. Recent thunderstorms had cleared out the heat and smudge of summer. The day was bright and pleasant, a refreshing breeze coming off Boston harbor.

As he strode into the computer studio section of Tucker the Terror's apartment, he knew immediately that something was amiss. While the place wasn't in complete disarray, it was obvious that the computer area had been gone through roughly by someone, and Johnny doubted it was Tucker. The main monitor was sitting at an odd angle, and a few desktop machines had been overturned, apparently in the haste of disengaging cables. Johnny immediately began looking for the pile of printouts he was after. Most everything was still there in the apartment. The printouts must have looked like meaningless code or the result of a system error. It seemed the perpetrator had left without successfully plundering what he or she was after, and without resorting to extreme measures to get it.

Johnny reached for his cell phone, and called Tucker's number. It was answered after a few rings. Tucker's voice was groggy and halting.

"Hello," Tucker's low guttural tone was obviously struggling from slumber.

"Tucker, it's Johnny. Where are you?" Johnny inquired.

"A few time zones away. Why are you calling me?" Tucker responded, still sounding sleepy.

"I'm in your apartment, I hope you don't mind," Johnny said. "I came over thinking I might take a look at those printouts while you were away, see if I could crack the code."

Tucker sniffed hard and cleared his throat, rousing himself with this information. "You thought you'd do what?" he said, a little agitated.

"I thought I'd look over the code, nothing major, but that's not why I'm calling," Johnny said. "Someone else was here before me, and moved a lot of stuff around on your computer desk."

"What?!" Tucker said, obviously alarmed. "What the hell is going on in my apartment? Why didn't I get any notifications? And who do you think you are just strolling into my apartment like you own the place?"

Johnny rolled his eyes. "Look, you can crack my head open later for being a presumptuous jerk, but right now we've got a bigger problem. Someone has found a way to circumvent your security systems."

Tucker laughed. "Oh they have, have they?" he mused. "Hold on, let me link up, and we'll see just who thinks they walk on water. My system logs everything, and I can review it from here. No cameras necessary, you see, but given the weight of the person, pheromones, breath, voice, and a few other little tricks, I'll know what went on, I guarantee you." There was the sound of keys tapping on a keyboard from Tucker's side of the phone.

A few moments passed, and Tucker came back on, sounding puzzled. "This is odd," he muttered. "Johnny, what time is it there?"

"A little before noon," Johnny responded. "Why do you ask?"

"And you say nothing seems to be missing?" Tucker asked.

Johnny looked around. "Well, now that you ask, I can't be sure. I really don't know your stuff that well. All I can see is that the laptop you were using the other day to analyze the hard drive data is still here, and most of your usual stuff is here, too."

Tucker paused before he spoke. "Johnny, the laptop with the hard drive data on it is with me. There shouldn't be any other machine like it there. It's the only one I have like this," Tucker said quietly.

Johnny froze. They'd been compromised. He didn't know to what extent, or what it portended. Suddenly, the meaning of the disrupted computer area was clear. It wasn't that someone had been searching for something, it's that someone had been hastily installing something, yanking cables and clearing desk space. And that new thing being placed in Tucker's computer system was the sleek laptop that now sat directly in front of Johnny, lid closed but powered up.

Tucker spoke slowly and carefully into the phone. "OK, Johnny, here's the deal. From here, I can't see into my network anymore. That laptop has been set up to absorb some key external access routes. That's why I asked about the time. The system time on that laptop is wrong, which indicates to me that it is a single-function terminal, probably intended to block my access into my own systems. Whoever put it there knows that it would take an entire machine with some severely disrupted hardware and software to thwart me, and that it would have to block me from my arsenal at the same time. And I'm not about to assume that it's safe to disengage it. It probably has a booby trap of some sort. So, what you need to do is quietly leave the apartment. Now."

Tucker's voice was so calm that Johnny became reciprocally alarmed. His friend was usually the more excitable of the two, capable of high hilarity, great enthusiasm, and ribald antics. To hear him steadily and methodically describe a perilous situation and completely suppress his fun-loving nature was signal enough to Johnny that the circumstances were grave.

Johnny began to back out of the room slowly, leaving everything untouched, including the pile of code printouts, his eyes fixed upon the alien laptop nested like a hissing snake in the tangle of cables on Tucker's computer work area. Each footfall made him cringe, as thoughts about proximity sensors and other fantasies about what might be going on pulsed through his hyperstimulated brain. Yet, through it all, the practiced Denovo mystique asserted itself, giving him on the outside a preternatural calm and a catlike grace as he slowly backed out of the apartment, phone held cavalierly against his ear as if he were listening to innocuous hold music. Inside, he was fighting fear, but his cool exterior wasn't in any danger of betraying that fact.

Once outside of the apartment and with the door closed behind him, Johnny dared to talk with Tucker again.

"Tucker, I'm out," he said, breathing a little harder than usual. "Was I in any danger?"

Tucker's reply was direct and serious. "I don't know. I can't see into enough of my system to tell. My worry is that whoever has done this physical hack – a crude but effective approach – might have been able to take over my security protocols, and if they had, they could have used them against you. But, apparently, that's not the case."

Johnny breathed not quite a sigh, but took a deep breath, relaxing. Tucker heard this and continued in his cold, professional approach.

"Don't relax yet," he warned. "If they couldn't hijack my security arsenal, they could still have taken over the surveillance reporting system. If that's the case, they may know you were in my apartment. And that, my friend, could be all they need to know."

Chapter 17

Broken

Johnny paused, the silence of the hallway outside Tucker's apartment suddenly palpable. Johnny wasn't superstitious by nature, but he respected his senses, and especially their synthesis in that instinctual center that guided most human behavior. When every sense he had was signaling danger, even if it wasn't immediately apparent, he proceeded accordingly. He knew the subconscious was the place where survival skills congregated. Their voice was inarticulate but strong. His survivalist brain was telling him clearly that something was not right. Whether this was a subtle dissonance in the noise levels caused by someone lurking around a corner, a silence that didn't square with his earlier transit of the hallway, a shadow or glint he didn't consciously notice but that registered like a pebble dropping into his well of self-preservation, Johnny could not discern. He only knew that there was something wrong. His skin crawled with anticipation and dread.

"Tucker, I'm going to hang up now," Johnny said quietly. "I'll call you back when I get to my place."

"Right," Tucker said. "In the meantime, I'll be working. I'm not due back for a while, but this is intolerable. Be careful."

Johnny had every intention of being careful. Closing his cell phone, he slid it casually into his pants pocket, ran his fingers through his hair, and started walking down the long hall toward the elevators.

Tucker's apartment consumed the entire floor of the building, Johnny realized. There were no other tenants here. He was alone.

The sun was nearing its apogee as Johnny came to the window at the end of the hall. The light seemed to coalesce into an other-worldly glow in place of the window, no shadow giving definition to the frameless glass. These tricks of the light made the window opening appear empty, tempting him to jump out through the gently beckoning fenestration.

Then, as Johnny stood looking out at the remarkable illusion, the lovely Boston waters at play in the distance, muted behind the pale layer of nothingness lit so wonderfully, there was a dull pop. In an instant the glass became a spiderweb as it eggshelled by the force of a high-caliber bullet striking it at an oblique angle.

Surprised only by the sudden change in the complexion of the glass, and spared anything more by the nearly complete lack of sound from the percussion of the bullet, Johnny startled only slightly. The point of impact on the glass was high up, above his head, suggesting that the shooter had been aiming downward.

The shock of seeing air shattered into a mosaic of crystallized silicate passed, and Johnny simultaneously realized two things. First, he realized that Tucker must lead a very interesting life to have bullet-proof glass layered inside bullet-resistant glass surrounding his apartment. The filigreed glass was not the only layer of glass. The bullet had lodged in the inside pane. Second, he realized that the shooter would have more bullets. He quickly ducked out of sight, rounding the corner and moving toward the elevators.

Isolated in front of the elevator banks, Johnny thought quickly. The shooter would probably be expecting him to emerge from the bottom of the building, and soon. That gave Johnny two expectations to disappoint. Given that his life was at stake, he decided he should disappoint both of them. He pressed the up arrow on the elevators.

Tucker lived near the top floor of the building, but not at the top. There were three floors above. When the elevator arrived, it was empty. Johnny selected the middle of the three remaining upper floors, and pressed the button. The elevator doors closed.

It only took a moment for the elevator to traverse two floors. As expected, the hallway he emerged into was quiet and empty. It was midday on a weekday in a building full of over-achievers. He decided to wait a while in the little lobby outside the elevators, think things over, and then make his way back downstairs.

He leaned against the wall and considered what had transpired. His first admonition to himself was that he had been playing the game against Winthrop so casually. He'd had many warning signs that should have made him anticipate worst-case scenarios. Tucker had suggested that the tracking beacons on the drives had been short-range, unless satellites had been repositioned. Johnny had felt comfortable assuming that Winthrop had used the beacons to isolate Johnny's trip to the airport, and that Winthrop had just guessed correctly from there.

Damn, Johnny thought. Winthrop had done more repositioning of satellites to confirm his hunch and learn more, such as precisely where the drives were taken by Johnny before being taken to the express mailer. Winthrop must have used connections in military intelligence to overcome Tucker's security system and install a laptop to jam Tucker's access from the outside. Winthrop would receive the full Denovo treatment from now on. This was not a game of cat and mouse anymore. This was a battle to the end.

Judging from the sound of the wind escaping the elevator shafts, the elevators were in use, and the building was still functioning normally. There was a muted ding from just below. Johnny tensed slightly.

There were two puzzles about Tucker's apartment invasion Johnny couldn't figure out. Whoever had done it must have been known to Tucker, or the security system would have had a holiday with them. And whoever had done it must have either known what kind of laptop to substitute, or must have had a standard-issue spook laptop to insert into Tucker's systems. Either way, it portended more trouble ahead.

Another ding sounded from below, a little louder than the previous one. Johnny shot a glance at the elevators.

Whatever the answer, underestimating Winthrop was something he would not do after today. He had allowed the lack of a client to influence his attitude, slow his reactions, lower his guard. It was his fault, and he accepted that.

There was only silence now. The elevators were not dinging or moving, and the floor he was on was still as the grave. Again, Johnny's limbic system tingled, apprehensive about something ill-defined in his conscious mind but definitely important to his survival. Using his instincts as a guide, he moved to stand near the door leading to the emergency stairwell. He stood against the wall and waited.

Moments passed, then suddenly there was a click, and the stairwell door began to open tentatively and slowly. Johnny's eyebrows rose and he tightened his muscles, but his affect remained calm, as if he had merely straightened up out of civility for the arrival of a guest. From this angle, he could not see into the stairwell. At the same time, he could not be seen, and felt that the person entering would be revealed sooner to him than the other way around, giving him a tissue-thin advantage.

The door opened more confidently, and a lovely young brunette strode out carrying a paperboard artist's portfolio. She was wearing long pants and her hair was pulled back severely. A brown smudge was apparent on her left cheek, and the opening of the portfolio was on the inside, nearest her leg.

The portfolio, the smudge, and how the opening of the portfolio was oriented gave Johnny's instinctual brain all it needed. He immediately bent his fingers at the first knuckle and punched the young woman hard in the throat.

She attempted to avoid the blow at the last microsecond, but due to the oblique angle Johnny had assumed relative to the doorway, she hadn't seen him until it was too late. She crumpled to the floor, the large portfolio hitting the ground with a clatter. A small sharp-shooter's rifle with a silencer and scope slid out of the portfolio and onto the floor.

Johnny knelt down. She was still breathing, he observed with relief. Experience had taught him that punching someone in the throat could have a different outcome. Broken windpipes were hard to fix. He quickly patted her down. There were no other weapons on her or in the portfolio, and she was carrying no identification. She had a cell phone, the type that operated as a walkie-talkie or radio as well. He put the cell phone on a table near the elevators, then removed the silencer from the rifle and put it in his pocket. He put the gun in the small trash can near the main hallway, a safe enough place for now, he reasoned. Then he leaned against the wall again and waited.

The young woman stirred after a few moments. She appeared to be of Greek extraction, fair complected and with the extra sheen of beauty Greek woman possess. The left knee of her pants was slightly dirty, something he should have observed when she'd come out of the stairwell, he chided himself. The discharge mark on her cheek revealed that she was prone to clutching her weapon very tightly. She was probably an excellent shot, and he felt grateful for Tucker's bul-letproof glass.

Coughing slightly, the assassin sat up, twisting her torso on the floor and rearranging her arms and legs into more natural positions. Propping herself on her elbows, the woman glared at Johnny. "That hurt," she said bluntly, and a little hoarsely.

"Yes, I'd apologize, but you were trying to kill me," he retorted sharply, nearly spitting the words at her.

The woman coughed more, and then peered more intently at Johnny's face.

"You're Johnny Denovo," the assassin said in genuine surprise.

"And you just took a shot at me," he said, peering closely into her eyes. They didn't look like the cold eyes of a paid assassin any more.

"I was told to wait for a signal, and then take out whoever walked out of that apartment," she replied. "If I'd known it was you, I wouldn't have accepted the job."

"Don't jerk me around," Johnny spat back at her. "You're a pro."

"No," she protested. "You've got to believe me. My family owes you. You saved my brother a few years ago in that case involving the bicycle mechanic and the Proust scholar. My brother was the cyclist they accused at first. You got him released. He was innocent."

Johnny laughed coarsely, remembering that case well. "I still think you're putting me on. You mean to tell me that someone who kills for a living, kills for money, has scruples about which targets she will and won't accept?"

Just then, the radio phone crackled, and a male voice spoke, "All clear on the top floor."

Johnny and the woman sat stock still, looking at the radio.

"Damn it," she spat, then looked at Johnny. "We're checking off alternating floors. He's moving fast."

"Who is he?" Johnny asked. Before she could answer, the radio crackled to life again.

"Angela?" the voice inquired.

"If I don't answer, he'll know something is wrong," the woman now identified as Angela said.

Johnny was already thinking the same thing, and had his hand on the radio phone before she finished her statement. He handed it to her.

"Watch what you say," he said.

Angela gave him a withering look, then held the radio up to her mouth.

"Nothing to see here," she said. "I'm on twelve. Sweep your last floor, then meet me in the lobby. He must have gotten away."

"I'm coming to twelve right now," the male voice answered. "I'll meet you there."

Before any reaction could be mounted, the stairwell door swung open and a powerfully built middle-aged man emerged, wearing a loose t-shirt and jeans. He glanced at Johnny and Angela, his radio clasped in his hand. A look of shock crossed his face, but vanished in an instant, replaced by the poise of a journeyman thug.

Johnny reacted simultaneously. He leaped across Angela's supine form, and ploughed into her accomplice with all his might. The blow jarred the radio from his adversary's right hand, Johnny's momentum propelling the man against the wall, pinning the man's left hand against the wall behind his back. He had been reaching for something.

A sharp blow struck Johnny's knee, and his leg buckled for a moment, allowing his opponent enough room to renew his efforts to reach behind his back. Johnny recovered and drove his shoulder into the other man's neck and jaw. Something clattered to the floor.

In the instant when both men's attention shifted to the sound of the fallen object, Johnny released his opponent's hand and drove the heal of his own hand into the other man's jaw with a dull crack, snapping his jaw back, forcing his head into the wall. His adversary grunted and seemed stunned for a moment.

Johnny saw a small automatic revolver on the floor. It was within range. He kicked it away, struggling to regain his balance at the same time.

His opponent recovered quickly and threw all his strength into a twisting move against Johnny. The torque whipped him around to the side and against the stairwell door. Luckily, the revolver, a smooth, compact gun, lay in his path while the impact forced the door open. His opponent punched him in the face, but Johnny focused on kicking the pistol backwards and over the edge of the cement stairs. There was no sound after it plunged over.

His opponent launched another punch, but Johnny ducked the blow, snapped upright, and pushed his adversary against the railing of the stairwell. Grabbing a flailing arm, he spun the gasping operative hard and smashed him face-first against the back wall.

"Come and get me," he grunted at the man, then turned and leaped down the stairs. Far below came the sound of the revolver striking bottom, its echoes resounding in the vertical cavern.

Johnny quickly reached the stairwell exit to Tucker's floor. He could hear his attacker in hot pursuit. He had not seen where Angela had gone.

Johnny flung open the door and raced down the hall, attempting to remember in his haste which door led to Tucker's computer room. It was easy to get confused, having only entered through inviting open doors on earlier occasions. Now, he had to remember, he had to think.

Reaching what he presumed to be the correct door, he waited a moment for his assailant to regain contact. He could tell from slamming and pounding sounds that his pursuer was closing fast. As he saw the man rounding the corner down the hall, he threw the door open and entered Tucker's apartment.

Johnny had guessed correctly. He was in Tucker's combination entertainment area and computer corral. He quickly crossed the dimly lit room into the brightly lit computer area, awash in fluorescent light. Nothing was amiss. The strange computer still perched there like a snake. But he was not attacked as he entered, and the machines hummed their sterile white noise. Johnny hoped Tucker wasn't all talk.

A moment later, his adversary was at the threshold of the room. Johnny must have appeared as if in a spotlight, standing in the glaringly bright room. Tucker's entertainment zone was still perfectly arranged. The plasma television and abstract artwork on the wall were undisturbed, the furniture soft and inviting.

"You're the one we want," growled his assailant, a military knife appearing in his right hand. "And now I get the other five hundred thousand." With apparent glee, the man entered the room swiftly and aggressively.

By the time he had wended his way through the furniture scattered around the living space, a few seconds had passed. Almost imperceptibly, three thread-like laser beams, each emanating from a point Johnny could not quite identify, had painted the intruder, triangulating on his position.

From his vantage point, Johnny could see the abstract artwork on the wall, the boxes filled with arcs and lines and ringed around an empty box. One of the squares had changed. Its lines had jumped to life and were converging on a single point.

"You're not even going to put up a fight?" his attacker taunted, apparently unaware that he was being stalked by Tucker's still-intact security system. "You're just going to let me kill you?"

Johnny smiled at his assailant with a smug, infuriating expression. A moment later, a small pop sounded, and two small, shiny projectiles trailing wires exploded out of the wall, aimed precisely at the intruder. Hitting his torso, the tasers sparked with decimating voltage, driving the knife-wielding thug to the ground in a paroxysm of gut-wrenching agony. The knife fell limply from his hand. Within a few moments, the man lay unconscious. The tracking lasers had vanished.

Johnny watched the proceedings in amazement. After silence reasserted itself over the scene, he muttered to himself, "Tucker, I owe you one."

Angela appeared in the doorway. She was empty-handed, Johnny was relieved to see.

"Don't come in," he warned. "I'm going to assume you're not going to try to kill me again."

"Right," she said. "This job is too messed up. I'm moving on."

"OK, well, whatever will keep me from being killed, I'll accept it," Johnny stated flatly, walking toward the door. "Care to help me drag your colleague out of here?"

"He's just a grunt I use sometimes," Angela noted. "But you said I shouldn't come in. You'll have to drag him out this far."

"You're right," Johnny confirmed, removing the taser points from the man's torso. As he did so, he glanced up at the abstract artwork on Tucker's wall. It had changed again. The square that had animated during the intrusion was no longer filled with arcs and lines. Instead, it had taken on the appearance of webbing or a net. Johnny thought he understood. This wasn't artwork, but rather a monitor of Tucker's security setup. It was now displaying its next setting for a room that was one trick down.

Smiling inwardly in deep respect for his far-away friend, Johnny returned to the task at hand. He grasped the unconscious thug under the arms and dragged him across the room. A whirring sound caught his attention. The taser lances were being reset into the walls.

Reaching the threshold, Johnny dropped the man back to the ground with a thud and turned to face the neutralized assassin.

"You need to answer some questions for me, like who hired you?" he asked, breathing heavily and trying his best to ignore the beauty the young Greek woman possessed.

"I don't know. It was a voice on the phone about 30 minutes ago. A half-million dollars had been deposited in my bank account," Angela revealed. "You don't get much prepaid work these days, so I didn't ask questions. And I live in the area, so I was able to get over here in a hurry."

"And now you're going to have to return the money," Johnny noted, closing the door to Tucker's apartment.

"Nope," Angela claimed. "That was the deal. I keep all the money no matter what, but I would get another half million if I killed the person leaving this apartment. It was a very strange offer, but I didn't see a downside."

"That is a pretty sweet payday," Johnny admitted.

"Now I just have to figure out whether to deal with this grunt or try to complete the job," Angela said with a smile, clearing her throat. "After that punch to my throat, I'm really thinking hard about this."

"Well, let's make a deal," Johnny suggested. "Take your silencer and the radios. Keep your half a million. I'll get rid of everything else here, and we'll just pretend this never happened. I'll make sure the bullet lodged in the glass disappears without a trace, and you still get 500K for one shot. Sound fair?"

Angela extended a hand to Johnny.

"Deal," she said as they shook on it. "Do you want some help dragging this loser to the elevators?"

"Sure," Johnny replied, and Angela moved to grasp the man's ankles while Johnny carried him by the shoulders again.

Reaching the elevator lobby, they set the man on the floor. Angela pressed the down button.

"What are you investigating?" Angela asked in an offhand manner.

"Eggs," Johnny said cryptically. The elevator arrived. Fortunately, it was empty. They placed the still-unconscious thug on the floor.

"Eggs," she repeated, smiling, her hand holding the doors open. "Well, I hope you crack the case. Thanks again for saving my brother. Next time, no mercy. We're even." There was a pause, and then she added, "And, by the way, you're not as tall as I'd imagined." With a toss of her ponytailed hair, she removed her hand, the doors closed, and she disappeared.

Johnny gazed after her a moment after the doors closed, then began to clean up. He walked upstairs to pick up the empty portfolio lying on the floor. He also retrieved the rifle from the trash, disassembled it quickly into its few components, and removed the bullets. He put the pieces back in the trash and pocketed the ammunition. He carried the portfolio with him.

Johnny opened his cell phone and dialed Tucker. When his friend answered, he sounded very alert.

"Tucker, it's Johnny. Any luck?"

"Not yet," Tucker responded. "Why are you calling again?"

"Well, for one thing, I can attest that your security system still works," Johnny mentioned.

"Are you OK?" Tucker interjected in a worried tone.

"Fine, but it helped save my hide," Johnny said. "Also, there's a broken window on your floor, at the end of your hall," Johnny added nonchalantly. "A very small flying object struck it. If you could arrange for it to be cleaned up, I'd appreciate it. And I mean, cleaned up – it, and everything in it, disappears."

There was silence on the other end of the line as Tucker assessed the words and the tone they were uttered with.

"Understood, I think," he replied dryly. "Talk soon."

Johnny pressed the down arrow call button and waited for another elevator, lost in thought. He still had a revolver to retrieve.

Chapter 18

Meringue

Johnny's mind was racing as he rode the elevator down. The encounter with a hired assassin instructed to kill the person leaving Tucker's apartment confirmed a few things for Johnny. The fact that this shooter's sugardaddy was willing to pay a significant sum for even a miss suggested that intimidation alone was an acceptable outcome.

It was also another inside-out arrangement – when the person inside comes out, kill them. It smacked of Winthrop, of his governing metaphor.

However, there was the remote possibility that this had nothing to do with the current case, that it was somehow tied to something else nefarious in Tucker's real life work.

This idea didn't hold much water with him. Johnny felt certain that the sharpshooter had been tasked to him because he was tightening the noose, closing it slowly, and this was an attempt to slash the rope. That meant that he was making progress, cutting off more air. Panic was edging closer to the surface.

The attempted hit also confirmed that Winthrop had most likely been dirty for a long time. He was willing to blow a million dollars to kill someone threatening him only obliquely, and to leave half a million just for effect. To have emerged from defense contracting with a horse farm and enough money to dispense it in large chunks on a whim – it all suggested that he'd compiled a massive hoard of cash, and that the stakes were very high indeed in the upcoming distribution of classified plans. This suggested a career to Johnny – a business, a process, and a network. You could only move up to the higher echelons of corruption by climbing the ladder. Winthrop had been climbing a while, and was in rarefied air.

Johnny decided that he was going to continue to tear at the insulation Winthrop believed protected him. He'd apparently made a couple of noticeable holes, and he wanted to open up a draft that would chill Winthrop and make him shiver and react again. The more pressured and distracted a mastermind became, Johnny had learned, the more mistakes he or she made, and the easier it became to unmask them and unravel their plans.

When the elevator arrived at the main level, Johnny stepped out and looked around nonchalantly. But his awareness level was at its maximum. If Winthrop were truly as evil and well-resourced as he seemed, Johnny might have met only the first threat of the day. Also, the fact that the assassin had received the call only 30 minutes prior to arriving suggested there was a lookout, that he'd regained his shadow. However, the few people in the lobby of the building were innocuous. Johnny quickly found the entrance to the stairs and retrieved the revolver that had fallen during the altercation. Johnny put the pistol in the portfolio and walked out into the blazing noonday sun, squinting hard as his eyes adjusted.

Walking down the sidewalk, now growing a bit crowded as workers finished their lunch hour routines, Johnny formulated a plan. All he wanted to do was let Winthrop know he could reach into his world as well. Nothing threatening, just a reminder that they had a connection Johnny was willing to use, and to signal back that he was not intimidated. He dialed information, and asked the operator for a phone number in Richmond.

The system connected him to the requested number, and he waited as the phone rang. A female voice answered.

"Hello," she said.

"Hi, Justine," Johnny said. "It's Johnny Denovo."

"Oh, hi, Johnny," Justine replied brightly into her cell phone. "Where are you calling from? Have you left Richmond yet?" Judging from the bounce in her voice, the slight sounds of a bridle, and the cadence of the horse's footfalls, Justine was riding.

"Yes, we just had a quick visit this time," Johnny replied. "But I think I left something down there, and wondered if you could look for it."

"Sure, I guess, what is it?" Justine asked.

"When we met with your Dad in his office," Johnny invented, "I gave him a sheaf of papers describing plans for a horse farm of my own. I wanted to get his advice on some plans I'd sketched out and some of the investment paperwork. The detective business has been good lately, but it's dangerous, and I'm thinking of ratcheting down while I still have all my limbs."

Justine was silent on the other end of the phone. "I can't get into his office," she finally replied in a constricted voice. "He doesn't trust anyone anymore. It all started after my Mom died. I think that scared him. Now, with the embezzling, his office is strictly off-limits."

Johnny was expecting a situation like this and continued the ruse undeterred. "Oh, I should have realized. That makes complete sense. Well, it's a little embarrassing for me, you know, but maybe I'll call your father directly and just tell him I forgot the papers."

Clearing her throat, Justine rallied herself, just as Johnny had hoped she would. "Well, you know, it is kind of silly. I'm his daughter, after all. If he can't trust me, who can he trust? Plus, he's out of town for the next couple of days. I know where he keeps the emergency key to his office. Can you tell me what the sheaf of papers looked like?"

Johnny remembered what he was after, a stack of papers inside a red folder secured by a thick rubber band. It had been a very distinctive item on the desk. It wasn't his, but it was a way to start a message that the Denovo reach and mystique were not to be trifled with.

"I had the papers in a red folder," Johnny lied. "There was a thick rubber band around the middle. I need to get those to the bank before the end of the week if I'm going to keep the financing rolling, so if you could overnight them to me, that would be great."

Her horse snorted loudly, and Justine spoke some soothing words to the animal. "Sure, your timing is great. The delivery guy usually drops off and picks up just about an hour from now, and I'm about done with my noon ride, so if I hurry, I should be able to get the papers in overnight mail today."

"Justine, you're a savior," Johnny said enthusiastically, only half acting. "Let me know if you want me to reimburse you."

"Don't be silly," Justine said warmly. "I'm glad I can do the great detective a favor. But you have to promise me that you'll go for a ride with me next time you're in Richmond."

"Done," Johnny said, providing Justine with his address. "Thanks again."

And the call ended.

Johnny felt a pang of guilt about the path he had set Justine on, but knew that because detective work was a contact sport, a collateral bruise on an innocent bystander was tolerable in the larger picture. He was sure that she would explain what transpired, withstand the anger of her father, and be forgiven as the anger returned to focus on Johnny Denovo. It was inevitable.

Johnny's cell phone rang as he climbed into his car, putting the pistol-filled portfolio on the passenger seat. He started the engine to get the air conditioning going, then answered.

"Johnny Denovo," he stated mechanistically.

"Mr. Denovo, it's Agent Ross of the FBI," spoke the person on the other end, in an very officious voice. "We need to talk. Where can I meet you, in-person and confidentially."

Chapter 19
Maps

Johnny agreed to meet Agent Ross, but first he grabbed a quick bite, disposed of the portfolio and its contents, and changed clothes. The summer heat had been more intense than he'd anticipated, and the extracurricular activities – fighting an assailant and avoiding an assassin being the highlights – had marred his calm, cool appearance. This was not good for his image, and he needed to rectify the situation.

Federal agents came with the territory but added little, Johnny had learned over the years. A few were excellent, broad conceptual thinkers who kept their eyes on the goal, but most were functionaries or worse, borderline personalities bounded only by the regimented existence that agencies like the FBI provided. He had never met this Ross before, and wondered which end of the spectrum he belonged.

The two men had agreed to meet in a small local bookstore's café. When Johnny arrived, the café was deserted and looked forlorn. Most people were either at work or enjoying a summer's day. The young female counter clerk was slouching against the counter and absent-mindedly wiping the counter with a pink-striped cloth.

Agent Ross was a compact man with short black hair who gave the impression of genuine politeness and wholesomeness. He was dressed inappropriately for the hot weather, a dark suit and tie with a white shirt, a stereotypical agent's wardrobe, but he appeared acclimated to the attire, not sweating despite the heat.

After exchanging greetings and handshakes, and after Johnny confirmed that Agent Ross possessed the proper credentials, they sat down at a small table meant to contribute to the artificial ambience of a sidewalk café, yet it only made perching on the chairs and resting their elbows an awkward experience.

"Thank you for meeting me, Mr. Denovo," Agent Ross said.

"Not a problem. What's on your mind?" Johnny replied effortlessly.

"Stolen military plans are on my mind, Mr. Denovo," Agent Ross said quietly. "Shall we call them 'items' from now on, as a convenience?"

"Items?" Johnny asked. "Why do you think I know anything about 'items'?"

"Let's not play games, Mr. Denovo," Agent Ross said in a tired, pained manner. "We know you know."

"Who is this 'we'?" Johnny inquired absentmindedly, seeking to provoke Ross. "The royal 'we'? You and your mother?"

"'We' are the FBI," Agent Ross asserted, bristling. "The F-B-I."

Johnny paused thoughtfully, carefully controlling his features to prevent any read of his next words.

"Go pound sand, Ross," he finally responded.

Agent Ross sat stock still. A slight rage began to percolate beneath his standard-issue countenance.

"Mr. Denovo," he finally and tersely responded. "What did you say?"

"Go pound sand," Johnny repeated in a lighthearted tone. "If you think I'm going to liquidate my detective agency to save the FBI some work, you've got another thing coming."

Ross studied him dumbly, a glaze of static for an aura. Johnny started to rise from his seat to leave.

"Sit down," Ross barked, and then quieted himself into a strained, measured tone filled with threat. "I should haul your ass in for non-cooperation, for some time in FBI custody. You think you're too famous, too well-known? You're wrong. There's too much at stake here. I can have your hide in an instant. Just push me one more time."

Johnny smiled grimly, standing now. "Ross, before you pop, just remember that the President and your boss' boss' boss owe me one."

Agent Ross tensed and flared physically. He looked as if he were about to react violently, then suddenly thought better of it and deflated visibly. "Please sit down, Mr. Denovo. Please."

Johnny looked down at Ross, pitying the agent's predicament, then settled back into his seat effortlessly.

Agent Ross looked more plaintive now.

"Mr. Denovo, let me begin," Ross intoned. "We know about the items, where they came from, what they are, and the threat to them. And we know you're also investigating, and that you're making progress."

Johnny had antagonized Ross enough to have regained the driver's seat, and was ready to play along. "And these items are the ones from Virginia?" Johnny asked.

"Precisely," Agent Ross said, sighing with relief at Johnny's cooperation. "You seem to have a passing familiarity with them, then."

"Only passing," Johnny said. "The items are incomplete. The central components are missing."

Agent Ross raised his eyebrows. "Missing?"

"Missing," Johnny confirmed. "The shell of the items is all I've seen."

Agent Ross ruminated on this news. "Well, that's a scenario we had considered. It's interesting that it's moving into the 'likely scenario' category."

Johnny felt it was time to drop some of the ruse. "Tucker Theisen helped me discover the items. I'm assuming you've been following us since we arrived in Richmond as part of the surveillance around Winthrop Stables. So you know about the computer drives."

"We know about the drives," Agent Ross nodded. "Mr. Theisen is top-notch, the best. What did he say about the items?"

"He said there's an encryption scheme on them like nothing he's ever seen before," Johnny related. "So, actually, the items are all there, but we could only see the exteriors. The contents are hidden away by an encryption we couldn't break."

Agent Ross leaned back on the little café chair and interlaced his fingers behind his head. Johnny could see his firearm in its holster under his right arm. Agent Ross was a southpaw, Johnny noted.

"Well, at least we have the items. Can we get them from you?" Agent Ross inquired.

Johnny sighed. "We returned the drives to Winthrop a few days ago. We have a copy of the data. Well, Tucker does, and right now he's a few time zones away. I'm not exactly sure where, but somewhere in Europe or Africa I'd guess. And someone just sabotaged his internal systems so that he can't get back in to use his main tool sets. His own network is set up to thwart him."

Agent Ross leaned forward sharply at this news. "Someone hacked Theisen's systems?" he said in surprise.

"Tucker called it a physical hack," Johnny recalled. "They installed a computer into his apartment network, and it's running things now."

Agent Ross shook his head in disbelief. "That takes some real skills," he breathed. "What can you tell me about it? Did you see it?"

"Yes, I was there about 20 minutes before you called me," Johnny recounted. "The funny thing was that the computer looked just like the laptop Tucker usually uses, so I didn't think much of it at first. The desk was in disarray, like cables had been shoved around and things knocked about, but the computer looked the same."

"Was it a silver laptop with a shiny streak vertically down the cover?" Agent Ross asked.

"That's the computer," Johnny confirmed.

Agent Ross contemplated this fact. "An inside job," he muttered. "This is bad. Those are standard issue portables for our data encryption experts, very durable, but unique in some important ways. Hard to hack. But who did it is the question. If this case has an inside component, we're bringing other scenarios to bear."

Johnny smiled. "You're really into scenarios, aren't you, Ross?" he quipped.

"It's the way we're taught to think about cases," Ross responded forcefully. "You have your methods, Denovo, and we have ours."

Johnny wasn't interested in scenarios. The FBI should have noted the right things before. The mind leaves patterns.

"Look, no disrespect Agent Ross, but if Winthrop is the catalyst in all this, then it's been an inside job for years, hasn't it?" Johnny asked. "He's ex-government, ex-contractor. This is no big surprise."

Agent Ross tensed. "Keep your voice down, Detective."

"Fine," Johnny said in a more subdued voice. He hadn't spoken loudly before, just in a normal tone. Apparently, this was too much for Agent Ross, who was growing jumpier by the minute. "But you can have multiple scenarios, or you can have what's actually happening. I'll pay attention to what's happening. And I can tell you that a lot is going on right now."

Agent Ross stopped fidgeting for a moment, and began what must have been a rote speech for an FBI agent. "Mr. Denovo, please let the professionals handle this," Agent Ross said. "The FBI has been following this case for months now, and we are well aware of the variables and scenarios we are facing. The reason I wanted to speak with you was to first learn what you knew of the stolen items, and second to ask you to cease your activities in this case."

Johnny was insulted that they'd sent a mid-level agent to deal with him, and unhappy that he'd just faced a threat on his life only to have a flunky with a rudimentary understanding of events and a simplistic way of viewing them try to divert him from his work. But he knew better than to confront Agent Ross at the moment about the shortcomings or foolishness of the cookie-cutter FBI approach.

"I don't even have a client in this case," Johnny stated coolly. "Why would I continue to pursue it?"

"Thank you, Mr. Denovo," Agent Ross said with obvious relief, and pride that his little speech had worked so quickly. He had failed to appreciate the fact that Johnny had promised nothing, only asked a rhetorical question. "Here is my number if you need to reach me." Ross scrawled a phone number on a small café napkin. "We will be in touch with Mr. Theisen, and we'll take things from here."

The two men rose from their chairs, and Johnny extended his hand to the agent.

"Shall I assume I'll continue to be under surveillance?" Johnny asked as they shook hands.

Agent Ross blinked hard. "Um, why, I suppose you should," he responded, a little flustered by the question. "Yes," he said, regaining his bravado, "in fact, you can count on it."

Ross shrugged his jacket straight on his shoulders, and walked away from Johnny. It struck Johnny as a bit comical to watch the agent, in a full dark suit, leave the bookstore and step into the city-sized furnace outside. It took a certain mentality to tolerate the monkey-suit life, Johnny thought.

He also noted to himself that while Ross wore his gun like a left-handed person would, he wrote with his right hand, had a strong right-hand handshake, and wore his watch on his left wrist. It would be fascinating if he were ambidextrous. Johnny knew from his neuroscience days that these individuals were fodder for controversial discussions and studies. The brain lateralization they seemed to possess might lead to better memory or linguistic skills. Others speculated the opposite. It was hard to tell, but Johnny's academic curiosity was piqued slightly. One thing was certainly true – it didn't seem that ambidexterity predicted good judgment. Ross had the means of the FBI at his disposal, but was using them foolishly.

After taking his leave of the possibly ambidextrous Agent Ross, Johnny flipped open his phone and called Tucker. His friend answered with a growl.

"Tucker, it's Johnny."

"I know that," Tucker said, the sound of typing still in the background. He was wrestling with the virtual nemesis that had taken over his home, Johnny speculated.

"An FBI agent just had a nice talk with me," Johnny said. "I'm under surveillance, and you have been, too. I thought you'd like to know."

Tucker laughed uproariously. "Johnny, I am surveillance, so I'm in, under, around, and over it. Not a problem, no difference. You told them about my situation."

"Yes I did. They think it's an inside job," Johnny communicated.

"Oh, that's brilliant," Tucker snorted. "Did he talk about 'scenarios' or 'situation plans' or junk like that, too? These guys are classic. Only a friend or colleague could have gotten into my apartment without tripping an alarm, and only a spook would have access to a machine like the one they popped into my network, to say nothing of the know-how. Yep, it's an inside job for sure, and once I get back into my network, I'll know who it was."

"When are you due back?" Johnny asked.

Tucker was pointedly silent for a minute. "Not sure," he said. "But I'm primed for a fight once I get back, neighbor. And you can bet that the coast will be clear soon."

Johnny recognized the coded indication his friend was giving. The next prime number with consecutive or neighboring digits was the 23rd. Tucker wouldn't be home until then. It was important information, but likely concealed well enough by a shared understanding to be overlooked by their observers. Now that they knew they were under surveillance and that a mole was involved, winks and nudges were keys to survival. Tucker was also promising that the surveillance might soon be compromised. He was an invaluable colleague on cases that involved high-tech and communications. Many did these days. The world was becoming digital through and through.

"Well, see you when I see you, then," Johnny drawled, and the phone call ended.

Johnny had a fitful night's sleep, finally awaking far too early. Another sultry summer's morning was heating up outside. Inside, his domain was cool and comfortable, but the rippling air beyond his windows was suggestive enough to make his skin prickle with anticipatory sweat.

The morning was uneventful until the package from Justine Winthrop arrived with the early delivery man, as promised. A hefty overnight envelope landed on his desk with a thump, and remained unopened. Johnny didn't want to open it. In fact, his plan was to keep it sealed. The intrusion into Winthrop's office had been purely rhetorical, a ploy to demonstrate and destabilize. Attacking the domestic front was unfair but necessary. Since he'd been shot at, Johnny felt only an icy calculation, and upsetting the Winthrop clan paled in comparison with his ambition to provoke anger and mistakes. Right now, smaller provocations would help him retain the energy and motivation he'd need later to close this case with a hard slam. No need to exhaust his supply of retaliatory motivation. Revenge was an explosive best served swiftly.

Mona called after a Wei Chou lunch had been consumed to inform Johnny that their tickets to Paris, and from there to Montpellier, had arrived from the travel agent. He'd had his travel agent ship them to her to conceal his travel plans. He was to meet her at the airport Friday morning, in three days' time, passport and luggage in tow. Her voice sounded professional and courteous, with no personal warmth. It was the pattern of their relationship – warm and cold. For a moment, he hoped that someday it would move to hot, and perhaps stay there. Then he brushed the thought from his mind.

Tucker called again late in the day, at what must have been an ungodly hour wherever he was.

"Johnny, it's Tucker," he rumbled unceremoniously. "Want an update?"

"Hey, Tucker," Johnny responded, happy to hear from his stalwart friend. "Yes, update me, please."

"OK, I've given up on the apartment solve," Tucker informed him. "I actually asked the building superintendent to lock down my floor, so no elevator or stair access. The window will be cleaned up from the outside. And I would happily tell anyone else what I'm about to tell you."

"I understand," Johnny responded, indicating he also spoke as if others were listening.

"Right," Tucker offered. "I've looked at the data a bit more. Trevor is innocent. I can prove it. Winthrop used the embezzling scheme to create a fund for himself he could draw upon to finance this latest escapade, since I assume he's a repeat offender. The fund is pretty sizable, so he's probably diverting in or siphoning off money some other ways. The data has a real miasma in it, though."

Johnny was following his friend perfectly, and agreed with his judgment. By feeding the surveillance important information about the embezzling and funding of the operation, he was giving them something actionable. Tipping off the FBI in this way was also helping ensure that Winthrop would be made even more uncomfortable, wherever he was, and it might lead to an innocent man's release. But by making only a fleeting and strange reference to the UK emails, sent from the miasma.net domain, he was acknowledging to Johnny alone that he had also found evidence that Winthrop was in the email chain, a knowing participant. It was becoming a closed circle, a noose, and now they just had to tighten it. That was often the difficult part. The fight could be horrible, and if the drop was poor, the criminal could survive.

"That's interesting," Johnny noted. "Hey, I was just thinking, I was reading those maps backwards the other day. I would have been so lost if I hadn't caught that."

"Oh yeah," Tucker said. "It was a miscommunication."

"Right," Johnny responded. "By the way, I've been considering dropping this case. I have no client, and dying for nothing doesn't appeal to me. So, let's just leave it at this. Thanks for all the work, but you can move on. Sorry, my friend. You're a tower of strength. That message was an eyeful, and I need you sane."

"Fine with me," Tucker responded with a final ironic note to his voice.

Johnny knew that he'd been understood. Tucker knew he was headed for Paris and the "maps backward" comment he knew had been interpreted as "spam." This was the power of old friends. Word-play had been part of their relationship as they'd grown up, laughing at silly puns and jokes, making up new forms of pig Latin and similar substitution schemes as their facility with patterns and joy in the abstract emerged. It was fun and useful still, and a deeply embedded part of a long friendship.

The meaning was clear – they'd use a spam email connection to communicate, adapting the criminals' tactics for the forces of good.

Johnny hung up the phone. He began writing Tucker a message, disguising it as spam by forwarding a spam email of his own.

Chapter 20
Connection

Johnny was reassured the next morning to find another email from the plotters, using the same double-substitution scheme and rhyming couplets. He decoded it while eating some leftovers from the night before. He'd found his way into their heads, judging from the contents of the message: "The fox is in the henhouse, but the farmer scared him off. The eggs are safe, the farmer pleased, and having quite a laugh." The rhyme at the end confirmed that the author was British, since the couplet wouldn't quite rhyme in American English.

Despite a slightly triumphant feeling, it alarmed Johnny to see how quickly his apparent resignation of the case had been transmitted into the criminals' network. The mole must be involved in the surveillance. He wished he could have a glimpse at the source email, see who had transmitted the information. He had a feeling it was the same person who'd hacked Tucker's apartment. But patience was the key to finding the mole. It could be anybody. Agent Ross was a prime suspect, but others lurked outside his vision, he was sure. He couldn't reach any conclusion yet. Tucker had the information, and it would be just 10 days before he'd likely know the culprit who hacked his lair. It could wait.

Johnny's task for the day was simple – return the package to Winthrop. So far, there'd been no indication that Winthrop had detected it was gone. It didn't matter. Having it reappear, unopened, with the right kind of antagonizing message around it would be sufficient.

Johnny considered the sealed envelope for a moment, and decided that the best approach was to place some doubt in the head of his adversary, a bit of fresh paranoia to layer on to the assuredly sizable amount already driving the man. Psychology was his friend. As someone practiced in sustaining a mental state balanced between the ironic poles of outward indifference and inward passion, he understood how fragile pretense could be. The burdens Winthrop was balancing would be different, more like outward normality and inward criminality, but the equilibrium between these two forces would be more tenuous. By making it clear to Winthrop that his façade of normality could be peeled away, Johnny would disrupt the balance more and more, revealing the criminality.

Johnny turned over in his mind the metaphors of the case – spam, eggs, horses, inside, outside, center, chicken, and the like. Metaphors were how the limbic brain expressed itself, synthesizing complex, even unrecognized inputs and feelings into a representative package sufficiently distinctive and rich in form to be emblematic. He wondered which metaphors were meaningful and which disposable.

It had all started with spam emails. As a metaphor, spam was a weak contender. Appropriated from the processed meat used for a generation or two as a ham substitute and camping staple, the pejorative term as applied to email had a jocular ring to it, but was otherwise meaningless. There was no compelling conceptual metaphor here. Spam was a metaphor for ham, a metaphor for food or sustenance, and a metaphor for something that mimicked the real thing but lacked its essential integrity. These were all weak metaphors. He wanted to use metaphors that revealed the inner workings of the criminal mind. The spam metaphor was lacking. Spam had been used as a technical approach, not as an inspired choice.

The egg, on the other hand, had been an inspired choice. It was a rich metaphor. It seemed that Winthrop had acquired his Faberge eggs soon after his wife's tragic death at the hands of a drunk driver. The egg, being essentially a female image, a metaphor for mother-hood and fertility, fit very well into the psyche of a lost love. Winthrop may have been inspired by his wife's death to seek some-thing precious, unique, and feminine.

Suddenly, inspiration seized Johnny as well, and he decided that what he sent wasn't as important as whom he sent it to. So, with care-ful penmanship, all capitals with nicely weighted swoops, he addressed a large padded envelope, put the sealed package from Jus-tine inside, and went out to mail it, express, overnight.

As he left the lobby of his building, he was surprised to pass Mona coming in the opposite way in the revolving door. Realizing quickly as they revolved around one another that unless one held course a comical situation could arise, Mona stayed in the lobby and waited for Johnny to swing around another 180 degrees.

"Mona, what are you doing here?" Johnny asked once he'd spun around into the lobby again.

"I thought I'd come by to drop off your tickets," she responded. "I wasn't going to buzz you, just leave them at Wei Chou's. Where are you headed, and what is that?"

Johnny hoisted the package under his arm and considered it momentarily. "Just a package for a friend," he responded.

"Addressed to Janet Winthrop?" Mona inquired, arching an eye-brow. "You do remember that she died years ago, right?"

"Yes, I haven't forgotten. I'm doing a little remote disruption work, you see," Johnny drawled. "Nothing too severe, just a little psy-chological depth charge for our friend."

Mona gave a pained look, then thought better of sympathizing with Winthrop and smiled at Johnny in admiration. "I like how once you have your mind set on making someone miserable, you are like a dog with a bone," she purred. "I hope I never get on your bad side."

It was Johnny's turn to smile. "You never will, Ms. Landau," he assured her.

An awkward silence settled on the two as their eyes locked and their gazes deepened. Noises from the street receded into nothingness as the world resolved into a frozen memory for a fleeting instant, a diamond in time. Their connection was like a stab of lightning, manifesting even as it disappeared. Then, gradually, noises returned. Shapes re-emerged around them. They breathed again.

Neither spoke for a moment. Johnny's internal equilibrium was barely balancing on that blade of time. But he was adept at shifting his internal psychological ballast, and recovered nearly imperceptibly. Mona breathed out as if she'd been holding her breath.

"Here are your tickets, detective," she said abruptly. "Friday. Don't be late."

Johnny smiled in a pained way, and accepted the tickets from Mona. She began to move past him to leave.

"Here, let me walk with you," he uttered softly as she passed. "I was just going out anyway."

Mona paused. "No, I'll see you Friday, detective. I'm not going that way right now." And with that, she pushed out the revolving door and left Johnny, composed and calm on the outside, staring after her, his heart pounding fiercely.

Chapter 21
Flying

Recalling the tempest of desire and emotions he'd felt when last they met, Johnny was anxious about seeing Mona again. For John A. Novarro, this would have meant sweaty palms, nervous glances downward, and a practiced interaction, at least to test the waters. The well of emotions that Mona could tap was deep. But Johnny Denovo had shined a light into his emotional well many years before, and knew that the waters would only slosh and not escape, despite being shocked by a seismic event like the one in his building's lobby. Even possessing such over-developed self-awareness, he felt it was necessary to cap the well by screwing on a heavy dose of Denovo mystique and attitude. This meant sunglasses, his best black leather jacket, and one of his nicest shirts. He wanted to be recognizable, his image honed to match expectations, so he would have the frenetic atmosphere of celebrity about him as he traveled this time. Forcing him to tighten his act would help him control interactions with Mona. This was survival mode. It was a long trip far away. Something untoward, or at least complicated, might happen if he wasn't careful. Despite the extra harassment at security and gaping expressions as he walked through the airport, he was convinced going big was his best move.

Mona seemed to have read his mind, having adopted the antithesis of celebrity for her appearance. If she was wearing cosmetics, they were naturalistic and subtle. Her hair was pulled back in a simple ponytail, and her clothes were as close to bargain basement as possible. She wore a long coat like a blanket in the chilly terminal, pulled around her as she sat, concealing her body in what Johnny interpreted as another signal of reticence and reserve, even resentment. Ironically, Johnny took this all as a positive signal about how seriously she took her relationship with him. He felt reassured that if romance erupted, she would take care to preserve their friendship and professional partnership. He was glad for this, because he already valued both. Romance was a risky possibility.

Johnny was also relieved to find that while he was flying first-class as usual, his travel agent had wisely placed Mona in coach despite the duration of the flight. He made a mental note to thank her for this. The arrangement ensured separation and allowed Johnny to indulge in his favorite activity during a long flight: sleep. Years ago, with some self-conscious practice, Johnny had mastered the ability to shift into sleep as soon as the airplane began to taxi down the runway. He had not experienced a trans-Atlantic take-off in a fully conscious state for many years. Using this technique, flights of many hours were reduced to a few half-hours of wakefulness.

As he shifted his mind into a trance-like state, he tumbled through the facts of the Faberge eggs case thus far, and tried to weave together the themes and patterns he had observed so far. The world was in an unstable phase. Alliances were fragile, dealmakers few and far between, enemies unclear. It was a volatile age. With Winthrop's intimidation techniques, the coded messages, the valuable trinkets, the secret plans, and the deadly stakes processing in his limbic system, the dream Johnny lapsed into was thematically unsurprising.

As the plane trundled and accelerated and took flight, Johnny's dream center generated images of a large egg seated on top of a wall, drawn in ink and verging on tumbling off, a texture of old paper a fleeting backdrop. It was a picture of Humpty Dumpty from a childhood book, at first precariously clinging to balance atop a thick brick wall, and then lying broken, exposed, at the bottom. The image dissolved and new thoughts fought their way into his mind – going into Winthrop's office with him looking out over the pastures, the assassin firing into the apartment building as he came out of Tucker's, the rhyming couplets inside spam emails, the Faberge eggs in rough caricatures, some with visible insides. But the images of Humpty Dumpty persisted, the juxtaposed whole egg and the opened, crushed egg, a subliminal flash, or a dominant proscenium, asserting itself in the dream as the unifying element.

When Johnny awoke, a stewardess was asking him if he would like the hot towel she dangled at him with a pair of plastic tongs. Only a few minutes had passed since take-off, yet he felt like his head was full of a day's memories. He also felt slightly panicked as the dream's images and his hopes for interpreting their meaning began to falter and dissolve. He grasped at and gathered the remnants into his conscious mind as he accepted the hot towel from the flight attendant.

When he was done wiping his hands, he grabbed the flight magazine and a pen and began to write out what remained in his memory of the dream and how it represented his inductive reasoning. Clearly, the eggs were at the center, but were the least known part of the equation. He hadn't even seen Winthrop's Faberge eggs except in pictures. That they were caricatured as a childhood memory of fairy tale drawings was an indication to Johnny that in his mind they were abstract concepts, not specifically the Faberge eggs. Something or someone had another secret inside. Tucker had found a file in which the central part of the secret was missing.

Details, he needed details. Johnny felt like the eggs were the central part of this mystery, but he had neglected studying them. He needed to view their details, see them up close.

Sifting through the dream's images again, he thought he remembered Winthrop appearing here and there, especially when he remembered seeing eggs, and that in each display of the imagery juxtaposing

Winthrop and the eggs, he had seen Winthrop steal a glance at the eggs. His limbic brain was telling him something. The message was clear. Winthrop was the mastermind, and something was going to happen involving the eggs that would be part of his plan. Winthrop was not the victim, and the eggs were vital to his success. He was watching them above all else.

Johnny refused the meal offered by the airline and settled back into his seat. He scribbled notes about the dream on a page of the flight magazine and dog-eared it for future reference. He would take his notes with him as he left the plane. In the meantime, sleep beckoned yet again. It was a long flight, and he had eggs on his mind.

Chapter 22
Sunny Side Up

A hard impact startled Johnny awake, his head bumping against his seatback. Disoriented for a moment, he quickly realized that their flight had arrived in Paris. Squealing tires and the lurch of the plane braking confirmed his initial impression. The orange beacon of dawn was warming the sky. Misty patches clung to the grass between the runways as he gazed out the plane's window, blinking sleepily.

Arriving in France was always something special for Johnny. He welcomed the shift in culture and environment. In the jetway, the air was milder, matching the genteel sounds of French spoken by the people filing into the airport. Compared to the French being uttered around him, he felt as if American English sounded primitive and harsh.

Mona's choice of attire had worked perfectly. By dressing simply, she emerged from the long flight looking composed, her hair pulled back regally and her clothes seemingly unaffected by hours pressed into a cramped seat. The Charles de Gaulle airport was vast, its scale making them feel tiny by comparison. As night receded, de Gaulle was aglow in green neon and shiny aluminum grills offset by faded faux wood planks as a naturalistic contrast. The two bleary travelers made their way through the pack escaping their plane, down the long corridors echoing emptily, then through customs, barely speaking in their somnolence. After gathering their bags, they headed for a taxi stand.

Their schedule called for a few days in Paris to adjust to the time zone before flying down to the southern part of France. It had been his travel agent's idea, speculating that a groggy detective is a vulnerable detective. Johnny had agreed, because not only was he very susceptible to jetlag, but this arrangement placed him close enough to the action while preserving his options in case plans changed or new information was uncovered. He only hoped Mona had believed him when he'd explained. She had sounded skeptical, as if seeing through a ruse.

"Where are you headed?" the driver inquired in brusque French.

"To la Rue de Saint Germaine, please," Mona answered without hesitation in perfect French, settling into her seat.

"I didn't know you spoke French," Johnny said.

"There are many things you don't know about me, Mr. Denovo," Mona relayed. "I went to school in Montreal for a few years after studying French in high school. I became fluent there. I've never been to France, though, so I have to watch that I don't sound like a Quebecoise. The Parisians don't like that, I hear."

Johnny's own grasp of French was strong, but compromised by having grown up with Spanish-speaking grandparents and parents who would often lapse into Spanish when his grandparents visited. This was fine for John Novarro, giving him an easy fluency with Spanish that he soon took for granted, but it led to confusion when shifting to French or Italian. It was all too tempting to borrow vocabulary across these Romance languages, and he required some immersion to guarantee fidelity to the local language. He would let Mona take the linguistic lead for the first day or two, until his mind was giving French primacy.

"Well, I'm glad," Johnny responded at last. "I tend to get mixed up the first day or two between Spanish and French. I'll have the vocabularies straightened out soon enough, though."

Mona smiled. "It will be nice to speak it again in long stretches," she observed. "I don't get to use French much in Boston. That's why I like Maurice's. There's a little French spoken there now and again, and the menu and music help. I'm more than a little rusty myself."

Soon, conversation in any language became non-existent. Fatigue's heavy mud engulfed their limbs, and their familiarity with each other allowed a comfortable silence to absorb them. Traffic from the airport was crawling along many lanes simultaneously. The slow sway of the car as it inched forward compounded their dazed dispositions. Outside, a damp summer haze was forming as the temperature rose and the sun brightened.

As a counterbalance to their potentially awkward stay in Paris, Johnny's travel agent had arranged for them to be in separate hotels in the Saint Germaine district, near one another but not together, and almost adjacent to the Jardins du Luxembourg. Mona was dropped off first at her hotel, and Johnny was taken a half-block farther and deposited at his. He unpacked upon arriving in his room, hooked up his computer, and checked email. Aside from the raft of typical fan email and other items, a spam email from Tucker awaited him. Its message was simple: "Still no dice." The physical hack of his apartment – the computer placed like a dam in his information flow – was still thwarting Johnny's genius friend.

Over the next few days, Paris proved a happy respite for both the famous detective and his agent. The amazing Museum d'Orsay, their first stop, entranced Mona in particular, its rooftop café vaulting her into Parisian conceits with its views and cloistered embrace. They behaved as tourists, wandering the Louvre, climbing to the observation deck of the Eiffel Tower, walking the Champs-Elysee, and taking an evening boat cruise on the River Seine. The pulse of romance so often associated with the city remained at bay for no apparent reason, other than perhaps their mutual tendencies toward irony made it unlikely they would allow something as cliché as romance in Paris to become the flashpoint for them.

From news reports and Web research, it was clear that terrorist groups, renegade governments, and egotistical world leaders were holding their breaths. The silence was oppressive. The infamous "slow news cycle" achieved a nadir as even the most reputable information sources scoured the land for filler to avoid dead air. Something big was about to happen, and those who knew about such things were distracted by it.

Johnny went unshaven during their days in Paris, letting his beard grow out to begin to conceal his identity. The scruffy look might have also had something to do with the lack of fireworks between the two. But Johnny felt that this simple disguise might come in handy as the case entered the full-contact phase. It certainly began to work in Paris, allowing him to walk the narrow sidewalks around Saint Germaine without being recognized after the first day or two.

In this, the peak season, the streets were crowded, even when they were not full of wild parades celebrating pride of various groups cavorting in the summer heat. Johnny soon realized a beard at this time of year was not recommended for personal comfort. It was hot. Tourists were abundant, and bikes, cars, and pedestrians competed for space. Bastille Day had already passed, and the month of August in which the French themselves typically began to sneak away on holiday had not arrived, so there was a languid pace to the proceedings.

Walking the historic streets, gazing upon the broad lawns and geometric pathways, Paris was soothing to the mind of the pattern-obsessed detective. It made sense in a way other cities did not. He was especially pleased looking out from the top of the Arc de Triomphe – the radiating streets, the straight line from the Louvre to the new cubic Arc. The audacity of order gave him a thrill. It was a simple but elegant accomplishment, one for which Parisians should feel proud, he concluded.

No further news arrived from Tucker, no more spam emails emerged, and all seemed quiet during their adjustment phase in Paris.

In fact, during the entire stay, Johnny didn't register any shifts in the patterns he'd already observed, even though from this vantage point he was not in a position to observe much at all. This was definitely a risk in some ways, trusting in the patterns he'd determined from prior observations, and limiting his world to the known. He thought he might be making a mistake, but this was his neocortex, his conscious mind, talking, and it was often wrong. His limbic brain was perfectly comfortable, and that was the center of reason he trusted above all others. Being adjusted to the proper sleep patterns was probably more important than tracking every twitch of the conspiracy.

The morning of July 19th arrived, the day Mona and Johnny were due to depart for Montpellier, and Johnny awoke to another warm morning, soft daylight sneaking around the perimeter of his hotel room's draperies. In the dim light, he padded over to his computer and stretched while it booted up. Checking email, he focused sharply on another spam email caught by his filter. The same double-substitution scheme was being used. This was the first sign of activity from the conspirators in six days. The nefarious world had started to breathe again. It was about to begin.

Decoding the message, Johnny found another rhyming couplet, this time providing a strange juxtaposition of images: "The eggs have come, as have their squire. He has the charges if you have the wire."

Johnny sat back after decoding the message to consider its contents. He was clear on the meaning of the first stanza – the Faberge eggs had arrived in Montpellier along with Winthrop. It was the second stanza that had him confused. Was this a reference to explosives? Why would they be needed? Or was the wire something else, like an eavesdropping wire worn by an undercover agent, and the charges were legal charges? And who was the "you" the message mentioned? This was potentially a new player. Or had there been a broader audience for these emails all along? Decoding the messages technically was now fairly trivial work for Johnny, but understanding their precise meaning was fraught with uncertainties, even in a context he felt he understood quite well.

There was no more time to ruminate – he had to leave. After a few last throes of packing, he checked out and walked over to Mona's hotel, a route he now knew well after a few days habituating himself to the patisseries and cafes in the neighborhood. Nods of familiarity greeted him as he strode past in his increasingly hirsute state, his suitcase rolling behind him. Smells of cigarettes, verdant gardens, and baked goods jostled for his attention. The low rumble of small engines grew in the streets. Mona was waiting for him under her hotel's awning, and smiled upon seeing him.

"The great detective, reduced to hauling his luggage through the world's most romantic city," she chirped sarcastically. "Oh, how the mighty have fallen."

Johnny smiled at her joke, and basked in her beauty. She was stunning in the rosy and dappled morning light of Paris, her auburn hair aglow, her skin soft and exuding warmth, her figure sculptural and arousing. He felt no need to respond with words.

Mona smiled even more broadly. "And at a loss for words," she continued jibing. "My, is a catatonic state next for the incisive Mr. Denovo?!"

Johnny arrived at her side, and kissed her cheek spontaneously. "What I had to say was best said with action," he said cryptically, and he saw Mona's pupils dilate ever so slightly. The connection was not just lightning this time, but more sustained. He and Mona were extending the prelude as long as possible. It was enjoyable, excruciating, and tantalizing.

They rode in near silence to the airport, sitting close enough together that they touched whenever the taxi jostled sufficiently and making the smallest of small talk. Checking their bags for the Montpellier flight, they wended their way through security to the smaller and more cramped gates that national flights were relegated to. They settled into two chairs, facing each other. For the sake of privacy, Johnny sat with his back to the main flow of crowds passing by in the corridor. He'd only been recognized a few times in Paris, and his beard had filled, so shielding his identity here in the airport was more of a habitual precaution than a necessity.

"Johnny, I never asked you," Mona said suddenly. "In Richmond, we were being followed. But it's been days now in France. If we were being followed once, couldn't we be followed again?"

Johnny mused to himself for a moment. Mona had a right to know, and had certainly proven with the travails of the past weeks that she had grit. The fact that she had asked demonstrated a pragmatic view, not an amateur's tendency to withdraw into hopes for the return of normalcy.

"We're still being followed," Johnny revealed calmly. "I didn't want to bring it up again, but it's true."

Mona's eyes widened and she jutted her head forward in exasperation.

"I should have told you," Johnny apologized, "but you were pretty stressed after Richmond. I need you to be focused. If you'd known that someone on that flight, and here right now, were tailing us, you wouldn't have been thinking about the case, and you wouldn't have enjoyed Paris. You would have been worrying about who was following us, and why."

Mona struggled to get her next words out. "But, aren't *you* worried?" she implored.

Johnny smiled. "A little," he admitted. "I've figured out that our escort is a Federal agent. The FBI agent I met with pretty much offered up the information. Plus, the ease with which I detected the person tailing me makes it clear this guy is FBI."

Mona was still looking a bit stricken. "But these guys have fed information to Winthrop," she whispered harshly.

Johnny smiled. "Precisely," he said calmly. "This is a tricky situation. After we met with Winthrop, and we realized that our tail had supplied him with information, and I met with the FBI agent in Boston, I suspected a mole in the agency working for Winthrop. The question I had remaining was, how far was this mole willing to go?

After the incursion and computer hack at Tucker's, it's clear whoever is corrupt at the FBI is willing to go very far." Johnny paused. "Do you really want me to go on?"

Mona looked hard into his eyes, and nodded after a nearly imperceptible gulp. She was still toughening to the realities of intrigue and modern detective work.

"Well, because we're outside of the US now," Johnny elaborated, "our friend is apparently freelancing. This means, frankly, that constraints on his behavior are less than they'd be on home turf."

Mona let this interpretation sink in for a moment, silently processing the implications.

"Is this normal for you?" she finally asked.

Johnny sighed. "Fairly normal," he confirmed. "So far, this guy seems pretty mild, but for one exception." He had still not told her of the sharpshooter's attempt on his life coming out of Tucker's apartment. "Sometimes, as things heat up, these games get downright wild," he concluded with a smile, leaning back and dropping his arms languidly to his sides.

Mona looked at him piercingly and somewhat in disbelief.

"Mr. Denovo, you amaze me," she said. "I had no idea."

Johnny smiled. "And you wonder why my paychecks are so big?" he smirked.

A thoughtful silence settled between them despite Johnny's levity and calmness, and the noises around them intruded – flight announcements, lively conversations, the occasional drum beat of a panicked traveler running by. Mona was trying her best to conceal her worry. There was a constant murmur of sluggish discussions from jet-lagged travelers, a variety of languages and accents mixing into an international ambience. Finally, Mona asked the inevitable.

"Is he here at this gate?" she inquired.

"No," Johnny responded. "But don't look when I tell you that he's down the hall at the next gate, sporting an iPod and wearing a green sweatshirt. Last I saw, he was slouching in a chair."

Amazingly, despite facing the hall herself and therefore the chair in which their tail was seated, Mona was able to resist looking right away, and instead leaned back in her own chair and closed her eyes. Johnny could see that she opened them into narrow slits to peek then. He reflexively stretched and yawned, drawing attention to himself. He was sure that their follower was looking, perhaps from behind sunglasses or through similarly slitted lids, and he wanted to divert attention from Mona. It was an instinct now for him, he noted with bemused resignation.

They sat for the remainder of the wait in silence, observing the flow of strangers passing by and contemplating their situation.

The flight to Monpellier was brief and uncrowded. Johnny and Mona were seated in the same row, with a seat in between them, and they didn't talk much beyond the civilities necessary to negotiate seating and the sparse refreshments. Sharing the news of having someone shadowing them here in France had put a damper on their emotional journey, making the connection earlier in the day seem as distant as a fairy tale from an era long since past.

Chapter 23

Benedict

Montpellier proved hotter and breezier than Paris, a summertime destination a little off the beaten track but still popular enough to be crowded. Johnny had read that the large Languedoc-Roussillon region around Montpellier at one time had been a subjugated territory ruled by lords from Barcelona. Later, it had been a rebellious stronghold where the Cathars held sway. Observing it firsthand, Johnny thought the area had a patina of new money that had sprayed up from the hoses of wealth all around, from Marseilles down the coast to Spain. It was vibrant and exciting. Ocean scents floated inland from the Mediterranean, and seagulls cried, barked, and laughed. Little dogs were on leashes everywhere as vacationers with pets crowded the walkways and plazas. French dogs were a fashion accessory and a degree more comical in form and disposition than American dogs, Johnny thought. French dogs possessed more idiosyncratic personalities and often puzzling haircuts.

This time, Johnny's travel agent had arranged for them to have separate rooms while sharing the same hotel. Johnny was grateful for this change in their logistics, most likely made simply because hotel rooms were less plentiful in this smaller city. But Montpellier was going to be more dangerous than Paris because the action was about to move into high gear. He wanted Mona close by.

The air was tropical here in the early morning at the edge of the Mediterranean. Palm trees were scattered about, large and small pleasure craft were moored in harbors dotted along the coast, and horse farms were small and more clearly equestrian, as if transferred from the Caribbean. It was a pastiche of many cultures, an admixture of land and sea, new and old, modern and traditional.

Adding to the sense of randomness was that the Tour de France, the large bicycle race, had been through town just a week before, and Johnny and Mona saw signs from its visit still scattered about as they were driven by taxi to their hotel, remnants of a high-speed party of enormous magnitude.

They were dropped off near the Place de la Comedie, the large plaza at the heart of the city. Montpellier had recently made dramatic changes to its town center, banning automobiles from much of the area. This made for a quieter and more sedate zone, and easier walking and human communication. It was a pleasant trend, Johnny noted, breaking the addiction to the automobile. He wondered how far the movement against cars could go in America, given the metaphors the marketing mavens had absorbed into their products (freedom, power, and sex) along with the devotion to convenience that permeated his homeland.

After settling into their rooms, the two met to conduct some local reconnaissance. They invested a couple of hours walking about to observe the fountains, statues, cathedrals, citadels, and villes in the historic areas of the city. It was about noon when Johnny and Mona left the town center on their way to find the small hall where the Faberge egg exhibit was to be held.

Faberge eggs were of interest, but the town's large Parc des Expositions was too mammoth and sprawling for such a niche exhibit, so a smaller hall closer to the city center had been chosen. As they passed in front of a sparkling little fountain, Johnny's cell phone rang. It was Wei Chou calling from Boston.

"Wei, why are you calling me? It must be the crack of dawn there," Johnny spoke into his phone after the two had exchanged greetings.

"Yes, Johnny, it is very early," Wei responded. "But I am what you call the early bird, and this morning I got a worm."

Johnny's eyebrows rose involuntarily. "Would you care to elaborate?" he said to Wei.

"As usual, when you are gone, I went up to your condo to make a phone call or two, keep the wires live so you have an alibi, all that. I also water the plants, check things out, you know," Wei described in more than enough detail. "This morning, when I was walking up to your door, it started to open from the inside."

Johnny stopped walking under the shade of a large tree with a barrel of flowers at its base. "Are you OK?" he asked.

"Oh," Wei laughed. "It is not me who is hurting, Johnny. It is the guy coming out!" Wei was chuckling quite hard by this time, but paused to restore his serious demeanor. "I had time to hide by the elevators, and when this guy came around the corner, I dropped him. He wasn't a very good fighter."

Wei sounded disappointed. Johnny knew that in addition to running a fine restaurant in his condominium complex, Wei also taught martial arts on the weekends, and had been an accomplished international competitor until just a few years ago. This was another reason he was a good friend – food and security.

"Who was he?" Johnny asked.

"No clue," Wei said. "No ID, nothing. He had a gun, but he never got it out of its holster."

Johnny had a sudden memory. "Wei, was his gun in a shoulder holster?"

"Yes, under his right arm," Wei confirmed. "Which is weird, because he didn't fight like a left-handed person," Wei observed.

"What do you mean?" Johnny asked.

"Oh, left-handed people in fighting and sports are the same," Wei explained. "They do things like lefties. He did things like a righty sometimes, a lefty other times. Weird, but he wasn't very good."

Johnny smiled at Mona, who, by this time, was studying him for signs that everything was all right.

"Wei," Johnny said wearily. "Let me guess. Did this guy have black hair cut short and look like he came out of a deodorant commercial?"

"That's the guy!" Wei responded brightly.

"Wei, do me a favor," Johnny said. "Don't go into my apartment at all until after I get back. No need for the usual ruses and games. The plants can wait. Just lock it up and leave, OK?"

"OK, Johnny," Wei said. "I already locked it up, and I put Mr. Intruder out in the dumpster. He will feel right at home, especially after I emptied last night's garbages on him. Busy night. Busy night!" Wei laughed again, and his jubilance was such that even with grim news and across such a distance, Johnny found himself laughing along.

Johnny and Wei signed off, and Johnny closed his phone.

"What was that all about? And what was so funny?" Mona asked.

"Oh, just trash talk," Johnny responded nonchalantly. "As to what the call was about, I think we now know that our Agent Ross of the FBI has been in on this, too."

Mona looked a little ill at this statement. "Is there anyone we can trust?" she asked.

"Plenty of people," Johnny assured her. "We can trust each other, Tucker, Wei, Daniel, Natalie, and many others, even some we've not met yet. We just know that we can't trust Ross, the guy who's tailing us, or Winthrop. And that's why we hunt criminals. They're pains in the ass. C'mon, let's get to the exhibit hall."

Once they emerged from the car prohibitions around the city center, the streets of Montpellier were thrumming all about them, the ubiquitous sounds of motor scooters now attended by noises from four-cylinder cars, with the anachronistic clicking of bicycle gears blending into a cascade of noise they soon acclimated to. Groups of pedestrians would jostle past them on the walkways, while conversations from cafes and shops swept through the air, along with increasingly enticing scents. Johnny and Mona stopped to buy sandwiches and sodas, and continued walking. The exhibit hall wasn't far, but getting there through the winding streets and multiple crosswalks of Montpellier took time.

As they neared the site, banners began appearing on small flag-poles, touting the exhibit in both English and French, a picture of a green Faberge egg on the field of yellow. The show was due to start in a few days. The summer sun was broiling, and the plaza leading to the exhibit hall had only sparse shade from widely spaced trees. On the narrow streets, shadows from buildings and trees had been more plentiful, so the baking sheet plaza was a blinding and unpleasant change. Fortunately, the hall itself was open for other shows that were underway, and they entered the air-conditioned lobby with relief.

The cool tiles of the exhibit hall lobby were gray and untrammeled. Very few people were evident. It looked like the mid-week set up period preceding a major show. Smaller events were going on, mostly on the upper levels of the three-story complex judging from the signs and noise.

The entrance to the main hall was positioned centrally on the ground floor. Signs for the Faberge eggs exhibit were placed near a set of triple doors, tall banners on poles promoting the upcoming event. Security guards were positioned near the entrances, standing mostly at attention and looking quite alert. Johnny noted how different this was from the US, where security guards usually slouched on tall stools and looked more asleep than awake. Security in France obviously paid better. The machine guns at the airports had already signaled the difference. He wasn't sure this was a good trend. It wasn't good for weapons to become metaphors for security.

Mona and Johnny walked past the banks of doors and then out the adjacent side of the hall into the summer sun. By now, their sandwiches and sodas had been consumed, and they were on an afternoon constitutional, or at least that was their story. In fact, they were checking out the venue from a number of angles. Johnny had already used a mapping program that provided satellite imagery to do some reconnaissance, but walking the actual space was much more revealing and informative. Satellites only provided snapshots, not movies, and from a poor angle. And when the pictures were out of date, real problems could occur.

The streets bordering the exhibit hall were busy, with one relatively large street down the left flank of the building, widened apparently to accommodate the trucks necessary to deliver exhibit materials. Fresh pavement and cars bounded the edge of the roadway. As they walked along this broad street, a welcome abundance of trees shaded their way. They made for the back of the building.

The entrance to the rear of the building was controlled by a high gate and a guard booth. A single armed guard sat inside the booth, a small handheld radio on his desk. Other structures across from the loading docks imposed themselves, older housing and commercial buildings that pre-dated the exhibit hall and likely would persist long after. Glancing down the wide alley leading to the loading docks, Johnny was struck at how narrow the passage was. This must have been an architectural necessity.

"It must take some real skills to put a truck down this alleyway, turn it, and get it back out," he remarked. Mona nodded in solemn agreement.

Looking above the alley, Johnny noticed that windows from the adjoining buildings had bars on them, a flimsy and easily defeated security measure. The rooftops had loops of razor wire along their tops, but placed below the roof line, meaning they were installed to discourage climbing or descending from the roofs. He couldn't see what was atop the exhibit hall as far as security measures. He had to stop peering about, as they were nearing where the security guard was stationed. He was beginning to give them a wary look.

Walking around the block, turning to stroll along the fronts of the buildings abutting the exhibit hall area, Johnny noticed that many were cafés with apartments above them. This worried him. To his mind, this was a major vulnerability to the security of the exhibit hall. Simply renting an apartment and finding a way to defeat the bars on the windows would give someone easy nocturnal access to the hall. A bribe to a willing confederate on the inside, a door left ajar or a latch left unsecured, and the first lines of defense would be defeated.

But given the profile of the case so far, the threat Johnny sensed was from the inside. If Winthrop were the mastermind, there was something more like embezzlement going on. It was clear the embezzlement charges against Trevor were bogus, and that Winthrop was a personality accustomed to dealing from the inside out – embezzling his own funds to pay for something else nefarious, stealing from his government to make himself rich, penetrating an agency from the inside by corrupting susceptible members, embedding messages inside messages, hollowing out a center of the code from stolen plans. An incursion from outside a building to the inside was not Winthrop's style. This was an inside job, Johnny was certain, and the external defenses were meaningless.

Chapter 24
Candling

The next two days were filled with ruminations and research on Johnny's part. The inside-outside motif consumed his thinking about Winthrop. He believed it was Winthrop's governing metaphor. Deducing the personality of a criminal by identifying the way they thought was akin to holding them up to the light and seeing how their thoughts flowed. For Johnny, metaphors were the light.

Johnny pondered the significance of Winthrop's metaphor engram, his imprinted habits. The inside-outside metaphor was a conceptual metaphor, the most flexible kind. It was essentially a spatial metaphor, related to being inside or outside of a structure or container. But as it became less literal and more metaphorical, its meanings multiplied, to social structures, personality types, risk assessment, and other domains. For Winthrop, it seemed to govern his style of interacting, and how he thought of himself and those around him. You were either inside or outside his trusted circle. If you were outside, you were a threat, which suggested an unhealthy level of paranoia. Winthrop probably felt under siege nearly all the time. He ringed battlements around himself, and from there launched attacks.

If this were as he suspected an inside job, and if Winthrop's way of thinking were so predictably patterned on an inside-outside conceptual metaphor, then what was inside the Faberge eggs might be the secret at the center of this mystery. If not, it was closely related in kind if not precise detail.

Johnny had brought along the folder of materials his insurance friend Daniel had given him about the Winthrop collection, and had been reviewing it in a leisurely fashion since his dream on the flight to Paris. Parceling out the information like this wasn't unusual for his technique. He was willing to give his own metaphor center information in small aliquots and plenty of time to process. He knew better than to rush it. Metaphors were layered concoctions. They were not one-dimensional, linear creations that responded to deadlines. They had to be cultivated.

Out of nearly 100 Faberge eggs in existence, Winthrop possessed a half-dozen, a valuable and important collection, distinguishing him as an important individual collector. Johnny sat at the desk in his hotel room and began sorting through the pages of the packet once more, this time feeling it was time to make some decisions about which of the Faberge eggs would matter most to what might transpire.

Karl Faberge, Johnny read for the umpteenth time, had started making the eggs upon royal commission in the late 1800s. Each was thematic, and both the exterior and interior were hand-crafted marvels. Winthrop held several eggs that immediately grabbed Johnny's attention when viewed through the hypothesis that the inside mattered more than the outside.

The Windflowers Egg was a beautiful red enamel egg with gold decoration wrapping it ornately. Inside was a basket of flowers created from platinum, enamel, diamonds, rock crystal, pearls, and green, yellow, and white minerals. The pictures from Daniel's packet were detailed and exquisite. This egg intrigued him because if he was right and the eggs were purchased initially as an unconscious metaphor for Winthrop's lost wife, then the addition of a feminine basket of flowers inside might make this egg especially and subconsciously appealing to Winthrop. He placed the pages for the Windflowers Egg on the bed.

An egg named the Diamond Trellis Egg also intrigued Johnny, first for its magnificent bejeweled beauty, but mainly because the listing revealed that the central "surprise," as these items in the Faberge collection were called, was missing. This fit his hypothesis of Winthrop's pattern too well – the invisible, missing center. He put these papers on same pile.

The four remaining eggs didn't have the right set of attributes to capture Johnny's limbic sensibilities. The Czarevich Egg was too morbid, the Napoleonic Egg had art at its center which Johnny found too self-referential to fit, and the Colonnade Egg was too formalistic. There was something about the interlacing filigree of the eggs he had set aside that attracted his mind, the pattern-seeker. The transparent egg also didn't fit Johnny's outline of what made Winthrop tick. He was opaque as a person, even as a father.

Johnny's mind turned to Justine Winthrop. He thought perhaps he should check on her. He'd set her up for conflict, certain she could handle it, but he wanted to be sure that all was well and that he hadn't created resentment or an additional adversary. After all, she was the remaining feminine presence in Winthrop's life. It was not unheard of for helpless rage provoked by the memory of one thing to be targeted at the most available similar thing. Associative rage was entirely plausible. He didn't want Justine to suffer for this investigation. Checking the time zones, he waited until it was mid-morning in Virginia, probably a good time to call a horse farm, he rationalized. He dialed Justine's cell phone number. She answered immediately.

"Justine here," she barked into the phone, obviously expecting a business call.

"Justine, it's Johnny Denovo," Johnny said tentatively.

There was a pregnant pause. "And what do you have in store for me today, Mr. Detective?" she said snidely.

"Yes, sorry about that," he replied. "I had to confirm something, and I did."

"Why don't you tell me what you confirmed?" she responded tartly.

"Detective stuff," he said condescendingly. "I just wanted to make sure you were OK."

"Oh, Mr. Great Detective, I'm fine," Justine said witheringly. "But maybe I know more than you think. Did that ever occur to you?"

Johnny stopped and wondered what kind of information she might possess. She was an extremely smart and capable young woman, and seemed like the lifeblood of the stables. Because of the strength she projected, he was intrigued by what the next few exchanges would yield.

"To tell the truth, Justine, nothing of the sort had occurred to me. I have to be honest," Johnny confessed. "Usually, the family is the last to know." He thought this statement opened the door wide enough without revealing what lay behind.

"Well, Mr. Denovo," Justine said, warming her tone a bit, almost conspiratorially. "I know Trevor is innocent, that's what I know. And I know my Daddy set him up. I just don't know why."

Johnny was shocked to hear her speaking so openly about the situation. She certainly knew more than he'd expected.

"Where is your father now?" Johnny asked.

"He just called from his hotel in Montpellier, France," Justine answered confidently. "I just got off the phone with him. And don't worry, nobody can hear me. I'm out in the middle of a pasture."

It made sense that Winthrop would have arrived. The exhibit was due to open, and he probably took the same flight from Paris they'd taken, just on a different day.

"Well, Justine, I think I know something about why your father framed an innocent man," Johnny revealed. "I don't have all my thoughts together yet, but I'm trying to figure it out."

"Well, I hope you do," Justine said in a strong tone. "I'm glad we're seeing things the same way, and that you're a quick study. He's my father, but he's gone corrupt on me. I'm too much of a realist to wallow in a dreamworld. If there's anything I can do to help, you just give me a call, and you can count me in. I want my Daddy back, not the conniver he's become."

"I'll let you know," Johnny replied. "I have to say, I'm impressed by your moral clarity, Justine."

"Thank you, Johnny," she said softly. "You may call it moral clarity, but I call it knowing where he ends and I begin. The death of my Mom made that clear. I'll tell you about it someday. You call me if you need me, you hear?"

"I will, if I need you," Johnny reassured her. And with that, they concluded their call.

Johnny sat back and reflected. In the space of two hours, he had secured an unexpected ally in the home of his adversary, and settled on two candidate eggs.

Another detective might not have believed the luck or been confident that they were on the right track, but Johnny's limbic brain didn't protest. He trusted that his course was true, and what appeared as luck was the unavoidable outcome of patterns in motion, patterns established by neurons firing in the dark.

Chapter 25
Fried

Johnny awoke the morning of the 23rd after a restless night of dreams. The dream he had first had on the flight over to France was still invading his sleep, the images of the broken egg, Winthrop, inside-outside, and Humpty Dumpty becoming more prominent.

Johnny shook the dream away and immediately thought of Tucker. He was due home and would come face to face with the sabotage of his systems, the complexity of which Johnny could not even begin to imagine.

He began the day by checking email, and was not surprised when his filter caught another spam email from the conspirators. He was becoming numbed by the regularity of these events, fitting precisely the pattern identified more than two weeks ago. In fact, an involuntary sigh escaped his lungs as he realized that another tedious session of decoding a double-substitution rhyme lay ahead. Picking up the hotel pen and complimentary notepad, he set to work, slowly and sleepily. In about 20 minutes, he had another rhyming couplet to ponder: "The fox is near, awaits the sign; if none is given, it shall be nine."

Part of the meaning of this message was clear – the thief, whoever it was and whatever the motivation – was within range, ready to strike if given the order. If no order was given, the meaning of the message became less clear. Johnny began to think about the alternatives. It could be an hour, a date reference, or some other value. But what struck him was that the intended recipient of this message was clearly not the thief himself or herself, but the mastermind, who Johnny presumed was Winthrop. If this were the case, it was a clear indication that Winthrop was colluding in the theft of his own eggs, a puzzling situation Johnny could not yet fully explain.

But what did "nine" refer to? Johnny wondered. If it was a time, it wasn't specific enough, indicating neither a.m. nor p.m. nor the day. If it was a day, then which date with a nine in it? If August 9th, then this trip to France was just a long sojourn for no reason, as the eggs would be back in the United States before then. The next date with a nine in it was July 29th. With little else to go on, and his feeling that the crime would occur in Montpellier, where an exhibit could be blamed and a European, African, or Middle Eastern clientele for stolen plans would be more accessible, he thought the 29th had to be the answer. That is, unless supervening orders were somehow communicated. Plus, he recalled, an earlier message on July 7th had possibly referred to the 29th by adding 22 to the date the message was sent. It fit the pattern.

In his mind, while he attended to morning ablutions, Johnny stepped through the coming days, and everything that remained unclear or unresolved. He needed a breakthrough. Now that he had a timeline for the theft, or presumed he did, the countdown had started. He began to feel the pressure to perform, yet lacked the means. He couldn't just think his way into disrupting the crimes about to take place. He needed a physical presence, a way in.

After his shower, Johnny called Tucker's cell phone and left a message, asking him to call when he arrived home and had something to tell. He then went downstairs to the local patisserie for a roll and a coffee. He breathed in the morning's sparkling air. It was predicted to be hot again in Montpellier.

Almost unintentionally, he had left Mona to her own devices

today. There was nothing drawing them together, and a little time apart might do them some good. Constantly sharing the experience of an extended stake-out wasn't sufficient.

Sipping his coffee as he sat at the small sidewalk table, he relaxed and contemplated what to do while he waited for Tucker to call.

Johnny knew that he needed to take action soon. He decided his next move would involve some good old-fashioned detective work. After sitting in the cool shade of the sidewalk café and enjoying his morning repast, he rose and retuned to his hotel and searched out the concierge. He found her seated placidly behind a heavy stand strewn with maps and papers, half-lens glasses perched serenely on her nose. She peered over the lenses and smiled as Johnny approached.

"Good morning," she said in a husky voice. "How may I help you?" She rose from her seat, and showed herself to be taller than Johnny had expected, and very well-built for a woman her age. There was a nagging angularity to her features. In a flash, Johnny knew that the concierge had a story to tell.

"Good morning," Johnny responded coolly. "I'm wondering if you could help me."

"Of course, that is why I am here," the concierge responded.

"Yes, well, I want to surprise a friend of mine," Johnny said. "He's at a local hotel, but I don't know which one precisely. And I'd like to drop by and see if he's available for lunch."

The concierge gave a slight smile. "I quite understand," she said in a manner that suggested she had completely misinterpreted his intent, but in a way that probably ensured his approach would work. "You would like me to find this 'friend' of yours?" A hesitation in her statement clearly placed a pointed emphasis.

Johnny nodded. "His name is James Winthop," he stated. "He is likely staying at a high-class hotel."

Again, the concierge gave a smile that Johnny could only describe as conspiratorial. "Of course he is," she replied in her deep voice. "There are only a few in town. Give me a minute, and I'll call you over once I've found him. And don't worry, I won't reveal a thing," she finished with a wink.

Johnny smiled automatically in response, turned, and walked a short distance away, hiding his mild revulsion at the concierge's interpretation of his motives. It was crude and obvious, the kind of deductive reasoning that stems from an obsession, not from an assessment of the facts and motivations of others. It wasn't rare for Johnny to encounter someone so obviously consumed by personal issues, but when he did, he pitied them, for the world would always be viewed through a filter that deflected reality.

He kept the concierge in his peripheral vision while he feigned interest in the street and its pedestrian traffic. Soon, he was called over by the tall woman, a lanky arm waving at him.

"I have an address for you, but not a room number," the concierge exhaled in a nearly baritone voice, a slight chuckle underpinning the sentence. "He is staying at the Hotel Midi, just across the plaza and down the main boulevard."

Johnny thanked her, and slipped a few Euros into her strong right hand. He received another wink from his accomplice, and left.

At the Hotel Midi, Johnny saw that sleeping rooms didn't start until the third floor, and that the 12th floor was the club floor. Knowing Winthrop, he presumed the club floor would be where he'd find his quarry. He went straight up, the club floor being just a name and not an access privilege.

He began walking the hall. After turning the second corner, he found what he was looking for – a member of the cleaning staff. This woman was stern looking, middle-aged, and heavy set. Her face looked dour and humorless. Johnny smiled politely at her and passed. He kept walking, and at the opposite side of the floor, he found a petite young cleaning woman who was rather pretty but also possessed, he thought he could discern, a malleable moral status. As he grew near, he felt more confident in his assessment – she looked downright shifty to Johnny, and he was glad to make her acquaintance.

"Mademoiselle, excuse me," he said to her.

"Yes, Monsieur," she replied, looking him up and down as if appraising a window display.

"Would you like to make 100 Euros today?" Johnny asked.

"Are you propositioning me, sir?" she asked in mock horror.

Johnny laughed slightly. "Not in that way, I'm afraid," he replied. "It is rather early, you see."

She smiled in return, relaxing. "Besides, 100 would not be enough," she huffed.

"Well, all I want is the contents of a guest room's trash," Johnny stated. "But I don't know the room number. Is 100 enough for that?"

She pretended to think hard about this. "Fifty now, fifty later?" she said.

"Certainly," Johnny responded, digging out a 50 Euro note. "The guest's last name is Winthrop. Do you have that? Winthrop. He can't know I've done this. Top secret, OK?"

The cleaning girl kissed the 50 Euro note, and assured Johnny, "Top secret. Come find me at 2 o'clock, and I will have what you want from your Mr. Winthrop. The back door of the hotel, by the garbages, OK?"

Johnny smiled and shook her hand, then left the hotel, feeling pleased that he would intrude into Winthrop's life again, this time without leaving a trace.

As he walked back around the town center toward his hotel, his cell phone rang. It was Tucker.

"Johnny," Tucker uttered, breathing heavily. "I just landed. Redeye from LA. Very tired. But, I got your message, and I have news for you. Let me get home, and I'll call you right back."

"Great, old friend," Johnny replied. "Everything OK?"

"Oh, it's all good," Tucker reassured him. "I want to reclaim my space, and then I'll get you some news you can use!" The phone call ended with Tucker's enthusiastic response.

For the mid-day, Johnny wandered the streets of Montpellier. The main plaza was slow to fill, and only now was hitting its stride. Montpellier was a college town most of the year. But it was summer now, so tourists were the main inhabitants amidst the jigsaw of white-washed plaster houses and more modern, and in some cases galling, architecture.

Traveling the world always reminded him of how expansive and complex humanity was. These lives, which he had never experienced before, were on trajectories he could only get the briefest glimpse of. These people were layered upon stories, heritages, and relationships he'd never know or understand. Yet, meeting the eyes of a passerby, he felt the indelible human connection shared around the world and throughout the ages. Details may differ, he thought, but humanity was built of the same stuff in deep and important ways. This was what he depended upon to make his living, the predictability of humanity across cultures and places. Even when he encountered someone only briefly, and they provided only slight hints of intentions and habits, he could profile them. Discerning significance subtle expressions of mental patterns was his gift.

Just after lunch, Tucker called back.

"Peace has been restored," he informed Johnny. "The evil-doers have been thwarted yet again."

"Good news, compadre," Johnny replied. "Any idea of the perpetrator?"

"None at all, except it was an inside job, which we already knew," Tucker groused. "Very nice work. High caliber job. Really first-rate. I'm stumped. But, let me tell you what I've found."

Johnny was puzzled. "You mean that you, Tucker the Terminator, can't figure out who came in and messed up your place?"

"Nope," Tucker said. "It was obviously someone I trust, but my security records were wiped. The last entry was Mona, and then there's a gap in the record. Totally wiped clean, erased, destroyed, dropped. I'm stymied. I may figure it out some day, but not right now. I'm too tired, and you need to know what I found in Winthrop's files."

Despite wanting to know who had breached Tucker's security fortress, Johnny realized that talking about anything but the files was a wild goose chase.

"OK, lay it on me," he told Tucker.

"All right," Tucker said, taking a deep breath. "Most of the other files on the system were mundane, pedestrian, uninteresting. But there were two files that resembled the stolen data files in certain respects – same type of encryption on them, some other hallmarks that would bore you. The two files look, I don't know, symmetrical or twin-like in important ways, like mirror images of each other, but with nothing connecting them. I think the encrypted portions tie them together."

Johnny was perplexed. "So, why does this have you so excited?" he inquired, uncertain why news of more encrypted files was so important.

"Don't you see?" Tucker implored. "There is a system here, and the key unlocks more than just these files. It gives access to something bigger. It's a layered system, too, so there might be two similar keys, one to unlock these files, which can then be used to unlock the plans or find the second key."

Now Johnny understood. "So, this means that I have to find two things, possibly, and that they're related?"

"That's right," Tucker confirmed. "And, by the way, this encryption is completely unknown to me. I can't fathom it. We're up against something unique here."

Johnny paused in thought, feeling his way through the next few words. "Well, Tucker, this is very useful. Just the other day, I was going through the files describing Winthrop's eggs, and two of them stood out from the half-dozen he owns, based on what I know about how he thinks and what they represent. An interesting coincidence, now that I hear myself saying it, but I'm not sure how it applies."

"Hey, bud, me neither, but I know the clock's ticking, and information is power," Tucker replied. "Use it wisely."

"Thanks, my friend," Johnny responded sincerely. "Good luck sleeping and untangling your mysteries. Call me with anything new, OK?"

"Definitely," Tucker said. "Solve this thing already, will you?"

"Si, Senor," Johnny laughed, and the two old friends hung up. Johnny recalled his words from what seemed eons ago, spoken with bravado to a detective in Richmond – by focusing on what doesn't fit, we learn the criminal's path. Tucker certainly had provided more things that were aberrant, abnormal, and perplexing.

Chapter 26
Hard Boiled

Two o'clock was fast approaching, and Johnny had a date with an untrustworthy cleaning woman. He retraced his steps to the Hotel Midi, and turned down the alleyway alongside the imposing structure, seeking the large garbage bins at the rear. A small door at the back looked like the right place to await his delivery. He verified that he still had 50 Euros to share with his source, and leaned against the unclean wall.

For a moment, he closed his eyes, relishing the coolness of the stone wall as it pressed through his thin shirt. It was quiet here, sheltered from the expansive noise of a city at mid-day. The distant sound of an approaching motor scooter barely caught his attention, but a tingle of worry raised his adrenaline level, heightening his senses. Still, he kept his eyes closed and body relaxed. The scooter was moving directly down the alley, and at high speed, coming from the opposite direction. Some auditory quality made it sound ominous. His limbic system was sparking. Yet Johnny measured his responses carefully, remaining in repose as if unconcerned or unaware of the approaching rider.

The scooter neared, getting very close, and then there was a slight shift in the engine noise, as if the driver were adjusting and revving simultaneously. Johnny's eyes flew open. Just then, the back door opened, and his friendly chambermaid appeared swinging a medium-sized plastic bag. She tossed this to the driver of the scooter, who caught it in mid-air, and roared away. Meeting Johnny's stare with a sideways glance, she shrugged and said casually, "Sorry, he gave me 200, in advance. Simple." She slammed the door and disappeared.

Johnny was taken aback for a moment. He'd been had. This demanded immediate attention. The scooter had been a beaten-up maroon job, nothing fancy, a bit downtrodden in its appearance, and driven by a wiry man in shorts and a t-shirt, wearing a white helmet with a smoked glass visor. No tattoos or other identifying marks. No distinctive suntan lines, jewelry, or mannerisms, and he'd not uttered a word.

Still, gathering his wits about him again, Johnny thought it could only be one person, the rogue agent shadowing them. Either that, or someone he had hired. Johnny had been followed to the Hotel Midi earlier, and it must have been a simple matter to have found the girl and paid her off for the delivery of the same item Johnny had wanted. Simple and effective. That was the problem with untrustworthy people. He'd not listened to his inner brain. It had told him she was morally malleable, yet he had trusted her. It had been fooled by a paradox.

Before he could take any action, the door opened again, and the same girl poked her head out into the alleyway, tentatively and secretively, peering around at Johnny.

"Is he gone?" she asked. "Is he quite gone?"

Johnny nodded slightly, wondering at her motivations. She should be off somewhere planning how to spend her 200 Euros.

"Monsieur," she said, emerging from the doorway carrying a small plastic bag pressed close to her stomach. "Here is what you wanted. I gave him only some scrap paper, along with all the tissues and wrappers and old newspapers, but these are the papers from Monsieur Winthrop's garbage. I know who you are, Detective Denovo. Your beard may fool others, but not me. Like you, I am sick of cleaning up after bad people, and if someone is doing an injustice, you will correct the situation, will you not?"

Johnny peered deeply into her eyes, which were rimmed with emotion. "Yes, if I can, I will," he assured her.

She kissed him on his scruffy cheek, pressed the plastic bag into his hands, turned, and disappeared back through the door again.

Johnny looked at the bag momentarily, and then folded it down and tucked it into the back of his pants, pulling his shirt over top to conceal it fully.

Back at his hotel, Johnny inspected the contents of the bag, which consisted of a few sheets of paper of various sizes and types. Most were easily identifiable and trivial – a roster of hotel rates, pieces of Hotel Midi notepaper containing restaurant names and phone numbers, some receipts for charges and ATM withdrawals, and a ripped up breakfast menu door hanger. But one smaller sheet of paper contained information Johnny found compelling. It was a list of metals with two rows of numbers next to each. Even more interesting, the paper looked age-worn, tattered, and yellowed, and the names and one column of numbers were printed in dot matrix characters, suggesting Winthrop had held onto this paper for many years. The other column of numbers was jotted in ink by hand.

The list read:

Copper:

Hard drawn	89.5	6.53
Annealed	100	
Gold	65	7.23
Nickel	12-16	
Nickel silver	5.3	7.74
Platinum	15	
Silver	106	6.56 & 6.89
Zinc	28.2	5.19

Johnny couldn't make anything of the list, but tucked it away. Apparently, it was important, or it wouldn't have been worth 200

Euros to retrieve. But if it were worth more than the paper it was printed on, why was it thrown away? he wondered. It must have been discarded by accident, the mistake only realized after it was too late. Then, when the minion was sent back to retrieve it, and it was gone, the cleaning staff was interrogated, the fact that it was out for bid was revealed, and the price rose. That must be the explanation, Johnny concluded. It fit the facts.

After sorting through the papers and puzzling out this little mystery, he called Mona's room. She wasn't there, so he tried her cell phone. She answered after a few rings.

"Hello, Monsieur," she said in greeting. "Wonderful day for some shopping, wouldn't you agree?"

"Is that what you're doing?" he asked, going along. "Well, I have done some shopping as well, and I'm about to inspect what I've purchased. Meet me at the café downstairs when you get back. I want to run some numbers by you." And with that cryptic message, he hung up.

Chapter 27
Caged

"Well, I have jewelry made of this kind of stuff," Mona noted, examining the list. "But I can't figure out the numbers for the life of me. These aren't sizes, unless it's jewelry for elephants."

Johnny concurred. "Yes, I think this has something to do with the eggs, because these are jewelry metals, for the most part. But why are the numbers so different? And why is this so old?"

Mona turned the paper over in her hands. "It's been folded a few times, as well. When you found it, it was open, right?"

"Right," Johnny indicated. "Someone kept this for a long time and wasn't always concerned about it, but has recently been treating it with care."

"Winthrop kept this for a long time," Mona corrected him pointedly. "This was from his garbage, you said. So it's his. He must have thrown it away with some of the receipts you found, so I'd guess it was in his wallet. It was important, and useful to him here and now. But he threw it away by mistake, and when he went back to dig through his trash to find it, it had been taken by the cleaning crew. So he asked someone else who's here working for him to get it back."

"That's my thinking, too," Johnny murmured. "That old-fashioned dot-matrix printout makes me think this had to come from the late 1980s or early 1990s. Winthrop was working for a government contractor back then. He must have had some idea years ago that these numbers could be useful, meant something, factored into some vague plan. So, he printed this out, cut it down to size, and stored it. And the idea never went away. In fact," Johnny intoned, "it found an application."

"What do you mean?" Mona asked.

"The handwriting," Johnny said pointing to the ink numbers alongside the printed ones. "Winthrop had a vague notion that information about metals, some measurable property, might matter someday to a plan he was forming, and then found the application of this concept, which required the addition of some other numbers. And what do we know he's acquired since the 1990s that have jewelers' metals all over them?"

"They're measurements for the Faberge eggs," Mona gasped in an epiphany. "That's what the handwritten numbers are for!"

"Exactly," Johnny agreed happily. "So this little sheet of paper is about the metals in the eggs. I'll bet the handwritten numbers are lengths or diameters or some measurement of the physical eggs. But what are the other numbers?"

A frustrated silence settled over the café table. It was approaching sundown, the fading brilliance of the day resolving into watercolor tones, and a mosaic of shadows was falling across the ground. Condensing smells of the verdant parks around them suffused the air. The sounds of the street intruded into what had been an active private discussion, and the noise from outside only emphasized the fact that they had hit a stone wall.

"Tensile strength?" Mona offered tepidly.

Johnny shook his head. "It could be anything. Metals have a lot of properties. I should do some research tonight when I get back to my room. I'll bet I can find something online that will crack this."

They sipped at their coffees in silence for a while, each churning their own thoughts about what they had found. Suddenly, the blare of a motor scooter at high speed caught their attention, but not for the sound it was making alone. Their adrenaline spiked because of the screams, crashes of dishes, and shouts that seemed to rush ahead of the roar.

Johnny spun around in his chair, and Mona rose from hers part way, coffee still in hand. A scooter was charging down the sidewalk, headed straight for them. Winthrop's minion was crashing through the sidewalk cafes, apparently having spotted Johnny and Mona from an angle across the plaza, and was hell-bent on reaching them. He was wearing a jacket that was flapping open, and Johnny saw a gun in the waistband of his trousers, directly down his right side. He was left-handed. Johnny filed this fact away as he jumped up and around behind Mona, and pulled her away from the sidewalk and under the awning.

The scooter roared to a stop at their table, the menacing visor of the driver swiveling toward them.

"Give me the paper, Denovo," the driver said coarsely, a British accent embellishing his utterance.

Without thinking, Johnny lunged forward with both palms of his hands hitting the heavy table they'd just been seated at, thrusting it into the motor scooter and upsetting the driver's balance, causing him to nearly fall. In the tangle of twisted bike and struggle of limbs regaining their balance, Johnny picked up a wrought-iron chair and threw it at the driver's helmet. People nearby screamed. The contact between chair and helmet was solid, and the driver slumped even further toward the ground, hovered for a moment, and then leaned slowly to the pavement. He was stunned, but still conscious.

"Let's move!" Johnny shouted at Mona, propelling her forward with a push that matched the urgency of the situation. Her coffee cup dropped from her hand with a clatter. In the dim light of approaching twilight, the confusion seemed to resound through the square with shadows multiplying the uncertainty and chaos.

Mona ran through the tables and out to the sidewalk. The tone of the scooter, low and idling, had not changed. Johnny followed her, thinking hard.

"We need to separate, buy some time," Johnny shouted. "He can only chase one of us. And I'm the one he wants. So, here," he said, thrusting the paper into her hand, "take this, go into that big store down the street, and call Tucker. Give him the numbers, make sure he gets which ones are in pen, and then meet me out the opposite entrance. Go!"

Mona was stumbling slightly, running in heels and grabbing the paper, but she retained her balance and was soon headed directly for the store Johnny had indicated. The sound of the motor scooter had changed, becoming an urgent whine, and Johnny knew he was out of time.

Yard-long cement pots filled with flowers separated the plaza from the road, with an opening about six feet between the two to allow for foot traffic and to avoid a claustrophobic feeling to the landscape. With a daring leap, he cleared the nearest barricade, clipping a few flowers on the way over, and upon landing in the road quickly reoriented himself to running as close to the barricade as possible. Cars honked but easily avoided him. The scooter's engine grew louder, drawing near.

Johnny stole a glance behind and saw the driver bearing down on him. It was time to employ some tactics. By running just outside the barriers separating the road from the sidewalk, he had options. As the engine noise became unbearably loud, Johnny leaped up onto a barricade, then back into the plaza, his step into the flowers causing him to stumble. But with a heave, he retained his balance, landed inside the plaza, and spun around, doubling back. The scooter's tires screeched as the driver tried to respond to Johnny's sudden move, but the time his adversary needed to slow, reverse, and control the little bike gave Johnny some distance on his pursuer again.

In an instant the scooter was charging up the sidewalk again. It was time for a new tactic. When the noise was at what seemed its zenith, Johnny turned suddenly and stopped, the motor scooter nearly upon him. The driver, surprised at this apparently suicidal move, reacted instinctively to avoid hitting Johnny, steering hard with his dominant left hand to swerve the bike away. Johnny planted his feet, lunged forward with one leg, and straight-armed the driver directly in the shoulder with his open palm, a tai-chi move that turned the opponent's kinetic energy back on him. The scooter flipped out from under the driver as he fell to the ground. Johnny, feet planted on the ground front to back, found himself tumbling over the bike as the rear wheel struck his forward leg, sweeping around from the outside. He struck his side against the nearest large garden pot. Shaking his head and rising quickly, he noticed that the scooter's engine had failed, and the driver was slow to rise from the sidewalk, clutching his left shoulder where he had struck the ground. Johnny put weight on his leg. It was fine, but his pant leg was shredded by the impact of the scooter's rear drive wheel.

"Damn it," Johnny muttered at the damage to his appearance, rubbing his aching side.

Johnny took off again, this time intending to meet Mona. He ran back around the café area through the carnage of overturned tables, bewildered pedestrians, and scattered meals, to the store's other entrance, directly opposite of the one she had gone in. Mona was standing there, waiting for him.

"What happened?" she shrieked at him. He must have looked worse than he thought.

"It's still happening," he shouted back. "Did you get in touch with Tucker?"

"Just finished. I left a message," she said. "I read off all the numbers. We should have what we need."

"Good," Johnny said, reaching her side and pausing to catch his breath. "This is a hell of an evening thrill-ride, isn't it?"

"What do we do now?" she asked.

The sound of the scooter was evident again. It was spluttering to life, out of sight around the corner.

"Wait here with me," Johnny said. "When this guy rounds the corner, make it very obvious that you are handing me the piece of paper. Then, go back into the store and find the men's pants."

"Pants?" Mona asked. Johnny showed her his lower leg, and then she nodded. "I saw a rack coming through. I'll meet you there." Then, with a jerk of her head, she indicated to Johnny that the scooter was in view.

She held the piece of paper in her hand, high in the air, and Johnny accepted it from her, holding it aloft over his head.

"Now hide!" he said tersely, his concern for her obvious by the tone, uttering what sounded very much like a command.

Johnny held the paper aloft resolutely, and the scooter pulled alongside. He peered squarely into the helmet, the smoked glass visor obscuring the eyes he was seeking to intimidate.

"Here you go," Johnny muttered. "Take it with my compliments."

The driver clenched his fists and began to move a hand to the waistband of his pants, but thought better of it as the wail of sirens began mounting nearby. He reached out, took the paper, and put it in his side coat pocket, twisting uncomfortably in response to the pain from his injuries.

"You will pay dearly for this, Denovo," the driver said in his British accent. "I should have killed you on the spot."

Johnny didn't respond. He wanted the threat to feel as empty as it was.

The maroon scooter roared off, and Johnny stood there for a moment, resonating with anger and adrenaline. The sirens were fast approaching, their keening wail freezing his attention. He knew he would have a few hours with the police explaining away the events that had just transpired. Mona reappeared at his side. She'd been watching from the shadows inside the store.

"I guess we're going to have to face the music now," she said.

Johnny smiled. "No, we just need to sing the right tune," he said under his breath, turning toward the store. "But first, new pants."

Chapter 28
Cracked

Johnny was still puzzling over the incidents that had transpired, but fatigue and a low pain from his leg were draining his overwhelmed mind. It was nearly 2 a.m., and the exertions of the prior evening combined with the long session with the unimaginative Montpellier police had sapped his strength and fogged his thinking. In fact, his limbic brain had taken an intermission break during the time with the police while he used his cerebellum to explain away the attack at the café as an attempted robbery – famous detective on vacation, recognized by a street thug, nothing much more to it. The story proved sufficient for the obviously harried police detective.

As soon as he and Mona left the police, Johnny's dog brain went back into high dudgeon: What possible pattern did all the disparate elements possess, share, inhabit? They had to all be connected.

He slid his hotel key into its slot, and pushed the handle down. Inside, the room was completely dark. He reached for the glowing switch just inside the door, and then stopped. It was all connected, he suddenly thought. Then, the double meaning his limbic brain was advancing upward into his cerebrum became clear. Tracing in his mind back from the switch before him through an imaginary series of wires behind the hotel's walls, through to the basement, to what had to be a large set of electrical panels, from there to the service source for the building to the grid's major supply and from there back to the power generation facility, this switch, this little glow, was connected to it all, both receiving power from the source and closing the circuit by sending back negative ions that kept the flow alive, enabling the electrical system. This little switch, when he pressed it, would close another loop in the system, and illuminate his room. It was all connected. It was all connected by wires. The world was like a globe entwined with wires completing a massive connected electrical system.

Still frozen in thought, he saw in his mind's eye the eggs, the Faberge eggs, with their intricate gold patterns wrapping their enameled shells, like those imagined electrical wires strung around the globe, the connection complete and absolute, the only requirement a pulse of electricity to charge the system. The eggs could become conductors of a very distinctive and special variety. Realization filled his mind. Even the last couplet fit the emerging and cohesive picture. This also fit the inside-out metaphor Winthrop operated within – except that it was more complicated than that. Winthrop had moved on to encompass a related intrinsic-extrinsic metaphor, the eggs' wires possessing invisible traits within their natures, and these becoming extrinsic with the application of electricity.

In a flash, the references to metals and numbers made sense, the serpentine filigrees of the eggs he'd instinctively selected as his prime candidates fit a broader context, and he knew that the eggs represented a way to close a switch. And the switch that remained open was the gap at the center of the stolen plans, Johnny realized. The eggs were the key to unlock the files. Tucker had said information was power, but in this case, power could generate information. The eggs were the physical hack, the electrical tumbler that when aligned would unlock the secrets of the stolen plans and complete the transaction.

The theft of the eggs, and their subsequent return, would not be anything for Winthrop but a way of completing a transaction, with no risk. The Faberge eggs were of no immediate monetary value to whoever possessed them illegally – they were too hot to fence, too identifiable, and not valuable enough disassembled. It was a well-conceived plan. The eggs were integral to a system.

Now, the challenge was clear for Johnny: How could he foul up the transaction? He gazed at the switch again. And again, the answer appeared out of nowhere in a blinding flash of the obvious – cut the wires.

During these revelations, Johnny had stood in the doorway, his body holding the door open, his hand hovering over the switch, for a small number of minutes by now. Almost superstitiously, as if sudden movement might break a spell that had been cast, he moved his hand from the switch, turned, and walked back down the hall, his hotel room door banging shut and latching behind him.

The next thing he knew, he was rapping on Mona's door. A sleepy voice answered his tattoo.

"Who is it?" Mona said blearily. "What do you want?"

"Mona," Johnny whispered urgently. "It's me. I think I've figured it out."

There were sounds of shuffling and rustling, and soon the door was flung open. Mona stood there, hair tousled, hotel bathrobe tied around her, bare feet and legs protruding.

"Well, it took you long enough," she said, making a mock-seductive face.

Johnny groaned. "No, not that," he said wearily. "I figured that out a long time ago." There was an awkward pause as they both realized the significance of the moment. Johnny was the first to recover, and he pressed onward with his thoughts. "I've figured out Winthrop's game," he revealed. "It's all about wiring."

Mona cocked an eyebrow at this.

"Look," Johnny said in feigned exasperation. "Can you just get dressed and come with me?"

"Sure," she said. "Wait here. I'll only be a few minutes." And with that, she closed her door.

Johnny moved quickly down the hall to the house phone perched demurely on a table near the elevators. He needed something. He picked up the phone, let it ring, and asked the front desk to have a maintenance man come up. At this time of the night, he wouldn't have to wait long, he hoped.

Another problem sprang to mind – the renegade agent who had been tailing them for weeks now. He wasn't the driver of the scooter, Johnny had realized. They were not one and the same person. Johnny had continued to see him after they left the police station, and he was uninjured. Johnny doubted he was far off, even at this time of the evening. He probably knew that Johnny hadn't stayed in his room, and was waiting somewhere nearby to continue his assignment. It was time to shake him, and Johnny had an idea. Calling down again to the front desk, the pulsing ring was answered swiftly, and he asked to be connected with the local television station. Once the phone was answered, he quickly reported that he had seen Johnny Denovo entering the hotel he now stood in, and thought Mr. Denovo would be leaving again for a night of carousing, suggesting they should send a crew over. He added as a convenient aside that he believed Denovo had eluded identification so far because he had grown a beard. He knew that the grave shift was a close-knit community in journalism no matter the nation or municipality, and that one call would lead to others. It was time to wield his celebrity.

The elevator's chime sounded, a muted electronic tone, and a small older man stepped out wearing coveralls and sporting a large tool belt.

"Monsieur?" he inquired looking at Johnny, who was just placing the phone back in its cradle.

"Ah, yes, thank you for coming so quickly," Johnny spoke serenely. "I have a small problem. My girlfriend and I have, you see, been playing, and I cannot open the, well, the handcuffs. They are only toy handcuffs, but we are, shall we say, in a bind. Very embarrassing. If you had some strong wire cutters, I would very much like to borrow them."

The older man raised his eyebrows and began to laugh. "You Americans are very odd," he croaked. "But life is short and you are young." Then, reaching into his tool belt and chuckling to himself, he extracted a medium-sized set of wire cutters. "Will these do?" he asked.

Johnny smiled and accepted them from the maintenance man. "They're perfect," he acknowledged. "May I return them tomorrow, most likely after breakfast?"

The maintenance man pressed the down call button for the elevator, and waved his hand dismissively. "Monsieur, they are yours to keep. I have another set. Consider them a keepsake. And who knows? You may need them again," he finished, cackling slightly at his witticism. Johnny laughed as well, and turned, one hand raised in thanks while the other pocketed the wire cutters.

Mona emerged thirty seconds later to find Johnny leaning casually against the wall across from her room. She was looking quite fetching and chewing gum. "Morning breath," she muttered. "I was only asleep for 10 minutes, if that, but I have morning breath. Go figure."

"You had time to sleep? You must have a clear conscience and a simple nightgown," Johnny ruminated.

"Actually, as you've noted before, I don't have a conscience. And it might interest you to know that I don't wear nightgowns, either," Mona responded playfully, squeezing Johnny's upper arm. He swung his head over and his eyes widened. She could be a minx at times, he thought.

He cleared his throat. "Well, where we're going, you will need fresh breath," Johnny said. "You'll need to lay on the charm."

As they rode the elevator down, Johnny explained his revelations to Mona. He also realized one benefit of the timing of their adventure – even creeps need to sleep, and he was fairly sure the injured scooter driver wouldn't be around at this hour. Having one less thug to worry about bolstered his confidence another small notch.

"OK, OK, let me see if I get this," Mona said as they crossed the lobby to leave the hotel. "Winthrop stole plans, but encrypted them in such a manner that a physical object, conducting electricity only as that single physical object can, must be used to unlock the encryption? And that the way the object is designed, the metals interact, and their lengths could be used as an electrical signature?"

"That's right," Johnny confirmed, while indicating to the doorman that he wanted a taxi. At this hour, it would take a few minutes for one to arrive. In fact, he was banking on it.

"And Faberge eggs make a perfect choice, because they are unique, and they conduct electricity," Mona murmured, more to herself than to Johnny. "It's a pretty good plan."

"I agree. Now, what we need to do is foul up his plan," Johnny offered.

"How?" Mona asked. "Cut the wires?"

"You're ready for the advanced course," Johnny praised.

"But how are we going to get to the eggs?" Mona asked.

"Follow my lead," Johnny said cryptically.

Chapter 29
Hatched

The street was deserted while they awaited the taxi, only themselves and the doorman at this hour. The occasional car went by thumping with mega-bass and cloaked in smoked glass. It was clubbing hour in Montpellier, and the kids were out. Loud whoops from what sounded like a drunken Australian emanated from a car passing across the end of the street.

Johnny sneaked a look back into the hotel lobby. His shadow was approaching, walking slowly and surreptitiously but definitely toward them, attempting to remain in contact if possible.

"When the taxi comes," Johnny said in a normal voice, making sure his lips were not in a position to be read, "get in and ask the driver to go around the block, then come back and pick me up. I'll explain when you get back."

"All right," Mona said tentatively, but then held her tongue. She was getting the hang of this.

Just then, a battered old taxi pulled up, spluttering to, if not a stop, then a severe pause. The doorman said something disparaging under his breath, then smiled obsequiously at them and opened the rear door. Johnny went toward the taxi with Mona, catching in his peripheral vision the fact that their shadow was now moving swiftly toward the doors exiting the hotel. After letting Mona into the taxi in what appeared to be a chivalrous manner, he stepped back, slammed the door, and slapped his hand on the rear stanchion, indicating that the taxi was ready to depart. The little car lurched forward uncertainly, and then began to move off slowly and noisily.

Johnny turned swiftly as his pursuer emerged from the hotel's entrance, a mild look of puzzlement on his face. He was dressed in a black shirt and jeans, and his short haircut made him look younger than he probably was.

The roar from a number of approaching engines took over the scene before either could do more than lock their gazes. Two news vans, three motorcycles, and two small cars zoomed around the bend, and screeched to a halt near the hotel. The paparazzi leaped from their motorbikes, flashes ablaze, taking picture after picture and shouting, "Monsieur Denovo, Monsieur Denovo!"

Johnny glanced at his pursuer, and then strode quickly to his side, putting his arm around his shoulders. Johnny moved so quickly and confidently that his adversary had no chance to react. The dazzling camera flashes in the night and the frenetic activity of uninhibited journalists caused a momentary panic in the man.

Johnny turned to the oncoming photographers and television crews and smiled, his arm firmly around his new friend's shoulders. His adversary, unfamiliar with the media, began to smile reflexively as well.

"Monsieur Denovo," said the first true reporter to arrive, "we are so honored you are here! Yet we are worried. Why are you in Montpellier? What is the crime?"

Johnny smiled even more broadly. "Well," he responded, "I should have known that the excellent journalists here would learn of my arrival very quickly. I am impressed."

The reporter beamed slightly at his response. Johnny knew the media and he were symbiotic, and he treated the relationships with great care.

Johnny continued, "My friend here and I are looking into a case." He turned to face his antagonist, still smiling. "Why don't you introduce yourself and tell people why we are here?"

Johnny knew a lie was impossible. Tomorrow, his adversary's picture would be online in many places. There was no longer anything like a local news story. He had in an instant been transformed into a rogue agent caught by digital cameras capable of transmitting his image everywhere instantaneously. And that image would show not only his face very clearly, but also demonstrate that his cover had been blown by the quarry he'd been assigned to stalk, the man who now stood next to him, smiling and grasping him around the shoulders. It was his worst-case scenario – revealed to everyone who paid him as a liability.

"Well?" Johnny inquired when the silence became noticeable.

His new friend cleared his throat, and muttered in poor French, "My name is Howard Gold. I'm here to fight criminals." The reporters attempted to conceal their laughter at the awkward accent and limited vocabulary of Howard Gold, and turned their full attention on Johnny.

"So, Mr. Denovo, why are you here?" the female reporter closest to him asked again.

"Oh, I've been asked to prevent a crime this time," Johnny replied. "None has occurred. The Faberge eggs on exhibit are very valuable, and I was asked to make sure they remain secure. And I love France, so I couldn't resist such an assignment," Johnny concluded with a winning smile.

The female reporter stopped writing, then caught herself, and returned to her work, flustered.

"How long are you here? For the full exhibit?" another reporter asked.

"Yes, for the full exhibit," Johnny responded, noting a distinctive putt-putt sound coming up the street. "Now, if you'll excuse me, my taxi has arrived and I am off to rest after a very late dinner. Mr.

Gold has to investigate a possible lead. Perhaps you should work with him to see where he is going?" Johnny suggested.

The reporter smiled at the suggestion, and the small band of journalists, photographers, and TV cameramen swiveled their collective attention and powerful lights on this morning's new media darling, Howard Gold.

Johnny collapsed into the back seat of Mona's pitiful little taxi, laughing so hard he felt like an adolescent again. Mona looked at him as if he she was worried for his sanity.

"What could possibly be so funny?" she inquired.

Johnny wiped his eyes and dispersed the last few swooping chuckles. "Oh, Mona, sometimes, this job is too much fun. I'll tell you on the way. Let's just say, that cockroach who was following us won't be bothering us any more. He just had the light of a thousand days thrown on him."

The slow and deliberate taxi provided a serene early morning ride, with no bumps or troubles, only the occasional wheeze making them anxious about its mechanical abilities. Yet, it proved unfailing. When they finally arrived at the exhibit hall, the neighborhood looked desolate. Everyone was asleep at this hour. It was as if the area were breathing hardly at all. They walked across the dimly lit plaza and around the corner toward the security gate by the loading dock. A guard was seated in the booth, and a thin beat of music dribbled out from a small radio perched on the windowsill. It had to be difficult to stay awake with monotonous work, a quiet street, and early morning hours. Bad French rap music would have been just the ticket for Johnny as well.

Johnny and Mona approached the guard shed, and as soon as they entered the perimeter of light thrown by the overhead street lamp, the guard jumped up and barked at them from behind the glass to stop where they were, clicking off the music as he rose from his chair. He certainly seemed alert, and was out of the booth in an instant, speaking and not shouting, but exhorting them to stop.

They obliged, stopping without protest.

"Good morning, Monsieur," Johnny said calmly and quietly as soon as the guard was within earshot. "My name is Johnny Denovo. I'm a detective from the United States. You may have heard of me. This is my assistant, Mademoiselle Landau. We were awoken about an hour ago and asked by our client, Mr. James Winthrop, to inspect his Faberge eggs, which are part of the exhibit here now, as you may know. He has hired us to look after them, and we have been given information that we believe warrants our attention."

The guard listened attentively to Johnny's long introduction, reading the calm body language as non-threatening. He did not detect that it was a lie.

"I see," he replied. "And could I see your identification?"

Johnny and Mona produced their passports for the guard, who inspected them with the practiced movements of a former passport agent. He handed them back after a minute.

"Yes, I know of you, Detective Denovo," the guard confided. "But how can I confirm that you are here on official business? May I call Mr. Winthrop to confirm?"

Johnny shook his head. "No, he's now asleep, and would view it as a failing if I were not able to do my job without waking him. If you'd like confirmation, you can call his daughter. She's in the United States, and is most certainly awake. She's aware of our engagement by Mr. Winthrop, and can confirm that the situation is as I've described." Johnny produced his cell phone as he spoke, offering it to the guard as a source of assistance.

The guard looked askance, but thought things over, then agreed.

"Yes, please dial the number. You have her in your index?" he asked. "I would like to see that you have called her number."

"Of course," Johnny answered, dialing Justine Winthrop's cell phone from his call log, and handing the phone to the guard while keeping both feet firmly planted, underscoring his non-threatening nature and awareness of security protocols. "She does not speak French," Johnny offered.

"I speak very good English," the guard said in clear English.

The guard waited, then said, "Hello, Ms. Justine Winthrop? Yes, I am a guard at the facility exhibiting your father's Faberge egg collection. Yes, in Montpellier. A Mr. Johnny Denovo is here, claiming that he was hired by your father to protect these eggs, and that he was asked to inspect them this morning. There may be a problem. Can you confirm this?"

There was a long silence through which Justine's voice was barely audible, but Johnny could tell that she was being very convincing, explaining and confirming energetically and in detail. The guard nodded solemnly at Johnny and Mona as he listened, signaling that everything was making sense.

"Thank you, Mademoiselle Winthrop," the guard said. "I wish you a good evening. Goodbye." He closed the phone, and handed it back to Johnny.

"I will allow you in," he said crisply. "Let me radio to my supervisor inside, and he can escort you to inspect your client's property."

Johnny and Mona were soon inside the gate leading to the loading dock. The guard had indicated they were to proceed to a small door. A bright modern light, flush-mounted and sleek, burned above it. These exhibit halls were doing very well, Johnny thought. Even their loading docks were well-appointed. He knocked at the door with hollow bangs that sounded as loud as fireworks in the quiet morning. Footsteps were soon audible from the other side. A burly man in his 50s opened the door, and said, "Monsieur Denovo?"

"Yes, it is," Johnny replied. "And Mademoiselle Landau."

"Ah, yes, come in, come in," the older gentleman said, pushing the door wider. "You have come to inspect some Faberge eggs?"

"Precisely," Johnny responded with a smile.

"I am Supervisor Largent," the man said by way of introduction as he began walking through the high-ceilinged loading area toward the exhibit hall. This backstage zone was crammed with empty boxes and large sheets of sliced plastic, heavy and derelict. As luxurious and well-appointed as the exhibit areas seemed, behind the façade, the detritus of modern showmanship resided. "You are not the only one with a nervous client," Supervisor Largent continued. "The owner of the hall is nervous as well. He visits every day. He's not accustomed to having a show containing so many priceless items, you see."

"I see," Johnny confirmed. They were now in a long hallway, moving toward a set of double doors. The supervisor pulled a set of keys from his pocket and unlocked the doors, pulling one open with some strength. He then reached inside and turned on a set of over-head lights. The room was nothing like a normal convention floor. Underfoot was what appeared to be authentic Italian white marble, and throughout the room were arranged elegant display cases, each aglow with muted halogen lights that illuminated their contents perfectly. This was clearly an attempt to create an environment that swathed the eggs in opulence. Johnny's instinctive dislike for ostentation was triggered, and his mind recoiled slightly from the scene.

Mona inhaled sharply and involuntarily at the sight of the exhibit alight and uncrowded. "It's lovely," she said demurely.

"Yes, Mademoiselle, it is," Supervisor Largent agreed eagerly, eyeing Mona with some consideration and reaching the same conclusion, Johnny thought, noting the leverage this gave him. Time was of the essence, so he moved in.

"Supervisor Largent, there are two eggs in particular that my client wished me to inspect first-hand, to see if any damage had occurred," Johnny said. "They are the Windflowers Egg and the Diamond Trellis Egg. May I inspect them?"

Mona felt it was her turn to help.

"And while he's doing that, I would love to see the Winter Egg," she said a little girlishly, her eyes alight. Supervisor Largent seemed to puff up with self-importance realizing that he could give this lovely young creature something she desired.

"Let me see," Supervisor Largent said in his deepest and most commanding voice. "The alarm system is active, but it can be turned off. Let me see where those two you want are located, Detective Denovo." He looked at a small stand at the head of the exhibit, and identified the two eggs in the schematic posted there. "Yes, they are both down this aisle, and the Winter Egg is over against that wall," he said, moving forward, his arm pointing off to the left, indicating where Mona and he were headed. "Give me a moment and I can open the cases for you, Detective Denovo."

Supervisor Largent strode off briskly into the dimmer areas of the exhibit room. Mona and Johnny exchanged a knowing look.

"Winter Egg?" Johnny asked in a soft, bemused whisper.

"I glanced at the sign. It's far away. Otherwise, it was a guess," Mona replied quietly.

When Supervisor Largent returned, he led them to the two cases in question, and lifted the glass from the pedestals.

"Usually, these are magnetically sealed, and strong enough to resist the strength of 100 men," he bragged mischievously. "But I can lift it now as easily as a small bird." He smiled at Mona, hoping this depiction of virility was being noted.

Johnny interjected, "Let me take a close visual inspection of the two eggs, and then look over more generally a few others in my client's collection. Then I'll be done. My client suspects that gems or precious metals may have been removed, a very unlikely circumstance, but I need to reassure him completely by looking inside, inspecting each egg. You understand."

Mona moved slightly closer to Supervisor Largent. "Perhaps after the Winter Egg, you could also show me which are your favorites. You must have one or two after having seen them night after night?" The supervisor smiled, and agreed to the extended tour.

As soon as the supervisor's back was turned, Johnny glanced about in a cautious and measured manner. Surveillance cameras were located in many spots he had noted coming in, but with a little cleverness, he could conceal his hands while he completed his right-eous vandalism. The wire cutters were already in his palm, their short handles tucked up his sleeve. By bending over for an apparent close-up visual inspection, and then standing erectly between the cameras and the egg, he could reach in and manipulate the delicate filigrees.

Because the metals were malleable – gold and silver primarily – he had to cut them quickly or risk distorting them. This meant tim-ing his aggressive move precisely with an equal countervailing force to leave the egg still and apparently untouched, and to allow for the swift snap.

Luckily, the eggs were open, the hinged top creating a natural counterbalance against the sheer forces he was applying, assisting him slightly in perpetrating the justifiable damage. As Johnny saw it, bejeweled decorative eggs, no matter how valuable or treasured, could be restored by a skilled metallurgist. National military secrets, once leaked, could lead to untenable consequences, including the deaths of young soldiers or innocent civilians. To have a rich criminal become richer in this manner and with such stakes was unacceptable. There was no debate to be had.

The first egg, the Windflowers, was the trickiest of the two because its design integrated the metals more completely. He had to circle the egg a few times, gazing at it from top to bottom, before he found his target – a small delicate piece of filigree near the base, which snapped with one hard squeeze of the wire cutters. Examining his handiwork, Johnny was pleased to see that the break was not appar-ent even upon relatively close inspection. It was a microscopic gap, sufficient for the purpose but concealed in a small forest of decorative goldsmithy.

He could hear a pleasant conversation ensuing between Mona and Supervisor Largent some distance away. This background noise was reassuring. He would only react if it stopped or drew too near.

The Diamond Trellis Egg was easier. The plentiful filigree was encrusted with diamonds and therefore had natural leverage points with which to grapple. His target strand snapped on the first attempt, the diamonds concealing the damage.

From there, Johnny proceeded to check the other eggs in the Winthrop collection, inspecting the eggs superficially, trying to look pensive and knowledgeable. Mona's voice mixed with Supervisor Largent's the entire time, but for one short pause, and they were drawing nearer as he gazed carefully at the final egg. Each Faberge egg was remarkable, he had to admit, each a work of art and craftsmanship worth preserving. The fact that they were part of a rich man's plot to get richer selling military plans was a travesty.

Supervisor Largent's voice broke his reverie. "Are you done, Detective?" he asked. He looked a little chagrined, and Johnny thought he discerned from a flicker of the eyes that Mona must know why. He would learn in due time, he reasoned.

"Yes, thank you," Johnny stated. "But I'm afraid I might have left marks on the cases when I removed them. My hands are not too clean."

Supervisor Largent laughed. "Do not worry. Before the opening every morning, everything is cleaned to within an inch of its life. Now, help me put the cases back on, please."

Cases restored, security reactivated, and Supervisor Largent left at the small entrance door, Johnny and Mona exited the gate and disappeared around the corner. Their rattle-trap taxi waited for them, as they had instructed.

Returning to their hotel, all was quiet. The press had departed, and the last sigh of night hung in the air.

As they walked through the brightly lit lobby, Johnny took Mona's hand and gave it a gentle squeeze. She smiled at him, and reciprocated.

They each fell asleep in their own separate room, exhausted.

Chapter 30
Easter

Johnny awoke. It was nearly noon. His room was ablaze with sunlight, and the warmth of the day was insinuating itself through the windows and past the air conditioning's attempts at control. He lay still on his stomach, blinking his eyes hard. On the nightstand sat a pair of wire cutters, reminding him of his recent exploits. He closed his eyes again and drifted off into a heavy doze, his mind trundling over the memories and bashing together rough scenarios of what might happen next. The dream from the flight over still dogged his mind. Images of Humpty Dumpty falling, crashing, were becoming clearer. The images were slightly grotesque, the way memories of a children's illustration can be, distorted and surreal, but they persisted. What did they mean? Ultimately, he knew he wasn't finished figuring things out. His brain wasn't at rest. Something remained unsolved, unexplained. Being subversive was only part of the job. The coup de grace was yet to come. The noose snap awaited.

As his mind emerged from its biochemical downtime, he knew the person he needed to update next was Tucker, who was at the nerve center of this case. Now that Tucker had a personal grudge to settle, Johnny's obligation to keep him apprised was all the greater. But the time difference factored in. He calculated the time in Boston, a little more awake with each passing moment. He remembered that Tucker would be strung out from jet lag after flying halfway around the world from wherever he'd been. He and his friend had always jibed somehow. Knowing when and how to show up was part of the friendship. Johnny could sense that it was not yet time to rouse Tucker the Trenchant, so he allowed himself to drift back to sleep.

It was early afternoon before Johnny finally roused himself completely and cleared his mind. He was glad he'd remembered to put the "Do Not Disturb" sign on the door. He decided it was time to lose the beard. After the encounter with the media last night, being recognizable was now going to help him more than flying under the radar. After a brief session with the electric razor and a quick shower, hunger struck, and he went downstairs and out onto the street. He quickly noticed that his constant companion, the surveillance shadow that had followed him for days on end, was gone. Exposure in the media had shed a beam too bright for the traitorous agent to withstand. Johnny relished the dilemmas he had created for that deceitful hack.

Ordering a panini, salad, and beer at the café, Johnny called Tucker. Passersby were now stealing glances at Johnny as he sat outside. It was clear that the media coverage and the shave were paying dividends. But he had accomplished more in the impromptu morning press event. In addition to revealing himself through the media, Johnny had also planted the suspicion that all was not well with the Faberge egg exhibit. This would make Winthrop's day more difficult, and Johnny liked that thought.

Tucker answered after a few rings. Johnny first thought was to see whether Tucker's lair was once again secure.

"Air tight," Tucker said confidently. "A few new wrinkles have been added. It sparked a creative rebirth in yours truly, I can tell you that. I'd probably gotten a little complacent. This was a monster wake-up call."

Johnny proceeded to detail the events of the prior hours, and was heartened to hear Tucker's slap of the forehead when he described his epiphany about the function of the eggs.

"Yes, my God, yes!" Tucker shouted in amazement. "I only had a few options for those numbers Mona recited into my answering machine, and electrical conduction was near the top of the list, but I didn't quite get all the way there. An electrical signature that unlocks encryption! Of course, that makes perfect sense. Let me see, which eggs were the ones your little limbic leprechaun identified? I think I can do something with that."

"The Windflowers and Diamond Trellis," Johnny confirmed. "What do you have in mind?"

"Reverse engineering," Tucker explained. "If I can find out some technical specs on these things – type of metals, length, other factors – I might be able to program a substitute for the physical objects sufficiently well to unpack the encryption, and then, watch out!" he finished gleefully.

"Well, Tucker, I was thinking, hacking code is all well and good, but we still need to peg Winthrop," Johnny reminded his friend. "Ideally, we could find a way to be more intrusive, but in just the right way – sink a bank shot he doesn't see coming, break him down with a good cross-over dribble, find a hole in the line and break free for a score, you get the picture."

Tucker was murmuring his assent as Johnny brought imagery and metaphor to the discussion, hoping to spark some creative thinking.

"Where do you think the files are now?" Tucker asked.

Johnny thought for a moment. "Well, let's see, there are two files he'll use, right?" Johnny asked.

"Right," Tucker confirmed.

"Let's assume that the files you discovered most recently comprise the starter set, the set that teaches how to use the second egg," Johnny speculated.

"OK, let's do that," Tucker murmured.

"And the larger files?" Johnny stated.

"The plans, as we know" Tucker said.

"Right, so let's work through the timing," Johnny said. "The eggs are here, and will get stolen soon. Winthrop has a few days from that point to share the files, according to the timing we've inferred from Ted's repair shop and the emails. So where are the files?"

Tucker thought for a moment. "They have to be there," he concluded. "There isn't time for Winthrop to get back to Richmond to retrieve them, so he had to bring them with him."

"Right," Johnny said. "So he transferred them to another set of drives and brought them with him. They were huge files."

Tucker clicked his tongue scoldingly. "Now, why would he transfer them? He had them on perfectly good and secure hard drives before."

"What are you getting at?" Johnny demanded.

"I can track those drives," Tucker revealed. "I still have the RFID information from the last time they crossed my path. I just need a satellite for a little while, but those are a dime a dozen over Western Europe these days. Would you like me to confirm?"

Johnny smiled. "Call me when you have something," he said, ending the call.

He didn't have to wait long for Tucker to call back.

"Easy as unscrambling a hex code," Tucker informed him. "The hard drives are right there, not too far from where you're staying."

"OK," Johnny responded, absorbing the information. He'd been dreaming up a plan, and now it was time to reveal it. He would turn Winthrop's metaphors against him. "Here's what we're going to do."

Chapter 31
Poached

Johnny knew that the timing of their plan was critical to its success. They had revealed many patterns emanating from how the criminals were coordinating events, and now they had to hit some precise timeframes so that vital elements of their plan streamed into established patterns without raising any alarms. First, Johnny composed a rhyming couplet, painstakingly rewrote it into the double-substitution encryption the plotters consistently used, and sent it to Tucker. Next, Tucker hacked a tiny file into an email designed to look exactly like the kind the system operator at miasma.net was used to seeing before a date with a prime number. Finally, they would monitor their listening outposts to detect activation of the small system file Tucker had crafted. He made it so the file would unpack exclusively within the IP addresses of the Hotel Midi.

Tucker was excited about his little creation. In a fit of prideful programming, striving to demonstrate to his adversaries precisely who was the greatest surveillance programmer on the planet, Tucker had created an ephemeral masterpiece of concept and execution, as he bragged in his joy. The code was designed to be undetectable by any email system or anti-virus software, and to reliably implant itself on any computer that accessed a storage drive, by writing itself onto the drive that was accessed. Once there, if the program detected a connection with the Internet, it would activate the computer's microphone, and broadcast like a phone call to Tucker's systems. Tucker would record what he heard, and keep it as evidence. What had tickled Tucker about his creation was the insight to make it activate when a drive was accessed, which wasn't novel, but which had fantastic potential for chaos in the criminal underworld when combined with turning on computer microphones as bugs. This meant that not only would it embed itself on Winthrop's computer when he viewed the email, but it would embed itself on the drives Winthrop distributed or on any computers that had the drives attached to them for even a few moments. If Winthrop was shopping the files around, Tucker's little workhorse would be installed on systems owned by some elite criminals. Tucker and Johnny both felt assured that at the very least Winthrop would be hooking the drives up to his computer before long if only to review his files like a nervous prima donna. The trap was set. Tucker was nearly beside himself with childlike excitement.

"This is going to totally freaking rock!" he exclaimed to Johnny. "I will be the Monster of the Midway in the netherworld I live in. Thanks for letting me in on this case, bro."

Johnny didn't want to reveal how grateful he was for Tucker's genius. "No problem, my friend. Just let me know when we're all ready."

Later in the day, as evening closed in and fatigue began to oppress Johnny, he called Mona. She had also spent the day recovering from a sleepless night. The call was brief. They agreed to meet for lunch the next day. No long afterwards, Johnny fell asleep, a dreamless, placid escape.

Johnny's cell phone rang early the morning of the 29th. It was Tucker, confirming that everything was in place. Johnny thanked his friend sincerely and hung up, flipping over and reentering sleep easily. Back in Boston, Tucker couldn't shut his brain down enough to sleep. The show was about to begin. He picked up his guitar and threw himself into a loud, joyous, and extended solo.

It was mid-afternoon when Johnny and Mona finally met at a little sidewalk café just off the main plaza. Over steak frites, warm and delicious, peasant food with French elegance, Johnny explained the plan he and Tucker had developed. As he finished, there was a moment during which Mona sat thoughtfully and silently. Then, suddenly and vehemently, she hit the table with the flat of her hand, knocking silverware askew with a clatter. "We're going to bust this son of a bitch!" she exulted.

"That's the idea," Johnny confirmed calmly.

"You and Tucker must have been terrible little boys," she laughed.

"Snips and snails and puppy dog tails," Johnny grinned in reply, picking up his wine glass. "Hearts of gold, though, hearts of gold."

Mona smiled over the upturned rim of her own wine glass. "That's clear," she said softly.

A burst of what sounded like gunfire startled them both out of the moment. A recklessly driven scooter zoomed by, close to the sidewalk, and they both flinched, remembering the events of the other evening. As the noisy scooter roared away, and normalcy reasserted itself, they both laughed nervously. Even Johnny had been rattled, and he reflected that this was a new feeling. He hadn't been afraid for himself, but for Mona. He had found himself instinctively positioning his body between her and the perceived threat. This was unusual territory for him, but he had to acknowledge the reality.

He felt uneasy about the change this might portend for his instinctual decision-making. Feelings like these may cloud or reshape his limbic brain. As a detective, he had the advantage of solitude and selfishness, so his survival and instinctual thinking was unaffected by considerations of how much others meant to him, or how they might depend on him or feel about him. If he and Mona were growing close, he had to compartmentalize those feelings, capture them in an area and not let them paint his perceptions. He had to remain Johnny Denovo, and not become a parody of what once was a great detective.

These thoughts passed wordlessly but definitely through Johnny's mind. His training and discipline around subconscious thinking allowed them all to register, and he could feel his brain responding with a remapping of the emotions he felt for Mona. They were still there, still intense, but now being placed in a display case, much as the Faberge eggs were, beautiful and precious and protected. Only an instant had passed.

Mona looked at him quizzically. "That was pitiful," she said. "We're a little jumpy, I guess. But you zoned out. What were you thinking?" She spoke these last words with tone of a therapist.

"I was thinking about the eggs," Johnny responded, with sufficient honesty. "They're in their cases, locked away. And tonight is the night."

Mona smiled. "Tonight is the night," she agreed.

Chapter 32
Speckled

Saturday morning, Johnny awoke yet again to the insistent ring-ing of his cell phone. He sprang out of bed, and threw on his slacks, which were in a pile on the floor, before grabbing the phone out of the pocket. It was Tucker.

"Hey, Johnny, hope I didn't wake you," Tucker nearly shouted. "It's happening! The eggs have been stolen, and I'm recording."

Johnny quickly transitioned out of a deep sleep and into a mode of anticipation and complete alertness.

"What have you heard?" he asked.

"Oh, it's Winthrop," Tucker revealed throatily. "He has the eggs, or at least the two you guessed, and is meeting his first buyer this afternoon outside of Montpellier. He's been on his cell phone for a couple of hours. I can't hear everything, but I can hear enough. The guy seems to be sitting right in front of his computer most of the time. He's been interviewed by the papers a couple of times about the stolen eggs, acting shocked and appalled and angry. He's a good actor. He's tested the drives, but not the eggs, so he's installed our listening device but doesn't know yet about what you've broken."

Johnny couldn't suppress a laugh. "Ha, that's great news, my friend. You're recording all of this, right?"

"Right as rain," Tucker confirmed. "Hey, I'll let you go, but I thought you might want to know. You and Mona have a busy day ahead of you."

"You speak the truth, friend," Johnny said, turning his head slightly to look at his bedmate, who was propped on her elbows, the sheet pulled up demurely and tucked under her arms. "Let me know when you have more."

Johnny closed his cell phone, smiling at his companion, who smiled warmly back. "It's working," he murmured, setting his phone down.

"Then you have some time to play," Mona purred, throwing the sheet back.

It was nearly noon before Johnny was interested in watching the news. The theft of the Faberge eggs was the lead story on both local channels and national channels. Even the lone international channel covered the theft in some detail. This had been one of the largest exhibitions of the eggs ever, so to have it spoiled by robbery was devastating. Speculation about the motives ran the gamut from money to crazed collectors, and some of the twisted history of Faberge fanatics was also shared. Johnny reflected on the predictable power of beautiful objects – they drive people to irrational acts.

He also realized that he had some egg on his face because he was mentioned time and again as having been in charge of preventing just such a theft. The media was beginning to ask as the news cycle wore on, "Where is the great detective Johnny Denovo now?"

Mona came out of the shower wearing a hotel robe, and Johnny hoped that he hadn't been driven to an irrational act by a beautiful object. Fortunately, Mona was not an object, but a friend, partner, and woman. And if he was being irrational, it wasn't unusual. He threw the superficial thought away.

"Can we listen to Winthrop?" Mona asked, toweling her hair dry.

"I don't see why not," Johnny murmured thoughtfully. He was curious, as well, to hear their mastermind in action. He opened his cell phone and called Tucker.

"Hey, Tucker," Johnny said brightly. "I ran into Mona, and we're here with my computer and phone. Is there any way we can listen in on Winthrop?"

Tucker sounded a little fatigued by this time, but responded enthusiastically nonetheless. "Sure, I can patch you in, but he's shut down his computer. I think he's going to meet one of the potential buyers."

"OK," Johnny drawled. "Well, could you call us when something starts happening?"

"I'll do you one better. Let's just set you up," Tucker replied, and instructed Johnny on how to set up his computer to also receive the feed from Winthrop's bugged computer. When Johnny had tested the setup, Tucker reminded him, "Now, this is only for Winthrop's computer. If others install the files, I'll have to set you up for them separately."

"Understood. Thanks, Tucker. This should be fun," Johnny responded.

"Oh, and by the way," Tucker added sheepishly, "Winthrop is gloating that Johnny Denovo looks like an ass because these were stolen right under your nose. Thought I'd tell you first."

Johnny smiled and thanked his friend. "I do look like an ass, he's right. But we'll see who has the last laugh."

Tucker chuckled. "And when it comes, the whole world will hear."

Chapter 33
Separated

It wasn't long before Mona and Johnny were listening to the live broadcast from Winthrop's computer. He was shopping his files around. Apparently he had advertised their availability fairly widely in an effort to drive the bidding and increase the price he'd receive. After the first few fascinating hours, a pattern set in, and Johnny and Mona began to listen less attentively, knowing that Tucker was recording everything.

Over the next couple of days, there were many supposedly secret meetings around Montpellier during which the encrypted files were demonstrated and shared after Winthrop had verified receipt of what, in effect, was a non-refundable deposit. Because he held the keys to the files, this was risk-free for him, but infuriating for Johnny, who had to listen to the man gloat as he became richer by the moment.

The Winthrop tour also meant that Tucker's listening files were installed on multiple computers belonging to covert agents from borderline governments. It was a nice side-effect of the approach they had taken. Cell phone calls placed near Winthrop's computer also identified important names and other details that Tucker said he'd be sure to share with the proper authorities at the right time.

But for Johnny, there was a case to close.

Early in the afternoon of August 1st, Winthrop found a buyer. Johnny and Mona learned through Tucker that Winthrop had delivered the drives and eggs to a person representing a government in the Middle East. The role of the eggs became clear from conversations – Winthrop was using the eggs to give pieces to his purchasers, and to secure payment while retaining leverage. If he only knew what was about to go wrong.

As the afternoon wore on, Johnny sat in his room, waiting. Mona and he were taking a respite from their blossoming relationship, comfortable now with a slower pace. Mona had just left on another shopping trip while Johnny hunkered down in his ad hoc command post.

It was late in the afternoon when his cell phone rang.

"Man, tell me your computer is running," Tucker pleaded.

"Yep, it's on right now," Johnny confirmed.

"Listen in on Winthrop," Tucker instructed.

With a few clicks, Johnny was eavesdropping alongside Tucker, shoulder to shoulder in a virtual sense.

"Look, Murat, I've said this before, and I'll say it again – I don't know! Did your engineers follow the instructions in the first file precisely?" Winthrop said, sounding exasperated, but with a striation of worry in his voice.

There was a pause while his conversant responded.

"The deal isn't off," Winthrop bluffed. "You have everything you need. It was all tested before the exhibit, and worked perfectly. The eggs were secure the entire time. The files were with me, and their integrity is beyond dispute. The problem is yours. Payment has been made, and I am done with this. If you do not return the eggs, I will collect the insurance money, so that is not a tenable threat. Don't harass me with your incompetence! Good bye!"

Winthrop closed his cell phone with a snap, and began cursing about the ethnicity and intellect of the person he'd been talking with. He also vowed in his worried rage that no matter what happened, he'd see to it that he got those eggs back. Johnny was still on the phone with Tucker.

"Looks like our little subterfuge has started to pay dividends," he said to his friend. He liked seeing Winthrop turning inside-out.

Tucker was more measured in his thoughts. "Johnny, this might go south on us," he warned.

"I think I know what you're going to say," Johnny contributed.

"I'm sure you do," Tucker agreed. "These people have paid tens of millions of dollars, if not hundreds, for these plans, and they feel like Winthrop has screwed them over. If he doesn't fix this, he's a dead man."

Johnny realized his friend was correct. "Well, then, it's time to lower the boom," he said.

"We've got him dead to rights," Tucker said.

"OK, let's do it," Johnny indicated. "Do you want to call Interpol, or do you want me to?"

"You should," Tucker said. "I'll be at the ready to send them the evidence we have. Just let me know. But you should get the credit for this. It's your case, your reputation. I'm just a computer grunt," Tucker said humorously.

"Hell of a grunt," Johnny smirked. "You saved me on this one, cuz."

"Thanks," Tucker murmured. "Now call the cops, will you?"

Johnny's next call was to Interpol. He had dealt with them many times before. They knew him and trusted him. He asked for an old friend, Investigator Floche, a young and ambitious Interpol agent who had great instincts and a flair for the unusual.

"Johnny," said Investigator Floche. "It's good to hear from you. To what do I owe the privilege of your call?"

"Floche, I have something that will make your day," Johnny replied, and detailed as quickly as possible the situation he was facing.

Investigator Floche paused to deliberate once Johnny finished. "You are telling me that the owner of some of the eggs stole them to unlock files he's selling to arms dealers from unfriendly foreign governments? Why should I believe your crazy story?"

Johnny knew that Floche inherently trusted him, but needed evidence before he could proceed and get resources.

"Where shall I send the recordings?"

"Oh, you have recordings?" queried Floche. "And how did you get these recordings?"

Johnny explained that Winthrop's computer had been turned into a listening device, and also how the files had been propagated to computers of interest. Investigator Floche was impressed.

"This is very good," he said. "We will have to work with a number of governments to complete the investigations coming from this. There will be paperwork, but this is very good. Congratulations, Detective Denovo."

"Floche, you have to pick up Winthrop now, though," Johnny indicated. "We sabotaged the eggs so they don't work as designed, but Winthrop doesn't know this. The purchasers are angry because things aren't working as promised. And Winthrop's becoming belligerent with the purchasers. There's so much at stake, we're afraid this might end badly."

"I see, I see," murmured Floche. "We will arrest him within the hour. In fact, I am in Montpellier myself right now, you know. We have been investigating the theft of the Faberge eggs for a few days. It is a very big deal for us. You are sure the files will give me the evidence I need?"

"There's no doubt," said Johnny. "Also, we can probably recover all the other missing Faberge eggs. You'll be a hero."

"May I borrow your cape, then?" Floche laughed.

Johnny and Floche concluded their call cordially, and Johnny began to pack his bags. The time to leave France was approaching. He called down to Mona's room, where he left a message. She was out.

Chapter 34

Beaten

Johnny had barely hung up the hotel phone when his cell phone rang. Tucker was calling again, and he was frantic.

"Johnny, listen in on Winthrop! Now!" he shouted into Johnny's ear.

Tucker's state of agitation was infectious, creating an equivalent sense of panic in Johnny. He could barely operate his computer for a moment. He fumbled with the pointing device, hit a wrong key, and then slowed himself down and calmly started over. Soon he was listening to Winthrop's room once more.

"Just grab her. If you have to take her out, she'll fight, but I don't care," Winthrop was shouting. "I need a bargaining chip, do you understand? I know Denovo is behind this, and I'm not screwing around any more! I've done worse than silence some dumb assistant. Bide your time, keep up the front, and when I give the order, do your job!"

"They're after Mona!" Tucker bellowed through the cell phone pressed between Johnny's shoulder and ear. "Where is she?!"

"Not in her room, I just called there," Johnny said in a hushed voice, listening intently to Winthrop's continuing tirade and closing his eyes, summoning his deepest thoughts for inspiration. He took a long breath, and then opened his eyes again, staring straight ahead as if with a beam from his eyes. "Tucker, implement the fallback position in the plan, now!! I've got to go! I know exactly what to do!" With that, he snapped his phone shut and dashed from the room, his computer still broadcasting Winthrop's room.

In the lobby, Johnny looked around frantically. There was no sign of Mona. He had dialed her cell phone on the way down in the elevator, but it had gone unanswered. He hadn't panicked at this, however, because she often didn't answer when she was out – if her phone was buried in her purse and she was on a noisy street, she wouldn't be able to hear it. It had happened many times in France. He was hoping desperately it was the case again.

There was no other choice but to go to the source, which meant Winthrop. Besides, as Johnny understood well now, this was precisely what Winthrop feared the most –intrusion from the outside. He wanted control, from the inside out. Losing control because of an unexpected incursion, from the outside in, would throw him off-balance at a fundamental level and give Johnny the upper hand. The element of surprise helped, but the attack on Winthrop's weakest spot, his mental model of how he interacted with the world, was a savage blow.

There was something else, Johnny sensed, still a missing center somewhere. The intrinsic-extrinsic metaphor used on the eggs hadn't surfaced within Winthrop yet, but they were neurologically highly correlated. One begat the other. There was something more lurking inside the man Johnny pursued, a hidden, absorbed secret. It felt like a missing step in a staircase, hurtling him forward as he tried to fathom it.

Johnny dashed out of the hotel and ran toward the Hotel Midi, weaving an erratic yet acrobatic course through the pedestrians crowding the plazas and streets on this Saturday afternoon.

Forced to stop at a busy intersection, Johnny had another inspiration, and called Investigator Floche.

"Floche," he gasped when the Interpol investigator answered the phone. "It's Denovo. We need to change the plan."

Floche sounded perplexed. "What's to change? We have a criminal, we arrest him. My men are on their way now."

"No!" Johnny yelled, surprising himself. "No," he said more calmly. "There's a change of plans, like I said."

Floche understood that something of magnitude had changed. "OK, tell me please."

Johnny thought a moment. "I need a couple of your men to go to my hotel room and listen to my computer. It's tuned in to Winthrop's room at the Hotel Midi. I think Winthrop's going to try to hold someone hostage to get to me, to learn how I've sabotaged his plans." Johnny shared his hotel information with Floche.

"But Johnny," Floche continued. "I must also send men to the Hotel Midi at the same time. We cannot let this Mr. Winthrop get away."

Johnny thought a moment. "Fine," he agreed reluctantly. "Just make sure they stay out of sight, and are discreet and patient. Have them work with the men listening from my room. That way, you will know when to move in."

"I agree. That is wise," Floche stated. "I will go to listen at your room personally, Johnny. This is too important."

"Great," Johnny responded. "Just don't mess this up."

"We will do this properly," Investigator Floche reassured Johnny. "Now, go, and trust that we will be with you." The light had changed, and Johnny had already started walking toward the Hotel Midi, but once the conversation ended, he broke into a run again.

Taking the elevator up to the 12th floor, Johnny gathered his wits and began to think. Winthrop was an actor who hid his motivations and betrayed people with ease. He was also ruthless, and now was more like a cornered animal, which would mean that his higher brain functions would have degraded, leaving him only with base impulses geared toward survival and deeply embedded traits. Judging from the little snippet of conversation he had heard, Mona might not know she was being kidnapped at first, Johnny concluded. It would fit Winthrop's tendency to deceive. She might be met by someone passing themselves off to gain her trust, and then find herself at their mercy. He tried her cell phone again. This time, she answered.

"Hi," she said brightly.

"Where are you?" he asked desperately. "Who are you with?"

"I didn't see you as the jealous type," she laughed, but the way her voice shifted from the phone receiver, he envisioned that she had turned her head to look at someone next to her, confirming in his mind's eye that she had company. She confirmed his instinct. "I'm being driven to police headquarters by an Inspector Guichard from Interpol. He said you would meet us there. Are you coming?"

He was in a predicament. If he revealed the truth – that this Inspector Guichard was one of Winthrop's men – Mona may panic or react violently, and her physical safety might be compromised unnecessarily. If he played along, he might buy some time. And time was what he was running out of.

"Yes, but I might be a little while," Johnny mentioned. "Can you do me a favor?"

"Perhaps," Mona responded coquettishly.

"Whatever you do, remember that eggs are delicate," he stated, hoping she understood what he was suggesting. "And to make an omelet, you sometimes have to break some."

Mona was silent for a moment, struggling to make sense of what Johnny had just said. "Oh, I see," she said with mustered enthusiasm, a trace of uncertainty in her voice. The seed had been planted. She was on her guard at some fundamental level, at least.

"See you soon," Johnny reassured her. He closed the phone. The elevator bell's ding announced his arrival at Winthrop's floor.

Johnny stormed down the hallway, his vision blurred with anger. His carefully compartmentalized emotions for Mona had escaped their bounds, and he knew that since Winthrop would be in animal mode, he was best equipped to come at him like an animal, too. He purposely began to work himself up even further, preparing his mind, muscles, perceptions, and attitude to deal with a shape-shifter, a clever chameleon on the defensive, but one with venom and a prisoner he could bargain with.

Johnny's goal was to overturn Winthrop's mind.

A bit of luck turned up in the hallway as he approached Winthrop's door – his cleaning girl, the one who he thought had betrayed him but who had in reality been a turning point. She was approaching, looking frightened at the seething detective headed for her like a missile. She moved instinctively to hug the wall. Johnny dimmed his anger and stopped, cooling down with a smile.

"Hi there," he said quietly and a little breathlessly, but in as friendly a manner as he could given the circumstances.

"Hi," she trembled.

"I need a favor," Johnny stated bluntly. "Can I have your pass key? I have a case to solve."

The cleaning girl dug the key from her pocket and handed it to Johnny. "Keep it," she said timidly. "I have two."

Of course she did. Johnny smiled, turned, squared his shoulders, and went the last few paces toward Winthrop's room, his rage and intensity regenerated completely, the pass key gripped tightly in his hand.

Whipping the electronic card into the slot in Winthrop's door, Johnny paused for the beep, then slammed the handle down and threw the door open.

"Winthrop, what have you done with her?" Johnny demanded at the top of his lungs.

Winthrop spun around, cell phone pressed to his ear, eyes wide in astonishment. In a flash, his countenance changed to become calm and calculating.

"Well, guess who's here? It's Johnny Denovo," he hissed theatrically into the phone. "If I don't call you back in 5 minutes, kill her." Winthrop closed the phone with a click, a triumphant look on his face.

Johnny was on him before he could say or do anything more, torquing his arm behind his back and pushing his face into the wall. Winthrop's phone bounced to the floor, and the door slammed closed with a bang.

"Yes, I am behind your troubles, you asshole, and if you think you're the one who is done screwing around, you haven't seen anything yet," Johnny said, pressing his mouth close to Winthrop's ear, but speaking loudly enough to be both uncomfortable for Winthrop and audible to Floche and his men. "I think I quote you accurately, don't I?" Johnny asked.

Winthrop squirmed to see Johnny. "You've been listening?" he said in sincere astonishment, the realization shattering layers of his defenses in one fell swoop. This was the essential part of the outside-in attack Johnny had planned, a decimating blow revealing to Winthrop that his belief of control, of having an impenetrable inner sanctum to his operation, had been taken from him without his permission or awareness. Johnny needed to drive the point home, to break this villain down further.

"*We've* been listening," Johnny corrected him. "And we're still listening, so be careful, Winthrop. In fact, if I'm not mistaken, there are plenty of people listening right now."

"Who, Denovo?" Winthrop wheezed. "The police? The feds? The cops? You'd better be careful yourself. I've got Landau, and if I don't call them back in 5 minutes, they'll kill her."

Johnny grinned. "Care to say that a little louder?" Johnny taunted, pressing harder on Winthrop.

"I said," Winthrop stated coldly, raising his voice menacingly, "my men will kill Mona Landau in 5 minutes if I don't call them back."

Johnny's smile widened and he pressed harder against Winthrop's sweating face. "Well, I hope your daughter is proud of you now, you morally bankrupt shit. We didn't want to bring her into this. It was a last resort, our fallback position. She's been listening for a few minutes now, as well," Johnny revealed.

Winthrop's eyes widened and his face chalked to a pallor. "You bastard." he spat, his body writhing with anger. "I don't believe you."

"See your computer, not three feet from us?" Johnny indicated. "The microphone has been transmitting for days now. We have it all – the calls to the prospects, the gloating over the payments, the discussions of the eggs, and the meltdown because they didn't work. It's a virtual confession, and it's all been recorded with digital clarity."

Winthrop's limp body suddenly began to tremble, and sobs began to escape from deep in his chest. "Oh dear God, what have I done?" he blubbered. "Oh Justine, I'm so sorry. I only did this for you," he sobbed, his voice rising and his head turning toward his computer in an attempt to communicate. "Don't you understand? They were going to kill me."

Johnny tightened his grip on Winthrop, and pushed him hard against the wall again. "Drop the act, Winthrop," he growled. "I'm not buying it. You weren't doing this for anybody but yourself, your over-preening ego, and your endless greed. You tried to have me killed, you're threatening a friend of mine with death, you've betrayed your own government and people, and you expect pity? You rat bastard, you deserve punishments beyond all hell."

Winthrop's eyes changed yet again into stony orbs as he began to disassociate from the moment. Johnny had expected this, expected Winthrop to shut down when his animal instincts to shape-shift, to hide inside another mode of outside expression, were clearly ineffective. Even being revealed to his daughter as a death-merchant and criminal wasn't enough to overthrow his basic animal tendencies, his brain's bulwarks of survival. Johnny had to probe deeper, into a part of Winthrop he suspected had been suppressed in its raw form, so was therefore more apt to surprise, even usurp, its owner. He had to find the connection in Winthrop that would close the final circuit.

"Think of your dead wife," Johnny whispered violently. "*Think* about her!" he insisted more loudly, banging Winthrop's head against the wall.

Winthrop grimaced in pain.

"She was all alone, wasn't she?" Johnny hissed. "Driving all alone at night in the rain, hit by a drunk driver." He pressed Winthrop's face hard against the wall again. "And where were you, you bastard?!" Johnny screamed. "Where were you?! Selling government secrets again?!"

Winthrop flinched for the first time, a deeply involuntary twitch. Johnny's mind fired. In a flash, his limbic brain reviewed the dream he'd had on the flight to France, with Humpty Dumpty falling through associated sounds and images. Janet Winthrop's face appeared, and smashed when the giant egg fell. All the kings horses, all the kings men. Eggs were a metaphor for motherhood, but the smashed image was the key. This was the secret, the real meaning of the eggs, of the dream. They were a metaphor for his wife, but at their heart lay a terrible crime.

The images, the meaning, the insight, all of it happened in a few heartbeats, all while Johnny watched Winthrop disassociate even more severely at the mention of this incident. It was clear he had tripped the timebomb.

"She'd found out!" he gasped. "You miserable lowlife! You had her killed because she had found out that you were selling out your own government to feather the nest! She was going to tell, and you had her killed!"

Winthrop spat back, "I was trying to protect my daughter!"

Johnny wasn't having any of it. "From what? From you?! You miserable, puny soul! You aren't a protector, you're a destroyer! And you've lost! You have lost! Do you hear me?! It is over! Your daughter knows. Soon, the whole world will know. Call off your men, or I will make sure you lose everything!" Johnny instinctively moved his hand down from Winthrop's jaw to his windpipe and began applying pressure.

Winthrop closed his eyes tightly. He was controlling his breathing, trying not to choke, trying to ignore the pressure on his trachea.

Despite his nearly blind rage, Johnny used his mental discipline to maintain a rational observational stance above the physical confrontation. From this vantage point, he could tell that something deep inside Winthrop was at work, something urgent and painful was processing from his brainstem up. His survival instinct was battling to overturn his higher cognitive functions.

Johnny let the silence hold the moment, the only sound the pounding of their pulses and the ragged breathing as Winthrop fought for air. Johnny's own thoughts were racing. Had he broken down the façade? Had he truly found the secret inside Winthrop? Had Winthrop's fear of his own death finally brought about an internal reckoning, a survival paradox?

Suddenly, Winthrop screamed, a gnashing, horrible release, flecks of saliva flying out. The recoil was so violent that Johnny lost his grip on Winthrop's trachea. Gasping for air, Winthrop's eyes opened maniacally with the outburst, but this time, when his eyes opened, they were alive again. The analogy, the violence, the revelation of his murderous past, and the imminent threat to his own life had gotten through to levels that Winthrop had hidden from himself and the world. The real person was a withered, desiccated soul, but there was enough. He stood there, heaving with labored gasps.

"You're right," he finally murmured in a nearly inaudible admission, still breathing heavily, and a tear, a genuine, spontaneous tear, leaked from the outside of his left eye. "I've lost. I have lost everything. I lost everything the night I allowed my wife to be killed."

Johnny tightened his grip again on Winthrop's neck, mindful that his goals had not been met. "Call them off, Winthrop. The clock is ticking."

Winthrop sucked in a harsh breath. "I'll call them off," he rasped.

Johnny waited a moment, to see if he sensed any muscles in Winthrop's body tensing, if he detected him preparing to attack or spring. But he felt nothing, so he spun Winthrop around and forced him quickly to the floor, pressing his face to the carpet near the phone. Winthrop offered no resistance, hitting the floor hard, a gasp escaping him upon impact. Johnny put a knee in Winthrop's back and held his twisted arm, then reached out to retrieve the phone, which lay nearby on the floor. Opening it and pressing redial, he brought the phone up to Winthrop's face.

"It's me," Winthrop said into the phone a moment later.

"Are you OK, sir?" the voice on the other end inquired. Johnny had the receiver tilted slightly away from Winthrop's ear so they could both hear the person on the other end of the call.

"I'm fine," Winthrop responded, hiding the duress he was under. "Take the girl back to her hotel. Drop her off at the entrance. Tell her there's been a change of plans, and thank her for her time."

"Yes sir," the voice replied with a trace of disbelief, and the call ended.

Winthrop sighed a shivering, emotional sigh, and stared blankly at the floor, every hint of bravado and arrogance drained from his demeanor.

Johnny pulled Winthrop to his feet and shouted at the computer, "Now would be a good time, Floche."

There was a momentary silence, and then the door to the hotel room burst open, two Interpol agents entering with guns drawn and Johnny's chambermaid friend standing behind them, replacing her second passkey card into her apron pocket.

"I love you, Johnny Denovo," the chambermaid cried, and then ran down the hall, eager to get away from the strange and violent scene she was witnessing.

Johnny smiled, and then spoke into Winthrop's computer again. "Floche, I'll tell you now that you can find the rest of the Faberge eggs by locating a maroon scooter driven by a man with a dented helmet and an injured shoulder. The injury will be only a few days old."

Winthrop was catatonic. The avalanche inside his brain – the dissolution of a massive amount of deceit and the truth its absence revealed – had overthrown his conscious mind. He was merely breathing, and trying to construct a new internal reality. He'd lost his wife, his daughter, and now himself.

Johnny's cell phone rang. It was Investigator Floche.

"Well done, Johnny," Floche congratulated. "But I have to know, how did you do this?"

"I'll tell you about it soon enough. But for now, let's just say, I made an omelet," Johnny answered cryptically. He hung up the phone, smiled at the agents, and left the room.

Chapter 35
Over Easy

Johnny met Mona back at their hotel about 20 minutes later. She kissed him on the lips, a warm and reassuring gesture that put his mind at ease. He sat her down and told her that Winthrop had just been arrested.

"I know," she replied. "I've been fielding some calls about it already. Congratulations."

"Thanks," he replied, smiling at her, still relieved nothing had gone wrong. "How are you doing?"

Mona then started to tell him about how the Interpol agent had located her and had said that she was wanted for questioning. Johnny feigned exhaustion.

"I think I'm going to lie down for a while," he told her. "Just to rest. I've had quite a day. How about we meet for dinner, just down here in the hotel restaurant? Say, 7 o'clock?"

Mona agreed, and reverted to her own professional demeanor.

"By the way, Mr. Detective," she said crisply, "don't take too long to freshen up. The media will be here for a press conference in about half an hour. You're going to be the top story in tomorrow's papers."

"Fine, fine," Johnny sighed. "I'll keep that in mind."

"And," Mona continued, "we will have to talk soon about how to divide the money."

"What money?" Johnny asked.

"Do you honestly think that I was just sitting around the past couple of days?" Mona asked. "Tucker helped me work the government, and I worked the insurance carriers for Winthrop's eggs and the others on display. All contingent on arrests and recoveries, mind you. You have a nice little sum on the way when you add them all up. And, therefore, so do I!"

Johnny smiled and gripped Mona's shoulder. "You are still the Mistress of Evil," he joked.

"You flatter me," she replied. They smiled at each other, shared a light kiss, and Johnny walked away to take the elevator up to his room.

He called Tucker first.

"Tucker, did you get all that?" he asked his friend.

"Yep, everything except for the stuff after you turned Winthrop over to Interpol," Tucker replied, breathing heavily. "Sorry, Johnny, but I had to get out. I sent everything over to Interpol right after they burst into the room, sent everything they'll need to spring that innocent guy in Richmond to that Detective Tin Man, and then I got out."

"His name was Timmerman," Johnny admonished.

"Yeah, yeah," Tucker gasped. "I wrote it the right way in the email. I'm just focused on my jogging right now."

Johnny was astonished. "You don't jog, my man!" he exclaimed.

"Oh, I read a book about fitness on the plane back from my last job," Tucker revealed. "I'm cleaning up my act. Only organic food, only real fruits, no white flour, and an exercise program."

"I give it a week," Johnny sighed. "I give it three days."

"You are so wrong. You wait and see. I'll be able to beat the fabled Johnny Denovo in a sprint before you know it."

"Tucker, Mona's fine, by the way," Johnny interjected.

"I figured," Tucker said. "I'm relieved."

"We'll be back in Boston late tomorrow afternoon," Johnny said. "Can we stop by to thank you?"

"Yes, stop by when you have a chance. Call first. I've got some new security measures, so you can't just walk in until I integrate you again."

Next, Johnny called Justine, and explained the situation in detail. This took some time, and Justine was emotionally shaken by what she had heard. But she listened attentively and completely.

Johnny had to ask the difficult question then. "Had you suspected he'd been involved in your mother's death?"

Justine answered with a noise like a mixture of a laugh and a sob. "You're kidding me, Denovo," she said after a moment. "That's what I meant when I said that I'd discovered where I began and he ended. That was the moment where we stopped being father and daughter, except for appearances. It's been terrible, but I take solace in the innocent purity of the horses here. They keep me sane and motivated."

"You're a remarkable woman," Johnny stated.

"Even if he is my father," she confessed, "he's a criminal. I can't deny that."

"I'm sorry this happened to you."

Justine sniffled, and her voice gained a stronger timbre. "Don't feel sorry for me. You were the one in danger. I'm actually very grateful this has reached its end. If you ever need riding lessons, just give me a call. Winthrop Stables is under new management, and you have a lifetime pass."

The call ended well, and Johnny was left with much admiration for Justine Winthrop, who seemed as solid in character as her father was lacking.

Johnny then looked at himself in the bathroom mirror, splashed water on his face, and decided to change his shirt. After one more look to ensure that the Denovo mystique was in full force, he went downstairs again to face the press.

A mid-sized conference room had been set up in a hurry for the media session, and Johnny found himself in the familiar position –

seated behind a cloth-covered table with a modesty curtain and a fabric backdrop, television and still cameras pointed at him, and a crowd of reporters with laptops and notepads asking questions. Mona introduced him briefly in what by now was very polished French, then left the room. Johnny wondered how much she really knew yet about what had transpired and her role in it.

During the questioning, Johnny learned a few new items himself. Judging from the questions, Interpol had found the rest of the Faberge eggs, which had been stored in a small house in Montpellier, and guarded by Winthrop's men, one of whom had a headache and a crippled shoulder. One reporter had learned that Winthrop had taken out a large insurance policy on his wife just prior to her death. It also became clear that the US government was being asked about its internal security measures, for not only had military plans been stolen, but one of its agents under investigation for espionage had been photographed in France while not on assignment and lost to authorities. Johnny thought he knew who slipped the background on this last revelation to the media.

Johnny was able to sneak in one of his trademark mystical statements, in French this time, which made it sound even more otherworldly. When asked how he had deduced that letting Winthrop steal his own eggs would lead to a bigger catch, Johnny responded, "He was showing us all what was inside of his soul the entire time. He put it on display. We must realize that we are living both in the world, and in other people's minds. How we appear in each is not the same."

Once the hour was up, Johnny politely stopped taking questions and posed for a few photographs shaking hands with Investigator Floche, who had just arrived and was next up in the press briefing. Then Johnny left for the sanctuary of his hotel room.

After packing a little more and tidying up some other loose ends with Interpol, the exhibit hall, and another insurance company who called to arrange payment with Johnny for recovering the eggs, Johnny met Mona at the entrance to the hotel restaurant as scheduled. She was dressed in a new lightweight summer dress with shoulder straps revealing her creamy skin, the cloth accentuating her curves and bringing an even more youthful glow to her satiny skin. She looked great, and was still buzzing from the events of the day.

They were seated in a secluded corner booth in the three-star restaurant, and once their drink orders had been taken, Mona started talking at a rapid pace, updating Johnny on the transactions she was handling, informing him of the media blitz she was arranging for him once he returned to the US, and telling her story about being escorted around by Interpol as if it were the most exciting thing of the day. After a time, Johnny began to elaborate upon some of the events that had been transpiring simultaneously, and soon the reality of her situation began to dawn on Mona.

"Wait," she interjected at one point in Johnny's delicate narrative. "Am I right in thinking you're going to tell me that my driver wasn't really with Interpol?"

Johnny paused, then nodded almost imperceptibly.

"He was working for Winthrop?" Mona gasped.

Again, Johnny nodded.

"Was I a hostage?" Mona asked in a hoarse whisper, the truth being reluctantly embraced.

Once more, Johnny nodded.

Mona threw her head back in disbelief, and looked at the ceiling of the hotel restaurant they were seated in. "Un-effing-believable," she uttered at last. "I'm such an innocent. I thought this guy was a fancy European law enforcement agent, and that I was going to help him bust Winthrop or something, but it turns out I was a stupid hostage. Damn," she finished, bringing her head back down and looking Johnny hard in the eyes.

"I'm afraid so, my dear," Johnny responded evenly.

"Fine, fine," Mona breathed, then paused portentously, as if weighing her next words carefully. "Thanks for saving me."

"You'll still want your share of the purse?" Johnny asked, smiling.

"Of course!" Mona responded hotly. "There is no savior discount, Denovo. And don't think that our new little relationship is going to change how I run the business side."

Their drinks arrived, a glass of local red wine for Mona and a gin, tonic, and lemon for Johnny. They glanced at each other, and Johnny raised his glass in a toast. His mind was at peace, satisfied after its efforts, open and willing again to accept whatever came next.

"To fate," he intoned. Mona raised her glass in response, then clinked it against his.

"To the human brain," Mona corrected, clinking his glass again and raising it to her red lips.

Johnny sipped from his gin and tonic, measuring his movements, monitoring his appearance, and manipulating his vibe. It was all part of the act. His eyes locked with Mona's as her words reverberated through all the chambers of his mind.

Printed in the United States
146490LV00001B/7/P

9 781598 588644